Hearth Stone

D1472886

Center Point
Large Print

Also by Lois Greiman and available from
Center Point Large Print:

Hope Springs Novels
  Finding Home
  Home Fires
  Finally Home

**This Large Print Book carries the
Seal of Approval of N.A.V.H.**

Hearth Stone

Lois Greiman

CENTER POINT LARGE PRINT
THORNDIKE, MAINE

This Center Point Large Print edition is published
in the year 2015 by arrangement with
Kensington Publishing Corp.

The text of this Large Print edition is unabridged.
In other aspects, this book may vary
from the original edition.
Printed in the United States of America
on permanent paper.
Set in 16-point Times New Roman type.

ISBN: 978-1-62899-729-3

Library of Congress Cataloging-in-Publication Data

Greiman, Lois.
Hearth stone / Lois Greiman. — Center Point Large Print edition.
pages cm
Summary: "After an injury shatters her chance at the US equestrian
team, Sydney arrives at the Lazy Windmill ranch angry and
heartbroken. When all seems hopeless, she discovers an injured
mustang. Seeing herself in the desperate wild mare, she feels
compelled to save the animal at all costs, little knowing that the horse
just might return the favor"—Provided by publisher.
ISBN 978-1-62899-729-3 (library binding : alk. paper)
1. Ranches—South Dakota—Fiction.
   2. Women ranchers—South Dakota—Fiction.
   I. Title.
PS3557.R4369H43 2015b
813'.6—dc23

2015024346

To Lona Pearl, who could identify a pinto
before she knew her primary colors
and who cries when she has to
quit riding . . . just like me.
I'm the luckiest grandmother
in the universe.

Acknowledgments

Special thanks to the one and only Tonkiaishawien Koemtiamleah, whose art and stories inspire me, and who, despite considerable evidence to the contrary, assures me he is *not* a flirt.

Prologue

"What's he doing here?" Sydney Wellesley kept her voice low, but it shook with emotion, with memories.

Golden light glistened on David Albrook's carefully tousled hair, glinted off his winning smile as he accepted a drink.

"I'll not have you make a scene in my home."

Sydney pulled her gaze from her fiancé's classic good looks and pinned it on her father. The knots in her stomach were yanked up tight, but when in her twenty-four years of life had she ever made a scene? "Why is—" she began again, but Leonard Wellesley spoke over her.

"We'll discuss this in private," he said and turned away. He was not a large man, but he was wealthy and he was a Wellesley. The fact that he was her father was almost inconsequential. Still, for a moment, she nearly bolted, nearly rebelled. But good manners, or maybe habit, made her follow him down the hallway's floral runners.

"Close the door," he ordered when she'd stepped into the room. His study was a caricature of a rich man's office. Dark paneling, sparse furniture, heavy silence. He turned away to pour himself two fingers of Royal Salute Scotch. "How are you feeling?" He didn't face her when he spoke, but she had become accustomed to talking to his back long ago.

"I'm doing well." She had learned to lie at the same time. "And you?"

He didn't respond. Apparently, his capacity for niceties had been stretched to the limit.

"David is here because I invited him," he explained and, rising to perfect straightness, took a quaff of scotch. "And because he's your fiancé."

David Albrook had professed his undying adoration. David . . . world-renowned equestrian . . . a god on horseback . . . but not so divine, it turned out, when it came to interpersonal relationships.

Still, Father insisted she proceed with the wedding. *Wellesleys stand by their word,* he'd said. But would that have been the case if he weren't even now trying to facilitate a merger with the Albrooks? And what about *David's* word? Was a little fidelity too much to ask of him? He hadn't even managed discretion.

Her stomach cramped at the memory of whispered words from a darkened tack room.

She squeezed her eyes shut against the unwelcome thoughts. Her fingers felt icy against the Austrian crystal. "I've been meaning to discuss that with you." She refrained from clearing her throat. Wellesleys were not throat clearers. One might just as well practice cannibalism. "I'm going to formally sever the engagement this evening."

Her father made no sound for several seconds, but his disapproval pulsed in the silence. It was a talent of his, passed down through generations of well-bred financiers.

"Because of that misunderstanding with the Ulquist girl?"

Misunderstanding. If she hadn't been such a coward, she would have laughed out loud. "I don't believe *misunderstanding* is the correct terminology for this situation." The memory of her humiliation was almost as painful as her injuries. But he breathed a dismissive hiss and took another drink.

"If I thought it was serious, I would have put a stop to his philandering long ago."

It took her a moment to catch his meaning, but suddenly her breath clogged in her throat. She stood motionless as tiny shards of reality tinkled quietly into place. "You knew about it," she said.

He didn't answer, but his brows were drawn low over saltwater eyes. Less dour expressions had silenced her in the past. But if ever there was a time to speak, surely it was now.

"How long?" she asked. "How long did you know?"

"Don't take that tone with me." He tightened his blunt, neatly manicured fingers against the cut crystal and pursed his lips. "I didn't spend a fortune on dressage horses and private tutors so you would become an insolent spinster," he said, then exhaled and softened his tone. He could play good cop/bad cop all by himself. Another talent not to be underestimated. "Listen, Sydney, I know this has been a difficult time for you."

Difficult? She had almost died in the fall. Had lost her nerve, her faith, her ability to ride, to do the one thing at which she excelled.

"And perhaps you needed a few months to . . ." He waved a magnanimous hand. "To rebel, as it were. But it's time to get back on track. To set a date with Albrook. His parents are as eager for this merger as I."

"The merger." David's father was almost as wealthy as her own illustrious family. She turned toward the blackness beyond the broad bay window. In the light of day it would boast a view of a church steeple purported to have been designed by Thomas Jefferson's favorite slave. Who said Southerners weren't forward thinkers? "And which is more important?" She kept her voice quiet as she studied that blackness. Her thigh throbbed in concert with her thoughts. "Finances or my future?"

At seven years of age, she had asked for a lemonade stand. After due deliberation, her father had commissioned a gazebo to be built on the edge of Arbor House's manicured grounds. She had manned the booth with terrier-like dedication. But there was little foot traffic in Middleburg, Virginia. By the end of the first week, tired and discouraged, she had been informed that she was $12,474 in arrears. In the future, it would be wise to leave the finances in more capable hands.

"There's no need for melodramatics," her father said. "I understand your . . . disappointment with David. But I've invested too much to change course now."

"Disappointment!" She twisted toward him, but pulled cautiously back from the terrifying brink of emotional release. "Is that what you call it when you find your betrothed fu—"

"Sydney!" It was the first time in her memory that she had heard him raise his voice. "I'll not have you using that foul language in my home."

"Your home."

"Yes, and if you hope to inherit one square inch of it, young lady, you will grant me the respect I deserve."

Her chest hurt suddenly. A strange raw ache near her heart. "Even though you've no compunction about marrying me off to the highest bidder?"

"I didn't know that living well had become so abhorrent to you."

"I believe there might be a difference between living well and prostituting oneself to—"

He slammed his glass onto the dark walnut of his ancient desk. She jumped, heart racing.

"What is this hideous racket?" The words were hissed. Gloria Wellesley had never reached the five-foot mark, but size had rarely mattered where she was concerned.

Silence, as usual, followed in her oppressive wake.

"*You* tell her," Leonard challenged.

Sydney faced her grandmother. By comparison, her father was as cuddly as a Labrador. Her throat felt tight, but she managed to push words past the constriction. "I'm afraid I won't be marrying David after all."

The faded gray eyes never blinked. "And what will you do instead? Find employment?"

Sydney gripped the crystal with both hands and tried a shrug. "I hear it's all the rage."

The old woman smiled. "Well, that's excellent then. I'm sure you will further the Wellesley name admirably. Perhaps you would like to try your hand at lemonade again. Or dare we hope Mr. McDonald is in need of another employee?"

Nerves tangled, stirring toward anger. "I'm sure there are viable options other than fast-food establishments."

"Viable options? Such as what? Becoming a dancer, like your mother?"

It had taken Sydney forty-three agonizing days to relearn to walk. She would never, the doctors told her, ride again. But the cruelty of her grandmother's words put steel in her spine. "Perhaps I will," she said.

Gloria watched her for several seconds, then turned mechanically toward her son. "I warned you, did I not?"

"Don't be a child, Sydney," Leonard snapped, but her mind had snagged on the other woman's words.

"Warned him about what?"

Gloria raised a single brow.

"Stop it. Both of you!" Leonard ordered. "Let's stay on track here. David has come tonight at my request. He's willing to forgive and forget."

"Willing to . . ." Sydney pulled herself from her grandmother's gaze and huffed a laugh.

"How many unattached millionaires do you think your father can scare up for you, Sydney? Do you believe yourself to be such a paragon that the numbers are limitless?"

"Maybe I don't want a millionaire. Maybe I just want to be . . . normal. To be happy."

"It's always about what you want, isn't it?" Gloria's voice was censorious, her expression mocking.

Still, for one crazy second, Sydney almost thought she was joking, but the apocalypse had not yet arrived. "I would think that where my marriage is concerned, my wishes could at least be taken into account."

"There are consequences to poor judgment. Your father learned that the hard way. Don't make the same mistake."

"What mistake?"

"Quiet, Mother."

"What does she mean?" Sydney asked.

Leonard remained silent. His mother shook her head as if bemoaning his weaknesses.

"I mean that if you continue to be a disappointment to this family, there are others who would be happy to take your place as heir apparent."

"Continue to be . . ." The words hurt her throat. She failed to push out the rest of the sentence. Instead, she remained as she was, frozen into immobility as a dozen painful memories burned through her. But finally she managed to move, to pivot away. Tears stung her eyes.

"Where do you think you're going?" The words were as sharp as razors.

Anywhere, Sydney thought. Anywhere but here.

Chapter 1

"Hey, grab the coffee, will you, Syd?" Colt Dickenson was Indian dark and cowboy lean. He had a take-no-prisoners grin and a rugged workingman's body. But none of those attributes was particularly surprising. What stopped Sydney dead in her tracks was his easy informality, the offhand camaraderie with which he seemed to treat every individual who crossed his well-trodden path . . . including paying guests.

This was Sydney's third day in South Dakota. Her second at the Lazy Windmill, the "anywhere" her favorite cousin Tori had found for her. A way to escape from the chilly disapproval of her family and a means of visiting the state of her mother's origins.

The Lazy was a strange place, more under-funded working ranch than cushy vacation spot. A place where they did not, apparently, have staff to fetch and serve.

"Not necessary," Emily said and reached for the coffee. Emily Kane, the African-American cook, had not yet reached her twentieth birthday. Sydney was certain of that. But the girl seemed to manage the weathered old farmhouse as easily as

17

she did motherhood. Even now, Colt stood near the table gently propelling Emily's mocha-skinned baby through the air like a slow-motion 747. The situation was disconcerting on several levels. Sydney, for instance, could barely manage being a *daughter* and had never, as far as she could recall, impersonated so much as a small-engine Cessna. "Have a seat. Breakfast'll be ready in a minute."

"No, I'll get it," Sydney said and bumped herself back to the here and now, though honest to God, the kitchen was as foreign to her as Tel Aviv. In the world of the Wellesleys, a lady *managed* the kitchen. She did not enter it. The battered coffeepot was as unfamiliar to her as the scarred, claw-footed table that stood barely five feet from the stove. But the dark bean fragrance that wafted from the coffee felt friendly and warm as she filled their cups.

"Thanks," Colt said and cuddled the infant against his flannel-clad chest. The baby was dressed in a nubby, parti-colored sweater that matched her mother's to oddball perfection. She did not, however, sport the kind of abused army boots that Emily seemed to favor. "You sleep okay?"

"Yes." The scene was surreal for a number of reasons. Rough-stock rodeo cowboy Colt Dickenson, for instance, had no blood ties to the child. And blood, Grandmother said, would always tell. Neither was he the mother's lover; his devotion to Casie Carmichael, the owner of this tattered-around-the-edges ranch, had been immediately apparent upon Sydney's arrival, making his dedication to Baby Bliss patently odd. Perhaps it was that very peculiarity that caused the pang near her heart. "Thank you." It was strangely difficult to drag her gaze from the pair; she had never liked children. Not even when she *was* a child. Or, perhaps more correctly, she had never quite mastered being one. "I slept quite well."

"So the bunkhouse wasn't too cold?" Colt settled the infant into the crook of his right arm with extraordinary casualness and reached for his coffee cup with his left.

Sydney shifted carefully into a nearby chair. Limping, Grandmother said, should be limited to decorated war veterans and panhandlers with cardboard signs. A Wellesley invited neither speculation nor pity. "It was fine."

"Good to know." He narrowed his eyes against the silvery curl of caffeinated steam as he raised the coffee to his lips. The clay mug was earth-toned and strangely misshapen. "We don't get many guests this early in the spring."

Outside the far-seeing windows, the temperature had not topped thirty degrees since Sydney's arrival. "So this is spring?" she asked and cautiously tested her coffee. True to form, it was strong enough to knock the uninitiated out cold and hit her with the gentleness of a stun gun.

"It's not always so balmy this time of year. Is it, Soph?" he asked and glanced up as Sophie Jaeger entered the room. The girl, once a paying guest like herself, was dressed in riding breeches and a sleek, long-sleeved tee. She was even younger than the Lazy's dreadlocked cook, but if Sydney understood the dynamics correctly, she managed the ranch horses as efficiently as the other girl cared for the house.

"Coffee," Sophie said robotically and poured herself a cup before sliding into a chair across from Colt. "And no, this isn't spring." She wrapped cold-reddened hands around her mug, sighed, and took a drink. "How did you get in here so fast?"

It was barely seven o'clock in the morning, but judging by their rosy cheeks and heat-deprived expressions, they had both been out of doors for some time.

Colt grinned. "Motivation. Heard Em was making Bacon Bake."

"With biscuits and rhubarb jam," Emily added and gave something inside the discolored oven an exploratory poke.

Dickenson lifted his shoulders in an "enough said" shrug. "You get chores done already?"

Sophie took a grateful swig of coffee and

didn't seem to care that it could surely erode tooth enamel from thirty paces. "The stalls are clean. The horses fed."

" 'They say she's grounded 'til she's dead,' " Emily crooned and plunked a pitcher of frothy goat's milk onto the center of the table.

They stared at her in wordless concert.

"Garth Brooks. What kind of cowpokes are you? 'Ain't Going Down ('Til the Sun Comes Up).' It was a hit single." She propped her fists on curvy hips. "Do I need to sing the entire song?"

"No!"

"Thanks anyway."

Sophie and Colt spoke in unison and with some alacrity.

Emily deepened her scowl, causing Colt to change the subject, perhaps more out of a sense of self-preservation than curiosity.

"So who had the honor of milking Bodacious this morning?"

Sophie grinned as she reached for the pitcher.

"You got out of it again?" Dickenson swayed, rocking the baby against his chest "What was the bet?"

"Listen . . ." Emily sounded honestly peeved and maybe a little impressed as she pointed a charred wooden spoon at the other girl. "There were, like . . . a *hundred* pancakes." She turned back to stir something on the stove. The house smelled like Sundays from a bygone era. "Nobody should have been able to eat that many. Not if she's human, anyway."

"Way to go, Soph," Dickenson said and gave her a fist bump.

The girl shrugged, pretty face smug. "It's a gift."

"And a curse," Em added grumpily. "Hey, Ty."

Sydney glanced toward the door. The boy who entered had the angular build of a teenager and the solemn eyes of an ancient. He nodded his shaggy head silently and took a seat across from Sophie. Their gazes met for one fleeting instant, then snapped hotly away.

Dickenson raised his brows at Sydney as if sharing a little-known secret about young love.

"How's Angel?" he asked.

The boy lifted a shoulder that was leaning hard toward manhood. "Hungry."

"If that mare eats any more, we're going to have to make the barn aisles wider."

"Like you should talk," Emily muttered.

The front door creaked and in a moment Casie Carmichael entered the room. Still shedding her well-worn outdoor clothes, the Lazy's owner was tall and lean, with nondescript hair and unspectacular features. She did not, to Sydney's way of thinking, possess a single outstanding physical characteristic. So why did both males watch her every move as if she might, at any given moment, yank a rabbit out of a hat?

"Morning," she said.

Emily, still apparently peeved about the hundred-pancakes wager, wordlessly pressed a cup of coffee into her hands.

Casie murmured her thanks and settled her gaze on Colt. "I can't believe you beat me in again."

"Em's making Bacon Bake." His tone suggested the casserole held the secrets of the universe.

"You didn't have no trouble out there, did you?" Tyler's eyes, always solemn, looked as worried as a hound's.

"No trouble." Casie cast a maternal smile over the rim of her coffee cup, though apparently there were no familial bonds between her and Tyler, either. "But we do have three new lambs."

"Already?"

"I would have checked the ewes," Colt said. "But . . ."

". . . there's Bacon Bake," Sophie finished for him. He chuckled as he pulled out a chair for his fiancée.

Emily nestled a basket of steaming biscuits between two mismatched plates. "I suppose the lambs are going to start coming for reals any time now."

"Like darts from a blowgun."

"I'll take the night shift," Tyler said.

"Don't you have an essay due?" Casie set her

mug on the table before pulling the baby into her arms and settling into a chair.

"For Mrs. Trembly's class?" Colt asked, and taking the adjacent seat, poured milk into her glass. It had the consistency and hue of fresh whipping cream.

Ty nodded and Colt shivered.

"Holy sh . . ." He paused, cast a wary eye in Casie's direction, and let the expletive die on his tongue. "Listen, I'll take night duty. What's a couple hundred sheep compared to Terrible Trembly? You just make sure you don't piss her off. She's been gunning for me for more than a decade."

"What'd you do?" Emily asked and set a bubbling casserole beside the crock of preserves.

"Nothing," Colt said, and slathering butter onto a biscuit, slipped it almost surreptitiously onto Casie's plate.

His fiancée's expression was an exasperated meld of gratitude and amusement. "Except glue her chair to the floor."

"Well, there was that. Help yourself, Syd," Colt said and indicated the Bacon Bake.

She took a modest serving and turned the handle of the spatula toward Sophie, who wasn't, she noticed, quite so cautious about portions.

"And hide her syllabus," Casie added.

Colt grinned and dished the entrée onto both of their plates.

Casie sighed. "And turn chickens loose in her classroom."

"That was probably my best . . ." he began, but one glance at Casie made him clear his throat and taste his breakfast. After the first bite, he cast a dreamy glance at the cook and thumped a fist against his chest as if the emotions there were too much to express in words.

Emily rolled her eyes as she lifted the baby from Casie's arms, but didn't quite manage to hide her grateful smile behind the child's buoyant curls.

Quiet settled in for a moment, broken only by the sound of clinking flatware and contented sighs. Sydney sampled a biscuit. It was unreasonably tasty, possibly because it consisted of approximately five hundred fat grams per serving.

Colt was the first to break the silence. "How's that palomino doing, Soph?"

The girl's milk mustache looked ad-campaign perfect beneath her polished features. "At riding or driving?"

"I don't know." He turned toward Sydney and raised his brows at her sparsely filled plate, but didn't broach the subject. "Which do you prefer, Syd? Saddles or carriages?"

"What?" She felt the muscles tighten like winched ropes across her shoulders and back.

"Horses," he said. "You do ride, don't you?"

"No!" The word darted from her lips. She

forced a smile, and abandoning the half-finished biscuit, pushed her hands beneath the table. She had been warned against stressing her still-knitting femur and fragile spine. But no one had said she wouldn't *want* to ride. That her hands would shake and her heart pound at the very thought of doing what had once made her life worth living. "I just came to relax." She tapped her thigh with a restless index finger. "I enjoy hiking." Walking was, in fact, highly recommended to hasten her rehabilitation. "I don't ride."

"Well . . ." Colt polished off a rhubarb-spread biscuit and reached for another. "We can fix that." He cut his gaze toward Sophie. "You've got some time for a lesson, don't you?"

Sydney entwined her fingers and felt sweat prickle her hairline. "That won't be necessary." The words sounded prissy and arctic cold against the farmhouse's cozy bonhomie. The room went quiet. It was Ty's muted voice that interrupted the silence.

"Soph's a real good teacher." The boy's tone was strangely soothing, as if he not only sensed her reluctance but understood her fear. "And you could ride Angel if you want. She maybe ain't as pretty as the palomino, but pretty don't pay no bills."

Casie's gaze landed softly on the boy. Colt pointed at him with a fork.

26

"Now there's an offer," he said. "Ty loves that mare more than . . ." He skipped his attention to the teenage girl across the table from him. Their gazes met before she snapped hers away with a disapproving scowl. "More than most," he finished and grinned.

Sophie's cheeks flushed prettily and Colt laughed again as if all was well. As if the world was good and right and unfettered joy waited just around the bend.

But Sydney knew better. Unfettered joy was not for poor little rich girls like her. Good-hearted men with knockout grins did not cuddle her like precious treasure against their work-hardened chests. Wounded youngsters didn't bask in her healing presence.

Disaster struck at mind-numbing intervals, leaving her with a disappointed father and throbbing limbs. She pressed a palm against her thigh and tried to breathe through the memories.

It was Emily's rendition of "North to Alaska" that brought Sydney back to the present. Sung to a rap beat, it was punctuated with a spoon against the countertop and performed without so much as a nod to any recognizable tune. Sophie groaned, Ty cracked a captivating grin, and Colt catapulted into a ludicrous story about the correlation between barometric pressure and bucking bulls.

And despite everything, their homey goodwill

seeped slowly into Sydney's bones like errant sunshine. As they talked and laughed and badgered, hope unfurled cautiously inside her battered soul.

So what if Leonard Wellesley wasn't going to be nominated for Father of the Year? So what if Grandmother bore a striking resemblance to Adolf Hitler, and David Albrook, her erstwhile fiancé, preferred the company of girls barely out of diapers?

The others gathered around the Lazy's battered table probably didn't come from perfect circumstances, either. Yet they had somehow forged this astounding warmth, this unheard-of contentment.

So maybe . . . Sydney's heart sped along in her chest. Her muscles trembled with anticipation. Maybe she could find the same thing. Maybe all she needed was a few hundred acres of South Dakota, a couple inspiring vistas, and a front porch.

The blossom of hope opened wider.

It was said that money couldn't buy happiness, but so far as she knew, the theory had never been conclusively proven.

Chapter 2

"Hello again." Philip Jaeger shared his daughter's glossy good looks. Like Sophie, he was tall and well built. More importantly, he was a Realtor who knew the area. A Realtor, Sydney hoped, who would find her a home in the deep hills of South Dakota.

Nerves jangled down her arms to her fingertips.

"Good morning," Sydney said and concentrated on moving smoothly from the Lazy's graveled drive onto the step of his three-quarter-ton pickup truck. Her thigh complained, but she ignored the niggle of pain. Sunlight warmed her face and turned the world a hopeful shade of impending spring. "Where are we headed today?"

"I thought we'd look at that property near Pringle first, then head over to Minnekahta."

"The place you e-mailed me about. The one with the brick silo?"

"It's got a house, too," he said and gave her a winning smile.

She tilted her regal head in a gesture that suggested she would reserve judgment on whether or not this particular structure deserved the title. They had seen more than a few that didn't warrant such an optimistic nomenclature, but she felt hopeful about the silo.

"Maybe it's not quite as posh as what you're accustomed to," he said.

"Maybe it's not quite as posh as the *silo*," she countered.

He chuckled. "I almost bought a farm in California a few years back," he offered.

"Almost?" Sydney asked and thought that could be the title of her theme song. Almost won the World Cup. Almost qualified for the Olympics. Almost got married. But things were going to be different now. She could feel it in her still-mending bones.

"When my ex and I were planning to get back together," he said.

She watched the country roll past. Long valleys sweeping up to red-rocked cliffs. Pines spearing toward the sapphire sky like ancient arrowheads. And peace. Everywhere she looked, there was that quiet peacefulness that spoke to some unknown place deep inside her.

"Monica." He pronounced the name with a long e sound and a fair amount of pain, she thought. Or maybe it was anger. Sometimes the two were almost indistinguishable. "Sophie's mother."

In Sydney's mind, she sat in her own kitchen in her own tidy little cottage. The broad bowed windows gave her a sweeping view of endless hills and far-flung valleys. Some might find it lonely, but not her. And not the openhearted people who would share her life. The dream man across from her had a cowboy's compact body and a crooked grin. Someone cracked a joke. It might even have been her.

"Here it is."

Jaeger's words dragged her reluctantly back to the here and now.

"Red Rock Road," he said and turned right onto a narrow thoroughfare. "They say you shouldn't get back together just for the kids. That it doesn't work out." He checked the notes he'd written on a steno pad in loose, sprawling letters.

Outside the window, the land had become rougher, broken into sienna bluffs and soft-shadowed valleys. A small wooden bridge spanned the gravel road where a stream, swollen from melting snow and a thousand meandering rivulets, wound eastward. She powered down her window. Tranquility whispered in. The hustling water chuckled quietly. Each ripple glistened like a diamond.

"I think this might be the place." He stopped the car and lifted a map from his lap. "Guess it borders Wind Cave Park. And . . . yeah . . . this is the west boundary of—"

But she didn't hear the rest of his words, because she knew where she was. She was home.

Chapter 3

"You what?" Casie Carmichael's tone was surprised.

Emily's was shocked. "You bought a ranch?"

Sydney laughed and glanced at her Realtor's daughter. But Sophie Jaeger seemed as uninformed as any of them. "I thought your father might have told you."

Sophie shook her head, unaware and unimpressed, it seemed. "Can you pass the beans?"

Emily did so without taking her attention from Sydney. "For reals? A ranch."

"Eight hundred and fifty-seven acres." Sydney could barely believe it herself. It had all happened so fast, but some things were meant to be. Tragedies could foster new beginnings. And she desperately needed just that. The papers were signed. The money distributed. She'd paid in full. There had been other options, Mr. Jaeger had said. Down payments, loans, mortgages that extended to the middle of the century. But she had no collateral, and there was another bid on the table. She had moved quickly out of necessity. Her father would be surprised at first—maybe even angry. But in the end he would applaud her decisiveness. She was sure of it. The fact that she had turned off her phone after the purchase had nothing to do with uncertainty. She just needed some time to think things through before discussing it with him.

"Where at?" Casie asked.

The door opened and closed. Colt stepped inside. "What'd I miss?"

"Green bean casserole," Sophie said.

He took his usual spot at the table and reached for the dish the girl passed his way.

"Sydney bought a ranch," Casie said.

"No kidding?" He scooped up some beans. "Here in the Hills?"

"Forty miles west," Sydney said and found it was almost impossible to suppress a childish giggle. Where on earth did that come from? She hadn't giggled even when she *was* a child.

Colt took an oat roll from the wooden bowl that was circulating. It glistened with a blush of butter. "What are your plans for it?"

"Well . . . I want . . ." Solitude, happiness, peace, maybe even love. In short, she wanted what the residents of the Lazy had, what they shared in this humble little tumbledown shack, but the words sounded silly even to herself. "I was looking for an investment."

"So you're not planning to live there?" Casie asked.

"Not full time, certainly."

"There's a house on the property?" Emily asked and handed scalloped potatoes off to Sophie.

"You might call it that." Sydney almost winced at the memory of the sorry buildings that occupied the acreage.

"What would *you* call it?" Emily asked.

"Prehistoric art?"

Colt chuckled as he accepted the potatoes. "We're very cutting-edge here in the Hills."

Sydney shifted her gaze back to her meal. "I'll have to tear it down. Build new." She sampled the beans. Some kind of fried onions were sprinkled across the top. They managed to be creamy, crunchy, and outrageously delicious all at once. "In fact, I was wondering if *you* might help me, Emily." She added a scoop of potatoes to her plate and didn't bother counting fat grams even though Grandmother had made it abundantly clear that overindulgence was meant for the masses. Like public displays of affection . . . and emotions of any kind. But Grandmother wasn't here. Sydney felt a giddy little kick of freedom. Or was it nerves?

"Help you with what?"

"With the finishing touches, once it's built. I'm told the bunkhouse is your brainchild."

"It was all her doing," Casie said. Pride hummed in her voice like a beloved melody. How surreal would it be to have that kind of support. That kind of acceptance. The idea was mind-boggling. "She handled all the decorating and most of the refinishing. Those are even her photographs on the walls."

"It's all very nice," Sydney said and realized she meant it. At first, perhaps, the old chicken-coop-turned-living-quarters had seemed a little chintzy. A little cut-rate and shabby. But her viewpoint had changed since her arrival. "I'd like to replicate that same rustic ambiance."

"Replicate?" Emily said.

Colt chuckled. "Em doesn't replicate anything," he said. "If the counter looks like it spent a decade in the cattle yards, that's because it spent a decade in the cattle yards."

"Really?"

" 'Fraid so." Emily nodded.

"Well . . ." Sydney lifted her milk; there seemed to be a dearth of mineral water imported from the Alps in these parts. "Here's to cattle yards."

They raised their beverages in unison and clinked mismatched glasses. Sydney took a sip, blinked, and didn't quite manage to refrain from coughing.

"Are you okay?" Casie sounded concerned, Emily winced, and Colt laughed.

"Some people think goat milk is an acquired taste." Reaching out, he swatted her on the back with companionable ease. "We actually thought Soph was going to die of dehydration before she took a shine to it."

"And look at her now," Emily quipped. "Begging to milk Bo every day of the week."

Sophie took another deep quaff of milk and shook her head. "I won fair and square."

The older girl scowled. "But you probably want to—"

"I don't."

"You didn't bet her again," Colt said and Emily erupted.

"There were a dozen sausages! No lie! A full—" The girl's harangue was interrupted by an ancient phone that hung near the stove.

"I'll get it," Casie said, but Emily was already turning away, eyes bright with anticipation.

"It's probably Linc," she announced. If she was trying to act nonchalant, she was light-years off the mark.

"Linc?" Sydney asked and returned her glass gingerly to the table.

"Bliss's father," Casie said. "He's spending a few days with his family in Detroit."

"Does he live here?" Sydney asked and Colt snorted.

Sophie rolled her eyes. "Dickenson doesn't think Lincoln's good enough to tie his little Emily's combat boots."

"I didn't say that," he argued.

"I believe what you said was *nobody* was good enough to tie your Emily's combat boots," Casie countered.

"Yeah." Sophie nodded at her employer while buttering her already buttered roll. "But I forget. Was that before or after he threatened to shoot off Linc's ear?"

"Both," Casie said, and Colt grinned.

"Maybe I was kinda hard on the gangly little—"

"Sydney . . ." Emily stood in the middle of the kitchen, spiraled telephone cord stretched tight. "It's for you."

"Me?" She actually shook her head, sure Emily was wrong. Who would have bothered to track her down? No one wanted to speak to her.

But the dread that suddenly curdled her stomach told a different story entirely. Tragedy had struck before.

"Hello?" Her voice sounded rusty, as if her trachea were being constricted. She tightened her hand on the old-fashioned receiver and felt her pulse beat a hard shuffle in her wrists.

"Sydney."

"Father?" A half-dozen emotions struck her at once, a tangle of feelings so complex, she couldn't sort one from the other. She glanced toward the people who watched her from only a few feet away. "What's wrong?"

"What indeed?"

She shook her head, confused, as images of black burned through her mind. Black veils. Black suits. Black dirt, thrown atop her mother's gleaming casket. "Is Grandmother all right?"

"I heard you made a purchase." A noise clinked in the background. Ice, she thought, languishing regally in his two fingers of Royal Salute Scotch.

"Oh . . ." Everything was fine. *Everyone* was fine. She tried to relax her grip on the phone and pushed out a laugh. It sounded breathy and false. "You scared me. So everything's okay?"

"Is it?" he asked.

Confusion swirled in her. "There's nothing wrong with Tori, is there?" Victoria Frances was the closest thing she had ever had to a sister even though her cousin and her father had barely spoken since Tori had colored her hair an unacceptable shade of ash three years before. Overall, however, Tori had toed the Wellesley line with old-world aplomb. Unless you considered the tiny tattoo inked behind her left ear, which Leonard invariably did.

"Was this your cousin's idea? Is that it?"

"What?" She glanced toward the others again. They had returned to their meal. Only Emily watched her, but certainly they all heard, all listened. "No. I mean . . ." She lowered her voice, then turned briskly and slipped around the corner. Faded wallpaper marched down the hall and up the stairs. "I just needed to get away for a while. She found me a place to stay, but—"

"So this fiscal disaster was your own brainstorm?"

She exhaled and lowered her voice even more, unsurprised that he had already learned of her purchase. "It's beautiful land, Father. You should see it. I really think—"

"I assume you obtained the mineral rights, at least."

"The mineral rights?"

He breathed a laugh. "If it weren't for the tests, I would swear we shared no blood at all. I knew you were irresponsible, Sydney, but I won't have you living in North Dakota like some back-woods hippie."

"South Dakota."

"What?"

"I'm in South Dakota." She sounded like a recalcitrant preschooler, but she couldn't help it. At five she had sounded like she was a thirty-year-old.

"Listen, young lady, I'm not going down this road."

"What road?"

"Is this an attempt to force me to prove my feelings for you?"

He couldn't, she noticed, even say the word *love*.

"No." She squeezed her eyes shut and wondered if she was wrong. Maybe that was exactly what this was. A shakedown to produce some sort of emotion, some sort of honest inter-action. "This isn't a lemonade stand, Father. I—"

"Come home," he ordered. "First flight out."

She huffed a breath of surprise. "I can't just—"

"First flight," he repeated, "or there will be consequences."

Chapter 4

"So . . ." Philip Jaeger had his Realtor smile firmly in place. Sydney simply stared in return, grappling with a dozen anxieties, a million insecurities suddenly laid bare to the world. Two days had passed since her conversation with Leonard. Three nights in a moldering motel room off Highway 16 had brought reality home to her in a tidal wave of regret. She must have been insane to buy this place, to think she could magically re-create what Casie and her crew had at the Lazy. Hell, maybe she was crazy just to *want* to. "You're thinking of living here now?" If he was trying to make it sound as if the idea wasn't entirely ludicrous, he missed the mark by a mile.

They stood in the kitchen of the log house she had purchased only days before. *Ramshackle* might have been one word for it. *Kindling* would be more apt.

"It'll only be for a short while," Sydney said

and slipped bumpily into her cool demeanor. Her stomach jumped. "Until I can start work on the new house."

Lies. All lies. The bomb her father had hinted at had made a direct hit. She had no money for reconstruction. The pimply-faced motel clerk had told her that much. Her credit cards, one in every precious-metal color, were no longer valid. Luckily, Tori had paid for her stay at the Lazy, but those blissful days were over. Her father had cut her off.

"I will say I'm a bit surprised," Philip said and glanced around the kitchen as if it weren't a short step up from purgatory. "I'm not sure this place is going to be up to your usual standards."

She almost laughed out loud. "They say hardship is good for the soul."

"Do they?" Jaeger asked and ran a finger across the blotchy yellow Formica that flowed like curdled milk over the countertop.

"Or some such tripe," she muttered.

He laughed. "Listen," he said, tone relentlessly upbeat. "I own a couple decent rental units in town. How about you stay in one of them until the weather warms up again?"

As if that was ever going to happen. It had snowed the night before, two inches of heavy accumulation that stuck to every surface like tar.

Out east the apple blossoms would be bursting to life and the foals skipping across pastures as green as shamrocks. But the pastures were owned by David Albrook, she reminded herself, and the foals belonged to a Chinese syndicate.

A pip of noise sounded from beneath the scarred cabinets.

Philip Jaeger made a face. "The rentals aren't fancy," he admitted. "But they're mice free."

"Mice?" The meaning of his words came home to her with a start. "There are mice here?"

He cleared his throat and looked as if he wanted to laugh, but managed sobriety with an effort. "To tell you the truth, Sydney, vermin might be the least of your problems."

He watched her mentally brace herself, watched her shore up her defenses.

"What are the worst of my problems?" she asked.

"Well . . ." He shrugged. "Like I said before . . ." he began, gently reminding her of his former caveats. He was all for camaraderie, but even more for covering his own ass. "No one's lived here for years. And you made it very clear you didn't intend to do so, either. So there might be a few things that make this property kind of . . ." He tilted his head. "Unlivable. At present, anyway."

For a second she was tempted almost beyond control to grab him by the lapels and tell him to spit it the hell out, but maybe she had made enough mistakes to last into the next millennium.

"Okay . . ." She gave him a prim nod, neat and crisp as if her life hadn't fallen into shambles around her ears. "What are the things I have to worry about first?"

"Well . . ." He nodded rhythmically. "Water."

She waited for him to continue. When he failed to do so, she still refrained from shaking him. A Wellesley did not shake. But maybe she wasn't a Wellesley anymore. Her people had always been tied to money, to power, to prestige. If that was gone . . . "What about water?"

"I mean, it *has* water," he hastened to add. "So you're in luck there."

She gave him the slightest corner of a scowl. It wasn't as if they were in the Mojave Desert; of course they had water.

"Lots of places around here don't," he added. "But I'm not sure the place was properly winterized before the previous tenants moved out. They were just renting, you know, and sometimes . . ." He shrugged. "Well . . . they may not have drained the pipes. They didn't take the best care of the place."

She waited several seconds, in case he wanted to laugh at the ridiculousness of the statement, but he resisted. Philip Jaeger had a good deal of self-control, too, it seemed.

"Very well," she said and wished she could throw up the yogurt she had eaten for breakfast. But that was another thing a Wellesley didn't do.

Bodily functions were inconspicuous and dignified, performed only when absolutely necessary. "What will it cost to drain the pipes now?"

He stared back at her. A half-dozen naked emotions skittered across his face. The first was humor, but it was rapidly replaced by something that looked suspiciously like pity . . . a feeling she detested more than the sliced beef liver she had been served without fail every Tuesday at Arbor House. "Listen," he said. "I'll give you a good deal on one of those rentals."

For a moment she was almost tempted to ask for a dollar figure on that "good deal," but all she had left in her checking account was a few thousand dollars. Practicality suggested she do whatever it took to preserve that paltry sum.

So she tilted her chin a little and steeled her spine. "I'm sure that's very . . . generous of you, Mr. Jaeger, but if you'll just tell me how to get the place winterized, I'm certain I'll be perfectly . . ." She intended to push out the word *happy,* but even Sydney Wellesley at the top of her game wouldn't be able to pull off a fabrication of such astronomical proportions. ". . . *content* here."

He refrained from glancing around. It probably wasn't a simple task. Train wrecks, after all, always invited interest. "Okay. Well, you don't have to winterize it now."

"Then why did you just imply the opposite?"

He opened his mouth as if to explain things, but finally smiled again. "How about I just try to get things working for you?"

"Well . . ." She spread her hands and focused her attention on the ragged nail on her right index finger. "If you insist."

"I do," he said, and glancing down the stairs, barely shuddered as he headed into what had surely been originally intended as a torture chamber.

Sydney watched his descent for a moment, then exhaled carefully and forced herself out of the kitchen. Not a single piece of furniture graced the family room. On the other hand, it was the proud owner of a stark white toilet seat. So perhaps the davenport was in the bathroom, she thought, and was less than surprised to learn that she didn't have enough energy to investigate. Momentarily comfortable with her weaknesses, she wandered into what might have been a parlor in some long-ago time. It was empty except for a half-rolled-up swath of like some-thing regurgitated by a love shack from the sixties.

The rest of the house was no better. The second stair gave way under her weight. The runner was half torn away. At the top of the steps, the walls were covered with stained paper and peeling paint. Up here there was no carpet, just yellowed vinyl flooring that curled at the corners and crackled if she dared venture across it. She turned away, but stark reality struck her from every angle. The missing doors, the pitted walls, the broken windows, the . . .

The windows. She found herself pulled across the floor, eyes glued on the center of the panes. The glass was cracked or missing completely, but beyond those shattered squares, the world swept away in an eternity of tree-lined hills and endless skies. From this vantage point, not another building could be seen. Only open land and gnarled evergreens. Red bluffs and pristine snow.

She drew a careful breath, and in that moment a deer stepped out of the brush. Delicate as a dancer, she lifted her muzzle as if testing the breeze. Her eyes were dark and limpid and in their depths there was both wisdom and wonder. She gazed into the distance as if contemplating the future, as if challenging the elements.

"Good news!" Jaeger yelled from downstairs.

The doe snapped her attention toward the house and then she was gone, leaping across the new-fallen snow like a sprinter, all speed and grace and wild optimism.

Goose bumps prickled along Sydney's arms.

"Ms. Wellesley?"

She turned toward the sound of his voice. "I'm up here."

His footsteps tapped toward her, tripped on the

second step, then hustled along. In a moment he breezed in. "I thought for a moment you'd hopped the four twenty-five back to Virginia."

She inhaled slowly, bracing herself, remembering the doe. "As I said . . ." She clasped her hands together, reaching for strength. "I'll be staying here."

"Well . . ." He smiled, but there was something about the expression that clearly questioned her sanity. "In that case, come on. I'll show you what we've got."

She followed him down stairs that moaned like ghosts. He glanced back. "You okay?"

"Of course," she said and picked up the pace.

"I thought maybe you were limping."

"No," she lied and stepped onto the orange-and-green carpet. It felt strangely crusty under her feet. What exactly would cause a carpet to be crusty?

"Okay." He led her into the kitchen. "Are you ready for this?" His tone was effusive, his smile a little too toothy as he reached out and turned the tap.

A choking sound issued from the faucet. It coughed, wheezed, and spat forth a sludge-like substance that was the color of urine and the consistency of mud.

Sydney stared, struck dumb, as a toxic-looking substance spattered into the stained porcelain of the sink.

"All right, it's not perfect," Jaeger admitted, optimism leaking a little from his tone. "But look. It's clearing up some already."

Panic squeezed Sydney like a sponge, but she forced herself to remember the hills that rolled like magic outside her window, the doe, the very image of independence and power.

"It'll be fine," she said and pulled her gaze from the pseudo-water with an effort.

"Sure," he agreed and turned off the tap. "Unfortunately, I wasn't so lucky with the furnace."

Her stomach twisted. "I beg your pardon?"

"I'm afraid you're going to have to hire someone for that." He winced as he glanced about. "And to replace the flooring. And maybe . . ." Taking the few steps to the stove, he fiddled with the knobs on the scarred face of the oven. Nothing seemed to happen. "Guess you'll have to have someone take a look at that, too."

"Well . . ." She tightened her fists, loosened them restlessly. Perhaps the doe *had* been a sign. But maybe instead of advocating independence and strength, it was suggesting that she flee from this place as fast as her crippled leg could carry her. "I'm sure you know someone who can take care of those things."

He cleared his throat and glanced at her before shifting his gaze uncomfortably back toward the oven. "I'm afraid you're going to need several different people."

"Oh?" Fear crept along her spine.

"An electrician and a furnace man, at least. I mean, I suppose you don't want to do too much to the house since you're just planning to raze it later, but if you're hoping to stay here at all, you're going to need someone to replace a couple windows and get the heat working."

"I see. Well . . ." She put as much enthusiasm into the word as she could muster. But after a lifetime of presenting a bored mien to the world, enthusiasm wasn't exactly in her wheelhouse. "I guess I'll need several names from you then."

He canted his golden head. "I'll see what I can do, but . . ."

"But what?"

"This isn't exactly New York City."

She forced a look of surprise. "Are you sure?"

He chuckled. "Okay, it's not even Sioux Falls."

"But South Dakota does have blue-collar laborers. Correct?"

"Well, yes, of course. But sometimes . . ." He shrugged. "Sometimes it's difficult to get people to come out this far. Especially if you don't know them personally."

She interlaced her fingers, tamped down the panic that coiled in her stomach and crept up her esophagus. "I'm told the Lazy Windmill was in rather poor condition just a short while ago. I doubt they had to mortgage their souls for a working stove."

"Well . . . Casie's always taking in kids, and that Emily . . ." He shook his head. "She feeds anyone who wanders onto the property. Have you tasted her blue beef?"

She stared at him. Seconds ticked into silence as she formulated words. "Are you saying I have to be a sous chef to get my furnace working, Mr. Jaeger?"

"Well, no." He laughed. "But it couldn't hurt."

Chapter 5

Sydney had purchased a used mattress while spending one more night in that depressing little motel room off Highway 16. It was lumpy and stained, but at least it was small, which meant it cost less to have it delivered.

Later, she'd called the car rental company and extended her agreement. But she wouldn't be able to afford that luxury much longer. Panic scratched at her spine, but she pushed it down. Everything was going to be fine, she assured herself. Father would come around in a few weeks. He could be vindictive. She had known that since childhood, but he was loyal. After her mother's death, he'd not so much as glanced at another woman. Instead, he had remained true to his wife's memory. Of course, he had hardly waxed poetic about her or lulled Sydney to sleep with amusing anecdotes regarding their courtship. But he wasn't an amusing anecdote kind of man. As was his way, he had merely assured her that Winona Wellesley was the epitome of femininity . . . lovely, graceful, and morally above reproach. Sydney would do well to try to fill her pointe shoes.

So what in heaven's name was she doing here?

Had she really believed she could *buy* contentment? Had she truly thought she could change who she was? *What* she was? She was a Wellesley, not some softhearted country girl like Casie Carmichael who could right wrongs and alter lives.

Reality felt sharp-edged and brutal, but she turned toward the mattress. Night was falling and her electricity was unreliable. Best to get things done while she could, to keep moving. Grasping the mattress by the lone handle that strongly suggested it had survived a wild dog attack, she tugged it toward the stairway. She'd put it in the bedroom to the right of the steps. It wasn't the largest, but it boasted the window with the best view. The view of the doe. The view that would help her survive until her finances were back to normal. Until the world had turned right side up.

Stumbling backward with the mattress held tight to her chest, she struck the wall with her thigh. Pain slammed through her body. She tried to right herself, but she was already falling, toppling sideways with a rasping shriek.

Self-pity screamed through her. She slumped to the floor, eyes squeezed tight.

Pain throbbed in her thigh. Apparently, when bone perforates flesh it is disinclined to leave a neat little hole. A scar jagged like a lightning bolt at the site of her injury. It turned out her father had been right all along. Unlike her mother, whose athleticism and grace had awed audiences on a hundred stages, Sydney was meant for a more placid role. While she had inherited dark hair and small stature from her maternal side, she did not have Winona's physical strength. Fragility had been handed down from her paternal grandmother, who strongly believed a lady need lift nothing heavier than a demitasse. Horseman-ship, however, was to be tolerated. Jacqueline Bouvier Kennedy had kept ponies on the lawn of the White House, after all.

Sydney had been told from the start, however, that she was not equipped to ride the more demanding horses used for eventing and jumping. Even when fueled by adrenaline following her discovery of David in another woman's arms, she should have realized her limitations, or so Father had told her. She remembered the conver-sation in vague wisps and staccato ellipses. The anesthesia from her first surgery had not yet worn off. Much more powerful were the other memories that flashed through her mind. Endless falling. Breathless pain. The labored wheeze of her mount's last breaths, then the long slide into unconsciousness. . . . "You need help?"

Sydney jerked to a sitting position with a quick rasp of surprise. Agony still pulsed like a heartbeat in her thigh, but fear was her overriding emotion.

A man stood in the doorway . . . or maybe it was a bear. Backlit by the fast-sinking sun, he looked as big as a grizzly, but somewhat less domesticated. His face was bearded and shadowed by low brows and too long, seal-dark hair.

"No." She snapped her gaze away and pushed ineffectively at the mattress. "Thank you. I'm fine."

"You alone here?" he asked and took a step toward her.

She stopped struggling and glanced toward the cell phone she'd left well out of reach. "No, I'm not. My husband . . ." Swallowing, she searched for a likely name for her fictional hero. Hercules seemed a little theatrical. Popeye a bit cartoonist. "Conan." God help her. ". . . will be here any minute."

"Conan?"

"Yes. He just . . ." If she only had her phone . . . or pepper spray . . . or the ability to stand up. "He just stepped out for a minute."

"Okay." In the doorway of the ramshackle two-story, Hunter Redhawk felt his lips twitch with humor. Phil Jaeger, the Realtor from Rapid City, had said Sydney Wellesley might be a little sharp-edged, but he hadn't mentioned mental illness.

She was dressed in varying hues of charcoal, making her face look winter white by comparison. "He just went to check on the . . . barn." She pushed at the mattress that half lay across her legs. "Is there something with which I can help you?"

He kind of doubted it and considered saying as much. Or at least informing her that Conan was a name reserved for Hollywood beefcakes and late-night show hosts. He should have remained in Hot Springs. But now that he was here, it seemed patently unwise to tackle the winding roads back to his point of origin; his truck's headlights were on the fritz again, and there was a storm brewing. Still, there was something about Ms. Wellesley's snooty demeanor that made him long to be anywhere but here, or at least to fire up every hayseed utterance he'd ever heard. Which was a pretty impressive number, he realized, and couldn't think of a reason in the world not to utilize some of that white-trash phraseology. "So your ol' man ain't here right now?"

She twisted fretfully toward the door as if her every desire lay in that direction. "As I said, he's just a short distance away in the barn. He'll be here any second."

"You sure 'bout that?"

"I could hardly be mistaken."

Oh, yeah, she was snooty as hell, but she was scared, too, and though she hid it well enough, that knowledge made Hunter soften against his will. "I guess Phil must have forgotten to mention him."

"What?" Her gaze skittered past him toward the window, making him wonder, with just a dash of unacceptable humor, if she was honestly considering an escape by that route.

"Phil Jaeger . . ." He paused, letting the name sink it. "He said you might need some help here. But . . ." He glanced around. Honest to God, he'd never seen such a rat hole in his entire life. And he'd spent his first nine years on the rez. "I guess he was wrong."

"You're a friend . . ." Her brow furrowed as she let her attention fully settle on him for the first time. "You're a friend of Mr. Jaeger's?"

"Just an acquaintance," he said and sighed as he let her slip off the hook. "But I am a friend of the folks at the Lazy."

"You know Colt?"

Did she say the name as though Dickenson were a living legend? Not that Hunt cared. Colt was all right as rodeo cowboys went. And he was a pretty good guy to know in a pinch, but he'd been turning girls' heads since they were in short pants and the scenario was getting a little old. "Yeah. I know him. You need help?"

She let her gaze skim down from his face, over his frayed shirt and patched jeans, then straightened her back and gave him a tight smile. It was a damned weird scene, her sitting there as if she weren't, even now, being crushed beneath that awful mattress. "It's very kind of you to offer, Mr. . . ."

"Redhawk."

"Very thoughtful of you, Mr. Redhawk, but I've no desire to impose on your time."

He raised his brows at her. He'd gotten the brush-off a number of times in a plethora of situations, but really, he thought, this one took the cake.

"So Phil was wrong," he said, just to be sure.

"Yes." It looked as if she was holding her breath. "He was."

"All right then," he said and turned to leave, but there was something about the image of her flattened like a rag doll under that god-awful mattress that would weigh on his conscience, and he had enough damned regrets to last a lifetime. Pivoting back, he strode over to grasp the ragged, cord handle. And damn if she didn't glower while he lifted the mattress from her legs to prop it against the wall. She looked as haughty as a duchess. Except for those eyes.

Those lost-child eyes. And then there was her scent . . . like peaches on a summer breeze. It was as disconcerting as hell.

"Thank you," she said finally and managed with marvelous aplomb to make it sound as if she had done him a favor. "That will be all."

He forced himself to ignore both her scent and her eyes. "So you've got everything under control here?"

"Yes. Thank you. I do," she said and wrestled herself to her feet. By the time she was upright, her cheeks had lost their last vestige of color. Was she sick? he wondered. It seemed a distinct possibility. She was as thin as the blade of the bone-handled pocket knife his grandfather had given him on his fifth birthday.

He glanced around, nodded once. "Planning to rough it here?"

"Actually," she said and gritted a vicious smile, "I'm planning to burn it down and build new."

"No joke?"

She brushed at an invisible mote on the lapel of her cashmere coat. Her left sleeve, he couldn't help but notice, was covered in dust from shoulder to wrist. "None whatsoever."

Was there an accent in her better-than-thou voice? A hint of Southern with perhaps a dash of Bostonian mixed in? "Who are you using?"

She stiffened even more, which, honest to God, he wouldn't have thought possible unless she'd been petrified for posterity. "I beg your pardon?"

"What contractor?"

"Oh." She pursed her lips. "You've probably not heard of him."

He watched her in silence.

"He's not from this area."

"Where then?"

"Manhattan."

"Manhattan?"

She didn't take it back, though he could see in her eyes that she realized her mistake.

"Now, if you'll excuse me . . ." Her tone suggested she was about to have tea and crumpets . . . possibly with the queen . . . certainly with someone more acceptable than a half-breed Indian with dubious intentions. "I have things to do."

"Yeah y' do," he agreed and prepared to leave. But damn it, he couldn't pull the trigger. Clenching his jaw against his own stupidity, he turned back. "You're not staying the night."

"I beg your pardon," she said again, but it seemed perfectly clear that she had never had to beg for anything in her life. Still . . . He glanced out the open door to the west. The sky was as dark as sin, bubbling with impending mischief.

"It's gonna get ugly."

"*Get* ugly?" She laughed, then sobered quickly. "I do so appreciate your concern," she said and damned if she couldn't deliver a lie. "But there's no need for you to worry on my behalf."

She was smack-dab on the money there, he thought, and tried to force himself back to his truck. Failed again. "You got the furnace working, right?"

She followed his gaze out the door. The wind was rising, whistling through the trees that surrounded the house, rattling the windows. She shivered. But apparently pride was all she had left. "As I said, you needn't worry," she repeated and shifted her eyes back to him.

"Please shut the door on your way out," she added.

He wanted to laugh, wanted to razz her, wanted to ask her if she had any idea how incredibly ridiculous she looked standing in the middle of the rubble in her thousand-dollar coat and her old-money attitude, but there was something in her eyes . . . something almost hidden behind that haughty façade. Despair maybe. He tightened his fists and glanced at the gathering clouds.

"I could take a look at it." He hadn't meant to say the words, but there was nothing new about that. He'd said a thousand things he hadn't intended.

"If you're referring to the furnace, I must assure you it's been taken care of."

"You got it fixed?"

Her right index finger tapped against her too

thin thigh. "I have a gentleman coming this evening."

"From Manhattan?" he asked and managed, somehow, to contain his grin.

She concocted a smile of sorts. "From Rapid City."

A branch scraped nastily against a nearby window.

"He's never going to make it in this weather."

"Oh?" Her left brow rose the slightest degree. "Are you, by chance, a meteorologist?"

"Hunkpapa," he said.

She gave him a head tilt accompanied by pursed lips and accented by one raised brow . . . clearly the full arsenal of her disdain. "I'm uncertain if I should offer condolences or con-gratulations."

He almost laughed. "Lakota," he said. "On my father's side."

"Oh." He could see the thoughts flittering like butterflies through her mind: What was in his maternal heritage? Buffalo? Grizzly? "Well . . ." She intertwined her fingers, effectively quelling the movement of that one rogue digit. "While I appreciate your people's . . . travails . . . I fear I can't offer you employment at this time, Mr. Redhawk."

Travails? Good God! He shook his head and didn't bother to stifle his chuckle this time. Some things weren't worth the battle. "Well . . . I suppose a woman like you is used to being cold," he said, and stepping onto the porch, closed the door behind him.

A minute later he was back. "My battery's dead."

She remained as she was, facing the wall. "Believe me when I say I will call the police."

"Believe me when I say I'd kiss them on the mouth if they'd give me a lift back to town."

"Assuming that won't be sufficiently motivating, you could always walk. It's only fifteen miles or so."

"You're not from around here, are you?"

"What gave me away?" She turned toward him finally. Her tone was polished, her expression haughty, but her eyes . . .

He felt the grin drop from his lips; he'd always been a sucker for little girl eyes. "Listen . . . maybe we can help each other out."

"I highly doubt it," she said.

"Then I hope to God your pipes have been drained."

"Why are you people so obsessed with my pipes?"

"The temperature's going to drop tonight. If you don't get some heat in here, you're going to have a hell of a mess to clean up."

She laughed, but there was fear in her eyes. "A mess?" she said finally. "In this palace."

He stared at her. "Maybe we can work something out, Miss . . ."

61

"Mrs." She straightened her back to ramrod stiffness. "Mrs. Wellesley."

He scowled, shuffled one booted foot. "As in the duke?"

"I beg your pardon?"

"Wellesley, as in the Duke of Wellington?" he asked.

"Oh." For a moment surprise shone through her careful façade. "Yes. The first duke was, in fact, my progenitor."

"Kept your maiden name, did you?"

"I beg—" she began, but seemed to remember her newly proclaimed marital status in a moment. "Yes, of course. How did you know of the duke?"

"I read," he said. Then, "How about fifty bucks?"

"Well . . ." Her fingers had escaped. She tapped one restlessly against her thigh. If he were a professional gambler, which he had been for five months in Atlantic City, he would call that her tell. "Fifty dollars seems a bit steep, but if you could repair the furnace, I might be convinced to . . ." She pursed her lips. They were full and bright in stark contrast to the rest of her being. ". . . give you a meal . . . if you agree to vacate the premises once the task is complete."

He stared at her. Maybe he was being punked, he thought. He had a couple of friends and several brothers who would sell their dubious souls to see this, but the broken-down old house seemed to be lacking the necessary technology. "How about I take a look at your furnace for a meal and a jump."

Terror flashed in her eyes. He scowled, bemused, until he realized his statement might have sounded somewhat sexual in nature. Then, although he managed to control his chuckle, he couldn't quite do the same with his next words.

"I got the necessary cables."

Her eyes widened to barn-owl proportions, and damned if she wasn't holding her breath.

"My truck . . ." he reminded her finally. "It won't start."

She blinked at him, and there was something about that guileless mannerism that almost made him feel guilty.

"If I give you this . . . jump . . ." She said the word as if she were speaking a foreign language. "Do you vow to leave immediately afterward?"

He chuckled quietly, no longer able to resist. "Yeah."

Her frown might have been considered intimidating under less amusing circumstances. "Was that your solemn vow, Mr. Redhawk, or some response to a gastric disturbance?"

"Both," he said and laughed quietly as he made his way down the death-trap stairs to the torture chamber below.

Chapter 6

It was dark in the basement, the ancient walls were crumbling, and the furnace was older than sin. Which, according to Mrs. Big Crow, Hunter's fourth-grade Sunday school teacher, had first begun over an apple.

Hunter considered original sin as he tinkered with the furnace's wires and limit controls, but really, there was no hope until he had better tools; he'd give his kidneys for a screw gun and wire strippers. Still, fiddling with the transformer gave his hands something to do while he thought about his next move. After rattling the pipes, he made his way up the stairs, avoiding the third one, which was missing, and the top one, which was broken.

He glanced around the empty living room. Some of the broad white-pine logs that made up the walls were beginning to rot near the windows and the ancient brass ceiling lights were tarnished and dented, but in its day this old house was probably a beauty. Filled with laughter and light and homey scents from the kitchen. Now the silence felt as heavy as old regrets, the cold as invasive as cancer.

Hearing a noise, Hunter followed the sound toward the front of the ramshackle structure.

Sydney Wellesley stood with her back to him and turned with a start as he entered the doorway.

Fear shone again in her eyes, but she hid it carefully behind a cool demeanor. "Did you get it working?"

He shook his head and wondered what she was running from. "Can't. Not tonight, anyway. But I thought . . ." He stopped as he caught a glimpse of the room behind her. "You've got a fireplace?"

"Oh." She twisted to the right. "Yes, I believe I do."

He'd been fiddling with that piece of broken *antiquity* for half an hour and she had a fireplace? He strode past her into the room. Perhaps it had been a parlor at one time. Now it was a pit, except for the far wall, which was a masterpiece. A neglected masterpiece. Still, made of native granite and crumbling mortar, it ran ceiling to floor. "Look at that," he breathed and admired it with breathless wonder. He should have guessed a levelheaded old beauty like this would have such a practical heat source, but he'd spent a fair amount of his youth in government housing; they'd been lucky to have *air.*

Sydney had followed him halfway into the room. He could feel her presence behind him, or maybe he had left the front door open again.

"Where's the woodpile?" he asked.

"What?"

"Firewood," he said and turned toward her. "Do you have any?"

She cupped her hands loosely in front of her as if about to recite poetry. "Perhaps it seems as if this is my ancestral home, Mr. Redhawk, but in actuality this is all new to me."

He ignored her sarcasm, though it was, in fact, pretty impressive. "If we can get this thing working, it'll feel like a sweat lodge in here before morning."

She watched him as if he were a foreign species. "Mr. Redhawk—"

"My friends call me Hunt."

She tilted her head the slightest degree, like a monarch amid peasants, or maybe like a queen bee among cockroaches. "What do the rest of your acquaintances call you?"

"Amazing."

She waited as if expecting another answer, but she could wait till hell froze over, which, judging from the plummeting temperatures and her frosty expression, might be any minute.

"Very well . . . Hunt. Yes, I do have a fireplace, but to the best of my knowledge, I do not possess any firewood."

"Sure you do," he said and paced toward the door. "Get some supper cooking, duchess. I'm going to be hungry."

"My name is not—" she began, but he had already stepped onto the porch.

It was fully dark now. A sharp gust of wind slashed his face, but he closed the door and leaned into the oncoming storm.

Sydney glared after him before turning restlessly toward the nearest window. What had she done? And what was she going to do next? A dozen harried ideas raced like frightened rabbits through her mind. Conventional wisdom insisted that she cry uncle. That she call her father and beg for a first-class ticket back to Virginia. To civilization. To home. But the thought made her stomach cramp. Pride, it seemed, was a difficult thing to surrender. Especially when it was all you had. On the other hand, she did have this house. She winced as she glanced around, started when the door opened.

Hunter Redhawk stepped inside, arms filled with timber.

She watched him move to the fireplace. "Where did you get those?" she asked.

"There's a lot of deadwood in the world," he said and knelt to settle his burden on the god-awful carpet.

She raised one brow and wondered if he was referring to more than the logs. She wasn't dead-wood, she told herself. She would have considered cooking supper, if she had had any ingredients . . . or the ability to cook. Neither of those things being true, she would have been thrilled to fix the furnace . . . except, for obvious reasons, she hadn't done so. Neither had she brought in the logs. She pursed her lips and entwined her fingers in front of her.

"Got any matches?" he asked.

"I wasn't aware we were planning a barbecue," she said and remembered a boy mocking her years ago for her ineptitude with peanut butter and jelly. She had assured her teenaged detractor that she knew how to ring for the butler; Oxbury would be happy to bring her whatever she wished, including the town car to take him home.

Redhawk snorted, rose to his feet, and returned to the out of doors.

In a matter of minutes he was back inside. "How about kindling?" he asked and, kneeling again, began tilting the logs against one another, wide on the bottom and narrow on the top.

"Kindling?"

He shrugged. From the back, he looked as broad as a bull. His neck, if he had one, was swallowed by dark hair that whisked over his collar and frayed near the ends. His beard could be seen from behind. "Newspapers?"

"I'm afraid I subscribe to the *Times* on my e-reader," she said.

"Yeah?" He didn't glance up. "You think it'll Kindle a fire?"

"What?"

He shook his head. "Got any tissues? Old books? Any kind of paper products."

Ineptitude gnawed at her self-worth, eroding her foundation, tilting her off balance; she hadn't even thought to purchase toilet paper. But she tightened her fingers against one another and straightened her back a half an inch. "I believe our agreement was that you would repair the furnace in exchange for a meal and a *jump* as you so charmingly called it."

He turned to stare at her, dark eyes steady beneath disapproving brows. "Maybe you whipped up a chateaubriand?"

She pursed her lips into a tight smile and wished she could threaten him with the butler, but Oxbury hadn't deigned to leave Arbor House for a sojourn into the eighteenth century. "I'll look for something to burn," she said and turned away.

By the time she returned, he had a pile of wood shavings started on the ugly-as-sin carpet.

"Anything?" he asked and continued stripping bark from the nearest log.

"I've got . . ." She managed not to wince as she stepped forward. "These."

He turned toward her. She hesitated a moment, then pushed a cardboard box into his hand and escaped as quickly as she could into the kitchen, but not before she heard his low chuckle.

"Tampons?" he asked, but she didn't answer. Instead, she closed her eyes and wished she were somewhere else. Anywhere, really. Anywhere at all. But wasn't that what had gotten her into this mess in the first place?

"Hey." He had to raise his voice a little to be heard. "You got any Vaseline?"

Vaseline? She wanted nothing more than to ignore him, but it would be just as easy to discount a hungry grizzly. She returned to the doorway and knew she was blushing. "I beg your pardon?"

"Petroleum jelly," he said. "Do you have any?"

"I didn't plan on . . ." she began, but he stopped her with a look.

"Chapstick maybe?" he asked.

Scowling, she pivoted away to retrieve her handbag. "I have lip gloss," she said, returning to the doorway.

"Yeah?" He glanced up, bearded face unreadable. "Got any Passionate Pink? That's my preference."

"I beg your—"

"Never mind," he said and reached out, but she hesitated.

"It's dull lips or hypothermia," he said.

She considered her options for a moment, then handed over the prize.

He humphed quietly, took a tampon from the box, and smeared it with goo.

In a matter of moments a fire was crackling in the hearth. It was small, but it was cheery. Funny how such a little blaze could lift her spirits. Still, it was sobering to learn that Resume Red looked better on a tampon than it did on her.

Chapter 7

"Perhaps we should eat by the fire," Sydney said. Her fingers had long ago gone numb and the cold had set a dull, throbbing ache in her right thigh. One bare bulb illuminated the kitchen. The rest of the house was dark except for the light of the fire.

"All right," Hunter said and eyed their meal. It consisted of a box of fancy crackers and four cartons of yogurt. A single spoon lay beside the delicacies. It was plastic. But she'd found a lone metal fork in one of the kitchen drawers. Judging from its bent tines and scratched handle, it might have been hiding there since the Great Depression.

"Please bring the flatware," she said, and raising her chin, picked up the yogurt.

He did as ordered and followed her into the parlor. The small room was warming up quickly. She handed him the yogurt and made a grand gesture toward the mattress. Pulling the foil off the first carton, he sat on the lumpy bed and scowled when he tasted the contents with the fork.

"Probiotics," she said and remained standing.

He glanced up.

"Yogurt," she explained and dipped her spoon into her own tiny carton. "It has probiotics."

"Fantastic." He was almost finished with his meal, but his tone wasn't exactly ringing with sincerity.

She peered into her yogurt. "And if consumed on a regular basis can help reduce gastric problems and abdominal fat." She took another spoonful and glanced at him. As far as she could tell, he didn't carry an ounce of body fat on his massive frame. Ergo, it was possible he wasn't concerned about the caloric content. Also, he might be considering eating *her*. Still, as sleet rattled the windows, she couldn't help but feel the tiniest sliver of gratitude for his presence. Gratitude tended to make her irritable. As did guilt . . . and embarrassment. Come to think of it, irritable might be her default mood. But she accepted that little factoid with an invisible shrug and spoke. "Help yourself to another carton."

He stared at his meal as if considering the remainder of her lip gloss as a viable alternative, then sighed and ripped open the next container before skimming the room with his hunting-bear eyes. There were plenty of cobwebs on the overhead light fixture, but no bulbs. Firelight flickered and quaked in the broad stone cavern, casting shadows under his eyes, dark dells into his lean cheeks. He lifted his gaze. She pulled hers rapidly away.

"She's got good bones," he said.

"Excuse me?"

"This house." His eyes skimmed the room again. "They don't build them like this anymore."

She raised one brow. "Decrepit and hideous?"

"Solid," he said. "Built to last."

"Might you be a drinking man, Mr. Redhawk?"

He chuckled. "It's a shame, losing these landmarks."

"It's hardly the Sistine Chapel."

"Not intended to be. But look at that mason work," he said and motioned toward the fireplace with one tine. The others pointed directly toward the window. "Native granite, every rock. And the floor . . ." He shook his head and nodded at the carpet. It was bunched at the corners, stained down the center.

"You've a fondness for urine?"

"There's solid oak flooring under there."

"Psychic, too, Mr. Redhawk?"

He stared at her, dark eyes unfathomable. "How did you know?" he asked, and honest to God, she couldn't tell if he was joking or not. So she put on a meaningful smile and hoped she looked all-knowing. Or at least as if she knew *something*.

"I'll make you a bet," he said.

"I'm not really the wagering sort."

He nodded slowly and caught her with his gaze. "How long have you been running scared?"

She felt her back stiffen and her lungs seize up. "Do you think you frighten me, Mr. Redhawk?"

"If I win, I spend the night," he said.

She made an indescribable noise, something like a mouse scrambling for its hole.

"On the floor," he added. "If you win I buy the necessary parts and fix that furnace."

"That's what this is for," she said and motioned regally toward their meal.

He raised a brow at her. She cleared her throat, but refused to back down.

"As I've told you, I have someone coming to remedy the situation."

"You also said your husband was in the barn."

Okay, so she had forgotten that little lie.

"If he's still out there, you may have to call the paramedics."

She tightened her grip on her yogurt, mind scrambling.

"Frostbite can be a real bitch if left untreated."

"Very well . . ." So he'd called her bluff. "As I'm sure you're aware, I happen to be here alone. But I had no reason to believe you hadn't come to rape and pillage."

A muscle ticked in his jaw. "Rape and pillage?"

She frowned. "You haven't, have you?"

"I'm a little tired right now," he admitted, assessing the room in which he sat. "And there's not much to pillage. Not until you tear this down and build your plastic mansion anyway."

She smiled at him. "I'm so sorry if good taste offends your sensibilities."

He rose to his feet, towering over her. "Snobs offend my sensibilities."

"Well . . ." She smoothed a pale hand over the coat she had not yet removed. "My apologies to rednecks everywhere." She stood as straight as grandmothers and riding instructors demanded. "Good-bye, Mr. Redhawk."

"I'll need your keys."

Fear raced down her spine at the thought of being stranded in that cold little corner of hell, but she raised a haughty brow.

"To charge my battery," he added.

She gave him a smug smile, but didn't move. "Of course you do."

He stared at her, dark brows lowered until her meaning dawned on him. At which time surprise, humor, and more than a little anger shone in his eyes. "You think I'm planning to steal your car?"

"The idea did cross my mind."

He gritted his teeth and tightened a mallet-sized fist against his thigh. "Lady, I wouldn't trade my truck for that foreign job you drive if it came with the factory it was built in."

"It's a BMW."

He gritted a carnivorous smile.

For a moment she considered calling him a liar, but he was as big as a Kodiak, and she liked to think she wasn't entirely lacking in common sense.

Turning, she retrieved her keys and dropped them into the palm of his outstretched paw.

Chapter 8

Hunter snorted and refrained from making a scathing rejoinder, but he couldn't quite stop himself from slamming the door as he stepped into the bitter elements.

Behind him, the kitchen light blinked, flickered, and fell into blackness.

He grinned into the slashing precipitation. Not only was Miss Fancy Pants Wellesley going to be cold and hungry, she was going to be cold and hungry in the dark.

Trotting happily down the teetering steps, he laughed as he popped the locks on the Bimmer. Tripping the tiny lever inside, he yanked up the hood, snagged the cables from beneath his truck's passenger seat and attached the clamps to the appropriate terminals. In a matter of moments he was seated behind the BMW's gleaming steering wheel. The engine purred to life. Stepping outside again, he hurried through the wind. The driver's door groaned as he pulled it open. He settled onto the ratty bench seat, then glanced back toward the house. And there, perfectly framed in the parlor's black window, was Sydney Wellesley. With the fire behind her, she was little more than a silhouette. Her features were lost in the darkness, and yet he could still see the fear, like a flame, banked but not doused.

He gritted his teeth and tightened his grip on his key.

Dammit, he hated damsels in distress. Especially rich ones with haughty attitudes and little lost-girl eyes.

He leaned back against his tattered upholstery, trying to convince himself to leave, to forget about her, to move on down the road. He'd become a veritable expert at that in the past few years. But what had it gotten him? An extra hundred thousand miles on his truck and leg cramps.

Exhaling heavily, he glanced out the window. The rain was mixed with sleet now and came at him at a sharp, driving angle.

If he had a brain in his head he'd leave and never look back. But like his Sara Bear had once said, *Sometimes really smart people are the stupidest of all.*

Lurching out of his truck, he yanked off the jumper cables and stashed them under his seat. Then, hunching his shoulders against the cold, he slammed the door and wished to hell he wasn't so damned smart.

He'd give her one more chance, he thought, as he stepped back into the house and watched her appear in the doorway of the foyer.

"Won't start," he said and jerked his head toward his just-abandoned bucket of bolts. It was an ugly truck. Had been since his old man had brought it to the rez almost two decades before. "Don't need pretty," he'd said and snagged his wife up close to his side. "Caught me my limit on that near ten years ago."

His mother had hushed her husband and pushed away, but not before planting a noisy kiss on his cheek.

Funny, Hunter thought, that he hadn't realized how rare his parents were. Surrounded by the dark squalor of the Rosebud Reservation, they had shone like a sacred fire. But somehow he had still lost his way.

"What do you mean it won't start?" Sydney Wellesley's voice was prim, her expression angry, as if she disapproved of such things on principle.

He studied her in the darkness. "There's a mechanism under the hood. It's called an engine. It makes the machine run. Mine doesn't."

They stared at each other. If she was thinking

she could give him a lift into town, she didn't make mention. Which was just as well. The rain was freezing on contact. Snot with an attitude, Dad would have called it.

"I only have the single mattress," she said.

For one crazy moment he considered asking if she wanted to share, but she didn't seem like the kind of woman who could take a joke. Or recognize one.

"I've got a sleeping bag in my truck," he said.

She was going to refuse. He could feel it, and half hoped she would. But thunder cracked, sharp and close. Lightning split the sky, like a melon dropped on concrete, and in that white-hot illumination, her eyes looked wild with terror.

"I suppose you could sleep on the floor." Her tone sounded stiff, but again, it was her hands that gave her away. She pried them apart and pressed them against her thighs.

He turned and she jerked.

"You okay?"

She lifted her chin and let her index finger bump once against her thigh. "Of course. Why wouldn't I be?"

Impossible to say, he thought. But his money was on mental illness. All those snotty European families marrying their cousins was bound to cause problems. "I'll get more wood," he said and turned back toward the door, but she followed him, jerking in his direction like a marionette just cut loose.

"Can you get the lights working?" she asked.

"I'm not a magician."

"Hunkpapa, I believe you said."

So she remembered. He couldn't help but be surprised that she was aware of anything that didn't involve her own interests. Her shoe size and the color of her favorite nail polish, maybe. But come to that, she didn't seem to have any color on her at all. What was that about? "And you thought that synonymous with magical?"

She shrugged, the slightest lift of tight-bound shoulders. "The way you said it, I could only assume."

He snorted as he turned away. Chuckled a little as he closed the door behind him.

Inside, Sydney paced back to the fire. She shouldn't have agreed to let him stay. Grandmother habitually disapproved of women who put themselves in compromising situations. Foolish girls, after all, deserved what they got, and it wasn't long before Redhawk reappeared. He was carrying a couple dozen branches the size of his arms. Which were, God help her, as big around as her neck. Squatting, he let them tumble to the floor in front of the fire, then straightened and disappeared. In a moment he was back, sleeping bag propped beneath one elbow.

Sydney gave him a head tilt that had sent better

men running for cover. "Surely you don't believe we will be sleeping in the same room," she said.

He turned to give her a steady look. "If you want to haul that mattress back out of here, be my guest."

She forced a smile. "You will be spending the night elsewhere."

"Then I'm going to be building a fire elsewhere."

"There's not another fireplace."

"I'm fully aware of that," he said.

She pursed her lips. "So you're an arsonist, as well, Mr. Redhawk?"

"As well as what?"

"That remains to be seen, but I'm sure if I call the sheriff he will be happy to enlighten me," she said and lifted the phone she had retrieved from her purse during his absence.

He watched her, gaze level.

"Last chance to choose another room," she said.

He didn't reply.

She dialed 911 . . . and shouldn't have been surprised when there was no connection. Reception here was sketchy at best. "Perhaps we can come to an agreement," she said and kept the phone to her ear as if it were ringing.

He didn't respond. Unless one counted the slight lift of his right eyebrow. But that might have been an involuntary reaction. Like a dog's twitching hind leg.

"You may sleep in this room if you swear on all that is holy that you will not touch me."

There was a long moment of silence, then a low, rumbled chuckle. "You got it."

She narrowed her eyes at his emphatic tone. "And you will . . ." She glanced around, eager to make him pay for that tone. ". . . repair the furnace."

He continued to stare at her, then nodded finally. "If you're sure you can trust me to resist your charms." The corner of his lips turned up a quarter of an inch.

She smiled grimly and ended her futile phone call. "Very well then."

"And pay me thirty dollars an hour."

"You jest," she said.

He shook his head and grinned.

"Twenty-four hours of room and board in exchange for every eight hours of labor."

"That's a lot of hours."

"How long do you usually work?"

"I meant twenty-four hours is a long time to spend with . . ." He paused, held her gaze. "This house."

He was implying, of course, that it was too long to be with *her*. But she was unoffended. She had entertained dignitaries and royalty without complaint. But a tiny voice reminded her that none of those posh individuals were with her now. She was entirely alone. Except for her pride.

Which apparently goeth before a fall. But she had already fallen, hadn't she?

"You're welcome to leave any time," she reminded him.

"Or I can stay . . ." he said. "And enjoy the lovely ambiance . . . not to mention your fine cuisine . . ." His lips curved again. "In exchange for free physical labor."

She clamped her teeth together. He had forgotten to mention her sterling company. "Yes," she said.

"Well . . ." Spreading his sleeping bag on the floor, he gave his head a single shake. "I'd have to be a fool to pass that up."

"But?" she asked.

He toed off his boots and slid into his bedroll. "But I'm staying anyway."

It was a long night. Sydney had never been a good sleeper. Countless nannies had complained to her father about her unwillingness to go to bed. But she had continued to resist, for once in bed, she was forbidden to rise until a prescribed hour. No water would be fetched. No lights turned on. Wellesleys did not believe in coddling.

Sometime well past midnight, Redhawk added logs to the fire and pushed them in with a branch. From behind, Sydney watched the flames lick higher. Father didn't approve of fires and had replaced Arbor House's ancient wood-burner with an electric unit to improve the quality of their indoor air. He had insisted that the lounge at Steeple Veil have the same kind of system. It flickered in her mind.

Down the carefully matted and meticulously groomed aisle, a horse nickered. Another answered. It was nearly time for their evening meal. Unlike your average backyard nag, Steeple Veil animals were fed three times daily to aid their digestion and pamper the relatively small size of the equine stomach.

Javier was already mixing the supplements that would be added to the grain. He glanced up as Sydney approached.

"Good afternoon, Miss Wellesley." He was small and dark and stood as straight as a soldier. "How did Bennie Bean perform this day?" Javier always used the Bean's full name and habitually employed formal, old-world English, as if every vowel must be correct, every syllable perfect. His American citizenship had been contested on more than one occasion. But he was David's favorite groom and what David wanted David got.

"Well enough," she said. "Do you happen to know where I can find Mr. Albrook?"

Javier nodded twice, as if once was too weak, thrice too dramatic. "He was in the tack room some minutes ago."

"Thank you," she said and turned. Her stacked leather boot heels were muffled against the rubber matting. A half-dozen hopeful horses turned to watch her walk by, but she didn't do the feeding and Steeple Veil mounts were not allowed treats. A door slid open down the way, emitting a groom and a big chestnut. Still saddled, Eternal Flame tossed his head. At four years of age, he was a potent mix of nerves, energy, and budding Olympic potential. Beside him, Emilio seemed scrawny and small. His mustache, the pride of his young life, looked sparse and desperate above his crooked grin. "Hey, Miss Wellesley."

She gave him a nod and continued on. It was best not to become too familiar with the help. She had learned that from Helena, the only nanny who had dared challenge the constraints of her bedtime ritual. Sydney had never heard from her again.

The tack room door was closed. She put her hand on the knob. Inside a girl giggled. There was something about the sound that made Sydney pause. Stable romances sprang up like jimsonweed every day of the week and she had no desire to surprise someone. She turned to walk away, but the voice from inside stopped
her.

"I love the way you laugh."

Sydney froze. The voice almost sounded like David's, but different somehow. Not bored, but engaged. Flirtatious.

There was a pause as something rustled on the far side of the door.

"What about your fiancée?" Missy Ulquist's voice was breathy.

"She doesn't believe in laughing. It's against her religion."

Sydney felt her cheeks heat, her breath hitch.

"I knew I was right," David said. "You do have an excellent seat."

"Better than hers?"

She was unable to turn away, unable to go inside.

David chuckled. "She's my secret weapon for reducing inflammation."

Missy giggled again. "She's not that cold."

"She replaced my ice maker. But you . . ." There was a breathy pause. "You're all passion. Hot. Here . . . and here . . . and . . ."

Sydney never opened the door. Never looked inside. Instead, she turned, face hot, hands unsteady.

Her footsteps were almost silent as she strode away, but they echoed in her ears. She turned the corner. Emilio was just about to fasten Flame to the elastic cross ties that stretched from the walls beside them.

"I'll take him." Her voice sounded oddly hollow to her own ears.

"What?" The boy looked immediately stricken.

"You've no need to untack him." She straight-ened her back. Their heights were almost equal. "I'll be riding him."

"But he is not full trained yet, miss." Emilio glanced to the right as if searching for a savior. "And Teddy's grooming the indoor ring. So you cannot ride there."

The gelding tossed his head when she took the reins. She crushed the braided leather between fingers gone numb and headed toward the door.

"Miss Wellesley, the weather . . ." Emilio called after her, but she ignored him.

Thunder rolled quietly in the distance, or maybe it was in her mind. The gelding danced as she mounted, but she welcomed his impatience, his speed, his power.

It began to rain even before she reached the cross-country course. She pushed the chestnut into a canter, lifted her face to the sky, and eased up on the reins. Flame lengthened his stride. The turf flew away beneath them. Autumn was bursting in on them, but artificial daffodils still bloomed in half barrels beside the first jump, an easy vertical spread.

Anger speared through her. But was she

surprised? Was she really? Or had she always known that love wasn't for families like hers? People like her? What would she do now? Bring her wayward fiancé to heel like a recalcitrant pup and forge on with the wedding plans?

Beneath her, Flame charged uphill. The second jump was more difficult, but she had a good seat, too. Maybe not as broad as Missy Ulquist's, but firm, well trained.

She smiled grimly as they approached the jump. It had a five-foot spread. Reaching gamely beneath him, Flame launched, soared, and recovered.

She would do the same. She would recover. In fact, she would thrive. She was a Wellesley, after all.

Rage mixed with embarrassment, spewing up a chalky bitterness. She gritted her teeth against it. Ahead, a water hazard was draped in tattered fog.

Flame raced toward it, ratcheting up resources lesser horses would never possess. Together, they soared over the heavy timbers toward the water below. And for a moment Sydney forgot her bitterness. Forgot the disappointment, the restraints, and the tedium. For a moment the old thrill pulsed through her veins.

And then something shifted. One moment

they were rising, flying, leaving earthly worries and cheating fiancés behind. The next they were falling, tumbling from the sky like felled sparrows.

Shock splashed through her. Water boiled up. Beside her, the brave gelding thrashed violently.

She awoke with a sobbing gasp.

"Hey! You okay?" Someone touched her shoulder.

She jerked back, jolting to full consciousness. "Yes." She said the word before she had any idea if it was true. "Of course." Her fingers trembled as she smoothed her hair behind an ear. No brave steed lay dying beside her. She closed her eyes to the burning memories. "Why wouldn't I be?"

Hunter Redhawk was crouching beside the awful mattress. "I'm not sure. Maybe because you had the mother of all nightmares?"

For a moment she actually considered denying it, but the evidence seemed fairly obvious. Her forehead was damp, chilled with perspiration, and her breathing was still uneven. "I'm fine."

"All right." He watched her from only inches away, dark brows lowered over skeptical eyes. "Could you be fine a little more quietly? I was just falling asleep."

"What time is it?"

"Three or so."

She tilted her chin in question.

"Sleep's overrated," he said.

She watched him. In the crackling firelight, his eyes looked deep-water dark and strangely haunted. "No," she said. "It's not."

He smiled and rose to his feet. "I'll get you something to drink."

"Really?" Her voice sounded weirdly breathless even to herself. He looked at her as if granting a simple favor was as natural as breathing. "I mean . . ." She lowered her gaze, found her center, and tightened her fingers in the single quilt. "That's not necessary."

"Probably true," he said and turned toward the kitchen.

She scooted back up against the wall behind her and rubbed her aching thigh while he was gone.

In a minute he was handing her a chipped mug. "Want to tell me about it?"

She took the water, managed a sip, and was grateful for the opportunity to lower her gaze, to break eye contact. "No," she said.

"All right." He didn't push, didn't prod, simply returned to his sleeping bag.

She finished the water, just because she could, then slipped back under the quilt. "Thank you." Her voice sounded ridiculously small in the darkness.

"No big deal," he said.

But she knew different.

Chapter 9

By morning Sydney felt drained and old and exhausted beyond repair. She sat up slowly on the bare mattress, mind churning sluggishly, like an engine too long in the cold. Tension strained across the back of her neck, stretching her shoulders tight.

Something scraped behind her. She twisted around with a start.

"Why not rent it out?"

Framed by the doorway in which he stood, Hunter Redhawk looked like nothing so much as an ancient, unkempt Viking.

"How long have you been there?" she asked and scraped her hair into a quick knot at the base of her skull.

He shrugged. "It is impossible to wake one who pretends to sleep."

"What?"

"Why destroy it?" he asked.

She shifted her feet to the floor, movements slow and stiff. "This house?" she asked.

"Ai, this house." He glanced around it, assessing the deterioration. "Just because she is old does not mean she has no value."

"You're right," Sydney said and slipped her feet into the boots she'd left beside the mattress. "It's the fact that it's an architectural disaster that makes it worthless. Did you get the furnace repaired?"

"Ai," he said again. "I but used the hide of an antelope and the juice of a prickly pear."

She studied him in silence for a moment, trying to decipher whether he was serious. "You're extremely amusing," she said finally.

"The Hunkpapa are revered for their sense of humor," he said.

"Which makes you what? Norwegian?" she asked.

He snorted. "I'll need some supplies from town."

"Supplies?" She wanted to sound authoritative, but worry had leaked into her tone.

"I need a new transformer."

She watched him, eyes assessing, mind churning. It had been a god-awful night. "What would *you* do with this house?" she asked.

"If I were lucky enough to own it?"

Sometimes she had no idea whether he was being earnest or facetious. Generally, she didn't care. "Yes."

He glanced around again. "I'd restore it."

"What would that cost?"

"It depends."

"On . . . ?"

"How much you want to preserve. How much

you want to add. How long you want it to last."

She forced herself to breathe. "What if I . . . on a whim . . . decided to live here?"

He raised his brows at her. "Indefinitely?"

She would have liked to laugh, but acting had never been her forte. "For the foreseeable future. What would it cost to make it . . . livable?"

He scowled, glanced around, and shrugged. "Ten, fifteen thousand?"

She felt herself pale. A few weeks ago that would have been nothing. Now she'd be lucky to scrape up enough change to buy lunch.

"If I did the work myself," he added.

She felt her stomach drop. "That's not including labor?"

"A pox on Lincoln," he said.

She scowled.

"Ruining a fine institution like slavery."

She didn't bother to deepen her scowl, didn't even consider glaring. Her mind was streaming. She had nowhere to go. No one waiting for her there. A dim memory of the proud doe settled into her mind. She tried to drive it away, but it remained, head high, eyes bright.

"What if I gave you extended room and board?" she asked.

She could feel his gaze on her. Hard as hammered steel.

"As much as my people like to sleep by an open fire . . ." He let the words lie.

93

She pursed her lips. "You could choose any room you like." The doe stepped carefully forward, perfectly framed in the shattered window of her mind. "Except the bedroom on the right. And you could eat whatever you wished." She refrained from clearing her throat again. She didn't need him. Far from it. "As long as you cooked it."

"You're offering me a job?"

"I'm not altogether heartless," she said and raised her chin without knowing she did so.

"So you've come to save the poor Indian."

It was hard not to squirm under his gaze. "I suppose in a way, you'd be helping me, too."

His snort was almost inaudible.

"I'm simply saying, perhaps you're right. Perhaps it would be wise to save this . . ." She willed herself not to wince as she thought of the catastrophe that surrounded her. "Structure. Live in it during construction and rent it out once my new house is finished."

"You said you were hiring a contractor."

She also had said she had a husband named Conan, but thought the reminder might not aid her cause. "Naturally."

"Then you can afford a crew for *this* house."

Tension knotted her stomach, but she eased out the coils and pasted on a smile. "The truth is, Mr. Redhawk, I'm in a bit of a financial bind momentarily. In fact, I will be stretching my budget to build my dream home even without needing funds to refurbish my . . ." She forced a laugh. "*Nightmare* home."

"A financial bind." He was watching her again, like a backwoods grizzly with nothing better to do than torment a sophisticated city mouse. "In Indian terms does that mean you're broke?"

"No. Not broke."

"Bent?"

She scowled.

He shrugged as if comfortable with the fact that she found him less than amusing. "What do you do?"

"I beg your pardon?"

"What line of work?" he asked. "Or are you spending your daddy's money?"

There was a moment's hesitation during which he was quite sure he had hit uncomfortably close to the mark.

"Do I look incapable of making my own income?"

"Yes."

She added a little more chill to her tone. Some would have thought such a feat impossible. "If I buy the necessary supplies, are you skilled enough to make the house livable?"

"My people are skilled at many things."

Clearly, those skills did not include conversation, she thought. "What about carpentry?"

The shadow of a smile lifted his lips. "Ai."

"What does that mean?"

"It's an affirmative in my ancient tongue."

"I'm not familiar with Old Norse."

She ignored his snort. "How much will it cost to make the house waterproof?"

"The *whole* house?"

"I don't want to seem uppity," she said. "But yes, that is my hope."

His lips twitched, but whether with humor or irritation, she was unsure. "I shall ponder that."

"Very well." She rose, stifling a wince at the twang in her thigh. "If you are still able to function after that Herculean effort, we shall purchase supplies."

Chapter 10

The lumberyard outside of Buffalo Gap was a large open building that smelled of fresh-cut pine and testosterone.

"Hey." The man who thrust his hand toward Redhawk was somewhere between thirty and seventy years of age. He wore two mismatched flannel shirts and jeans slung low under a belly trying hard to impersonate a rain barrel. "How you doing, Hunt?"

Redhawk met his handshake. "Milt," he said simply.

"We heard you was back. You going to be racing this year?"

Sydney raised her brows, but Redhawk seemed to see no reason to enlighten her. "Don't think so."

"Your little brother says he's got some horses could win the Derby if given the chance."

A light shone in Redhawk's eyes. "Tonk's deluded about many things."

Milt shoved his hands into the front pockets of his jeans, threatening their already shaky position on his nonexistent hips. "Listen, I was sure sorry to hear about Nicole."

Hunter nodded simply. Silence stretched uncomfortably between them.

They turned away in unison.

"How's business been going?" Hunter asked.

"Decent. Owen Crandell's building a house for his new bride out by the river. You remember Owen."

"Gabby's boy?"

"That's the one."

"He's married al—"

Sydney followed at a distance, mind churning, but the discussion had turned toward tools and hardwood. Neither of which she could afford. All of which she knew nothing about and had no interest in. But who was Nicole? And Tonk? And what was that about the Derby? Not that she cared. She had troubles of her own. How was she going to afford renovations? Or should she just hope she had enough funds for an airline ticket and—

"Which would you prefer?" Redhawk asked.

"What?" Sydney turned toward him with a jolt. He was already frowning at her inattention.

"Perhaps when my finances are back in order I shall buy you a new expression," she said.

He raised a brow a fraction of a hair.

"You're scowling again," she said.

"I hope I'm not boring you."

"Not at all," Sydney said. She *might* have been bored if she wasn't scared out of her mind. But she was miles out of her comfort level, light-years out of her element. Then again, what was her element exactly? "Talk of insulation and galvanized nails makes me practically giddy."

He continued to stare at her, as if he could see through her skin into the well of fear beneath. "Wait until you see the shingles," he said.

"I simply cannot."

He exhaled a quiet snort. "Like I asked before, do you want to pay the lumberyard extra to deliver the supplies or pay *me* extra to come pick them up?"

"How much will it cost?" She tried to keep the stinging worry out of her voice and thought she might actually have succeeded.

His shrug was halfhearted. "Couple hundred, maybe."

Relief flooded her. She hid that, too. "Well . . . that seems reasonable enough."

He narrowed his eyes a little as if trying to ascertain whether she was being serious. "For the delivery," he explained.

She felt her stomach cramp and tilted her chin, duchess to peasant. "Of course," she said. "And how much for the merchandise?"

"Four thousand and change."

For a second, she thought the news might actually crush her, as if it were physical weight dropped from above. But her mind scrambled. Too late to pretend the number was expected, she thought, and allowed an offhand question. "For a pile of boards I could fit in my car?"

"You changing your mind?" he asked.

She forced a sliver of a smile. The expression actually hurt her face. "About whether or not my house should be waterproof? No, I rather think it should."

He watched her a moment longer, then nodded and pressed a slip of paper into her hand. "This is yours then," he said.

She raised it to chest level and blinked.

"It's the invoice."

She couldn't seem to move. "Obviously."

"You pay at the register."

"I'm fully aware of what to do with an invoice."

He raised one brow, forcing her to clear her throat and goose-step to the front of the store.

But the word *store* was rather a lofty term. Half the size of Steeple Veil's training barn, it was peopled by men in overalls and muddy rubber boots. People who wouldn't have been in the periphery of her universe for the first two decades of her life.

The checkout boy was eighty years old if he was a day. He wore a fake brass name tag pinned to the strap of his work apron. Perhaps Cecil wasn't proof positive that ears and noses continue to grow after every other body part has begun to atrophy, but he supplied considerable evidence. "Milt didn't give you no trouble, did he?" he asked.

Sydney pulled her thoughts out of her quagmire of problems with a jolt. "Excuse me?"

He grinned at her. Gold glimmered on a corner incisor, mischief in his eyes. "Man thinks he's Johnny Carson. I keep telling him not to pester the pretty girls, but he don't listen. If he bothered you, I'll fire him right here and now," he said and stabbed a gnarled index finger toward the floor.

"Hey, Hunt . . ." He nodded at Redhawk. "Good to see you again."

"Cecil."

"So what do you say?" the old man asked, returning his attention to Sydney. "Can I give Milt the boot?"

"Not on my account," she said and wondered if

Hunter had spent his childhood there in Buffalo Gap, a tiny blip of a town that boasted 126 friendly people. It seemed strange suddenly that she knew next to nothing about him.

"You sure?" The old man tapped a few buttons on the cash register. "Cuz I've been looking for a reason to get rid of him since the day he first started hangin' around.

"That'll be four thousand and five dollars and seventy-three cents."

"Very well." Her stomach twisted brutally. But according to her online checking, she should still have a few hundred left after this purchase.

"Been here since eighty-two," Cecil said, not clarifying whether he was talking about himself or the slandered Milt. "Was a beatnik then and he's a beatnik today. Told him a thousand times to *cut his hair.*" The last three words were increased in volume and sent over Sydney's shoulder, but she barely noticed as she handed over her debit card. He tugged it away with fingernails as thick as turtles' shells.

"There haven't been no beatniks around for fifty years, y' daft old coot," Milt said and straightened a man-sized stack of tools proclaiming to be "as advertised on TV."

"Don't you use that language with ladies about," Cecil warned. "You'll have to forgive him, Miss . . ." He beetled his brows at her debit card, slid it through his machine, and gave

Sydney a sly wink. ". . . Wellesley, he thinks being my son-in-law gives him a license to be irritating."

She tried a smile. It was almost impossible to make her lips bend in the appropriate direction.

"Huh . . ." He scowled, propeller ears prominent beside the frayed antiquity of his John Deere cap, but in a moment he brightened. "Well . . . I guess it's a good thing you brought Redhawk here with you."

Her throat felt dry. "Why is that?" she said.

"Looks like there's a problem with your card."

"A problem?" She raised her brows at him. Felt the heat rise up her neck. "That can't be. Run it again please."

He did so, stared at the small screen, and shook his head. "Looks like it just don't like us today."

"There must be some mistake," she said, but her stomach felt queasy, suggesting the mistake was hers. That her life as she knew it had ended. Fear collided with embarrassment. But she took a steadying breath and assured herself that everything would be okay. Her father could be vengeful. She knew that. But he was loyal. He had loved her mother with undying devotion even after her death. Surely, he loved Sydney, too.

"Sometimes this machine can be crotchety."

"Like its owner," Milt said, glancing over a nearby stack of raw lumber.

The old man sent his son-in-law a snort before turning back to Sydney. "You got another card you want to try?"

She could feel Redhawk's attention on the back of her neck. Was there anger in his perusal? Or worse . . . pity?

"Miss?"

"Yes?" She jerked at the sound of his voice.

"You got another card?" the old man asked.

"Oh, of course," she said and handed him her platinum. Maybe there had been some mistake at the moldering motel. Or maybe her father had only wanted to send her a message and had restored her line of credit.

Cecil tugged the card from fingers that had gone cold with dread.

"So where you from, Miss Wellesley?"

It was almost impossible to follow the conversation as he swiped her second card, but she focused. "I just purchased a farm a few miles from here."

"Schneidermans'?"

She tried to read the electronic screen, but it was too small. "I'm sorry." She pulled her gaze back to the old man's lived-in face. "What did you say?"

"You didn't buy Lizzy Schneiderman's place, did you?"

"Oh. Yes. I believe I did."

"Well, for crying out loud." He shook his head,

expression distant. "A slim little drink of water like you bought the Schneidermans'."

She didn't bother to respond. Couldn't. Her credit card was still being held hostage.

"It's a sight, ain't it?" he asked and shook his head. "But you should have seen it in its heyday. During the holidays that place was lit up like a Christmas tree. Candles in every window. That was before your time, I suppose, Hunt. But we used to go sledding behind the house there when I was a boy. Folks around here call it Gray Horse Hill. No saying why. Had hot chocolate and macaroons in that big old kitchen. Later I sparked little Margie for a spell." He grinned, showing a modicum of the charm to which young Margie had probably succumbed. "Prettiest girl in Custer County. Looked a little like you," he said and winked before lowering his gaze to the machine again. "Hmmmf." The sound made her intestines twist painfully.

"What is it?" She could barely force out the words.

"We're just not having no luck today."

"There must be something wrong with your machine." Her lips felt numb when she said the words.

"Likely as not," he said and handed her back the piece of plastic that weighed nothing and meant everything.

Panic sizzled through her, but Redhawk nudged her aside.

"I got it."

She felt her body stiffen. "I assure you there's no need for that."

"I assure *you* I'm going to charge you a boatload of interest," he said, and pulling out a beaded leather wallet, handed over a card.

"I'm good for a paltry four thousand dollars," Sydney said and kept her attention riveted on the road ahead. Redhawk's truck rumbled like a tank despite whatever improvements he had made while in town. It was, without exception, the ugliest vehicle she had ever seen.

"So you said." His voice sounded a little like his truck.

"Are you suggesting that I'm being less than honest?"

"My people . . ." He shook his head once. "They are brave, but they are not foolish." His expression was as impassive as ever, but something shone in his eyes. Humor maybe.

She pursed her lips. "I didn't imagine old Leif was too timid to speak his mind."

He snorted. "I got you something."

"What?" Her tone was immediately jittery. She had never really known the proper way to accept gifts. When David had presented her with a two-karat square-cut diamond, she had declared it to be of fine quality. Perhaps it wasn't all that surprising that he thought her cold. "Why?"

He shrugged, then reached under the seat to retrieve a paperback novel. Sydney felt her brows wing into her hairline at the sight of the couple on the cover. They were physically perfect, half naked, and apparently being buffeted by the sort of wind gusts that sent their mutually glorious hair sweeping back in opposing directions. "What's this?"

"I was under the impression that it was a book."

"I know it's a book, but why . . ." She shook her head at the Easter egg colors. "I don't read this kind of . . ." She motioned toward the novel with a jittery hand. "Nonsense."

"Ever?"

Her cheeks felt warm just from holding the thing. "No."

"Then how have you determined that it *is* nonsense?"

"I just . . ." She shook her head.

"Think it wise to judge a book by its cover?"

"I like to improve my mind when I have the opportunity to read, not . . . not rot my brain with scenes about thrusting and heaving and—"

"There is thrusting and heaving?"

"I don't know what's in it!"

He didn't laugh, but his dark-magic eyes looked ungodly bright. "I just thought it might help you sleep if you had something to read that wasn't so . . . mind-improving. You look tired."

"Oh." She ran her fingers over the raised title.

Surrender My Heart. God help her. "Well . . ."
She cleared her throat. "Thank you."

"You're welcome."

She tightened her fingers on the book and glanced out the passenger window. In for a penny, in for a pound. "I'm sorry to make you pay for the lumber."

She could feel him turn toward her. Silence echoed in the cab. Tension jabbed her with nasty spurs.

"Stings like a wasp, doesn't it?" he asked.

She glanced at him with raised brows. "I've no idea what you're talking about."

His eyes glinted again. "It wasn't too bad for your first apology."

"I've apologized before."

"Did you want to kick the crap out of that guy, too?"

"I don't want to . . ." she began, then stopped and let her shoulders drop a sparse half inch. "Yes, I believe I did."

He was silent for a second before chuckling. The sound rolled in like a warm cloud, enveloping her, relaxing her.

She felt her lips twitch.

Their gazes met for a second before he turned back toward the road.

"Horses," he said.

"What?"

He nodded toward the south, where five mares

and two geldings lazed in the afternoon sunlight. Shaggy, with hips cocked and bottom lips drooping, they looked like nothing so much as overworked mules.

"Are you sure?" she asked.

He glanced at her. "You a horse snob, too?"

"Not at all. I just didn't recognize them as equine immediately."

"The mustang is a noble creature," he said. "As misunderstood as my own people."

"Really? I didn't know the Neanderthal were so unappreciated."

He chuckled again. "Nearly as much as the inbred aristocracy," he said, and though she had no idea why, she felt the last twist of tension slip from her shoulders.

Chapter 11

"Have you run away with any hot cowboys yet?" Victoria asked.

"Three or four," Sydney said. "I am, even now, trying to decide which one to keep."

"Waste not, want not," her cousin suggested.

"I'll take that under advisement," Sydney said and glanced at her bedroom door. Or what *would* be her bedroom door, once she had a bed, and a door. It was a mystery to her why this particular room was missing such essential pieces. She took a deep breath, bracing herself. "Tori?"

"Yeah."

"I need a favor."

The line went quiet.

"Victoria?"

"Yeah, excuse me, there must be something wrong with our connection." She tapped briskly on the phone. "I thought you said you needed a favor."

Sydney smiled a little. Cousin Tori was the closest thing she'd ever had to a sister.

"That *is* what I said."

"Really. Well, I'm all ears. And boobs." She sounded distracted for a moment as if watching herself in the gilt mirror that graced the sitting room of her New York condo. "Did I tell you I got enormous implants?"

"You're not serious!"

"Not as of today. But Howard's weakening." She and Howard Frances III had been married for nearly ten years. Most of that time she had spent trying to shock him out of his wealth-induced stupor. Apparently, the addition of big boobs was her latest ploy. "What do you need?"

Sydney shut her eyes and exhaled softly. It had been years beyond count since she'd asked for a favor. Defunct lemonade stands had taught her better. But cash was going to be necessary if she was going to fix up this place. In fact, she wouldn't even be able to afford her rental car much longer without a financial boost. "I need . . ." She paused, breathless. "The truth is, I'm in need of a loan."

"Ahh, good one, Syd. Did somebody die and bequeath you a sense of humor?"

A noise sounded from the hallway. Sydney tightened her grip on the phone. "It's, ummm . . ." She had no idea how to do this. "It's for a good cause."

"You're not serious."

As serious as bankruptcy, she thought, and cleared her throat. "I think I overextended."

"Overextended?" Tori laughed. "Did you buy a continent or something?"

Sydney tried and failed to chuckle. "A ranch."

"What?"

"I bought a ranch."

"You did not."

Tori was right. What Sydney had done was buy a catastrophe, a veritable nightmare. "It needs a few repairs." Such as a new house. A new barn. Fences.

"And Leonard"—the shrug was implicit in Tori's tone—"doesn't know about it?"

"I didn't want to bother Father until the property is up to his standards. You know how he is."

"How is he? Stuffy?"

"I thought that was how *you* were."

Sydney had always preferred the word *sophisticated*. "I'm sorry to ask—" she began, but Redhawk suddenly filled her doorway.

"I need you for a minute," he rumbled.

"Oh." She pressed the phone to her chest for a moment. "I'll be right there."

He nodded once and turned away.

"Who was *that?*" Tori's tone had perked up like a cockatiel.

"That was . . . you know . . ." Sydney tried to sound lighthearted. Constipated would have been closer to the mark. "Cowboy number three."

"Yeah? What's his name?"

She closed her eyes. "I guess that sense of humor should have come with instructions."

Silence.

"I was joking," Sydney explained.

"Uh uh. Unless you were imitating Sam Elliot on testosterone, someone just said he needed you."

Sydney turned to glance out the window, but whatever inspiration she had found in days past was noticeably absent now. "You know I wouldn't ask if it wasn't important."

There was a moment of silence, then, "Are you in some kind of trouble, Syd?"

"No. Of course not." Her throat felt tight, her hands unsteady.

"How much do you need?"

Not a stick of gum. She hadn't asked for so much as a piece of Juicy Fruit in the past fifteen years of her life. "Twenty thousand dollars."

"Oh, okay . . . if you tell me his name."

Sydney let her eyes fall closed and rubbed her temple. It was beginning to throb. That's what favors did. "It's Hunter Redhawk. But people seem to simply call him Hunt."

There was a pause. "I'd rather you told me to go to hell instead of lying to me."

"I'm not . . ." Sydney exhaled again. "Well, you know what they say, lie big or lie low."

It was a joke from their teenage years. Neither one had ever really known what it was supposed to mean.

"Hunter Redhawk . . ." Victoria chuckled. "If you give me your account number I'll transfer money this afternoon."

Sydney tightened her grip on the phone. "Could you do it right away?"

"You sure you're okay, Syd?"

"What? Yes. Of course. But . . . cowboys don't come cheap, you know."

"Really? That's exactly how I thought they came. You're killing all my illusions of . . . What?" Tori asked, attention obviously drifting. "Oh, that's right. I almost forgot. Listen, Syd, I'm supposed to help Howard's mom decide on the menu for his thirty-fifth. Can I give you a call later?"

"Of course. But . . . you won't forget, will you?"

"Forget what?"

Sydney closed her eyes. "The loan."

"Oh! Yes. I'm coming. Holy mother of God, you would think we were planning the inaugural ball." Sydney could hear Tori gather her keys, pick up her purse. "The last time I gave him a party, he was dozing on the putting green before he opened his presents. I'm thinking of having a half-naked girl jump out of a cake this time just to keep him awake. Are you sure you're all right?"

"Yes. I'm fine."

"Okay then. Have some cowboy on me, will you?"

"Sure," Sydney said and wondered if today was the day she would fail the Wellesley name and throw up like an un-pedigreed cocker spaniel.

Chapter 12

"Problems?" Redhawk was behind her again. For a man the size of a national monument, he could move with disturbing stealth.

"Besides the fact that this house looks as if it suffered an eight-point-nine on the Richter scale?"

Sydney asked and tore up another few inches of moldy carpet. For some ungodly reason, the previous homeowner had used industrial strength adhesive to glue down the flooring. Her arms pulsed like a jackhammer. Her back felt as if someone had taken a crowbar to it. And when had she begun thinking in terms of demolition tools? "None whatsoever."

"Good. Cuz you're going to want to finish up there before the new windows arrive."

"When's that?"

"About ten minutes," he said and turned away with a grin. It had taken her two hours to get this far.

She glared at his retreating back only to realize he was carrying a log the size of a Scottish caber. It was perched on his shoulder as if it was no more cumbersome than a paper clip. She curled her upper lip into a snarl. Damn barbarian, she thought, and yanking at the carpet, barely managed to avoid hitting herself in the head with the claw of her hammer.

And that was the best part of her day. By noon she thought she might die. By five o'clock she half hoped she would. Her biceps burned and her knees twanged with an intensity that rivaled the pulsing in her injured thigh.

But she had discovered that rhythmic walking helped alleviate the cramping that could seize up the muscles in her quadriceps. So once she had finished her self-imposed tasks for the day, she made her way down the plywood ramp that had replaced her defunct porch.

The sun was shifting toward the bare treetops on the western horizon. A robin landed on a listing fence post and warbled at the sky. The slanted shaft of late-day sun felt warm and hopeful against Sydney's skin. She tilted her face toward its friendly heat, then glanced east. The winding gravel road that swept away from Gray Horse Hill provided solid footing and a challenging climb, but her own land beckoned. True, she had no intention of remaining here any longer than necessary, but surely it was good business to know what she owned. Resolved to hike the backcountry, she shoved her hands into the pockets of the tattered coat Hunter had loaned her, and headed south.

The fences that had once partitioned off pastures and fields were mostly hidden beneath winter-browned weeds and tired snowdrifts. Still, her hip complained as she stepped over the remaining strands.

Off to her left, a cottontail leaped from some unseen sanctuary and bounded away, body arced and floating like a well-bred courser. Sydney watched its erratic path and noticed the shadow of a red-tailed hawk overhead, but the bunny had already dashed into a new haven.

Amazing, she thought reluctantly: the cleverness of the rabbit, the persistence of the falcon. She scanned the long sweep of distant hills, then lowered her gaze to a nearby cairn of stones. Tiny purple flowers, as fragile as hope, peeked through the remaining snow.

Goose bumps prickled along her arms, though she couldn't have said why. It wasn't as if Gray Horse Hill was one of the Seven Wonders of the World, but there was something here. An austere beauty that allowed her to forget the throbbing in her leg. That forced her to venture onward, uphill and down, around the next bend, until she lost her breath at the wonder of the place. Spread below her, Beaver Creek wound through bold bluffs and patient cottonwoods.

The hustling currents glistened like diamonds as they hurried toward parts unknown. High above, the hawk had found a mate. The pair soared on warming thermals, shadows racing over pine and prairie. It was, in a word, breathtaking. But time was slipping away, Sydney realized suddenly, and turned. It was then that a rasped shriek shivered through the still evening.

Pivoting back, she scanned the valley below her. A bird, she thought. It had been nothing more deadly than a grouse. Or maybe a pheasant hidden in the brush. When she had a spare minute, she would Google wildlife in the area and learn . . .

The sound came again, scraping along her nerve endings, skittering up her spine. Her eyes skimmed the red-rocked canyon, past the rusty bluffs to the pines below. It was there, practically hidden in a cluster of deep green boughs, that a flash of movement caught her attention. Something quick and small. She scowled, trying to make out the source of the noise. A cat, perhaps, or a fox? She took a few tentative steps forward. Maybe a weasel or a . . .

The sound came again, low and breathy. With anger? With fear? She glanced toward the house she had left far behind. But curiosity or something like it forced her to turn, to hurry down a winding trail made by unknown travelers. Keeping her attention trained on the spot where she had seen the movement, she hiked along, but when she had rounded the last bend, she could see nothing unusual.

Perhaps it had simply been the light playing tricks on her. Or maybe . . .

The raspy noise sounded again. She stopped, breath held. It was impossible to see through the tangled branches, but she was sure suddenly that no small creature had made such a noise. She had, she was certain, seen just a portion of a much larger animal.

A shiver of fear coursed through her. Something was hidden in the underbrush. A pronghorn, probably. The hills were thick with them. She took a few cautious steps closer. Stretched between the branches of two ponderosa pines, she recognized the leg of an animal. Too large for an antelope. And dark. A cow, most likely. Angus roamed these hills with impunity. Maybe a wolf had taken one down. She jerked to a halt when she realized what that implied and swung toward home.

But the noise came again, an almost defeated moan that stirred something inside her.

Exhaling carefully, Sydney fisted her hands and ducked into the trees. It was tough going. She pushed the branches from her face, wound through small, thorny bushes, and stepped into a clearing.

For a moment she couldn't even identify the species. Emaciated and filthy, the animal lay flat on its side. Its clay-colored hide was covered in mud, but it was the sight of its legs that made her stomach twist. Caked in dried blood, they were swollen at the hocks, slashed at the pasterns.

A horse.

The sound that escaped her lips was little more than a breathless hiss. Still, the dun jerked its head up at the noise. Its eyes, rimmed in white, opened wide. Their gazes locked, and then it tried to scramble desperately to its feet. But even as it did so, barbed wire tore at its flesh.

"Don't!" Sydney rasped, but the sound of her voice sent the animal into a panic. It thrashed.

Fresh blood sprayed onto snow plowed away by frantic hooves. "Stop!" she begged and lunged forward.

If she lived forever, she would never know what caused her to do something so foolish. Would never understand what she had hoped to accomplish. Maybe it was pity that drove her forward. Maybe it was sheer panic. Or perhaps it was something deeper . . . an intrinsic understanding of pain and fear and loneliness. But whatever her intent, she threw herself at the animal. It snorted and tried to jerk away, but it was weak, trapped. And in a moment Sydney found herself sprawled across the poor beast's head.

"It's okay! It's all right!" Her lies, of course, did nothing to placate the animal. It thrashed, nearly tossing her aside, but she grasped the upthrust branch of a nearby log and readjusted her weight until the horse finally lay still. "It's okay." Sydney squeezed her eyes closed and tried to catch her breath. "Don't struggle." She needed help. That much was clear. But from where? And in what form? Euthanasia was the obvious answer.

"I'm sorry," she whispered and, easing her right hand into the pocket of her borrowed coat, managed to pull out her cell. She could dial 911, pray her call went through. The police wouldn't have a sedative, of course. But they'd have a rifle. She'd seen a chart once that showed the proper way to shoot a horse. A single bullet to the brain and the animal would be out of her misery.

Her hand shook as she touched the button that awoke her phone. Beneath her, the mare paddled weakly, almost defeated, almost subdued, but not yet ready to give up.

Sydney gritted her teeth and punched a button on her phone.

"You okay?"

She had no idea why the sound of Redhawk's voice made her want to cry.

"I need help." Her voice sounded scratchy and scared to her own ears. "There's a horse." A sob tore at her throat, but she pushed it back, tamped it down. "Tangled in wire. It's bad, Hunt. It's really bad."

"I'll get my rifle. Be there as—"

"No!" She sounded panicked, near hysteria, but she massaged it into some semblance of normal. "You can't shoot her."

He exhaled quietly. "Listen, I know it's hard." His voice was calm, practical, but she'd been practical all her life, and where had it gotten her?

"*You* listen!" Her voice cracked. She ignored it. "She's not going to die."

He didn't respond.

"Hunter?"

"Where are you?"

"South of the ranch." She lay still, listened,

heard the sound of running water. "Close to the creek."

"East or west of Gray Horse?"

The sun was sinking on her left. "West. West, I think."

"All right. I'll be there as soon as I can get some backup. Just stay clear of the horse," he said and hung up.

"Hey, Hunt." Colt Dickenson grinned as Emily took a pan of raspberry crisp out of the oven. The kitchen smelled like warm sugar and contentment. "We were just going to have a little dessert before chores. Want to join—"

"Sydney's in trouble."

Casie turned toward him, sunny smile already fading as she cuddled Baby Bliss to her chest. "What's wrong?"

"Sydney needs help."

"What's going on?" she asked.

Colt repeated the question. Hunter's monosyllabic answer was nearly a dissertation by Hunkpapa standards.

"There's a horse in barbwire," Colt said.

Casie passed the baby off to Emily, expression already troubled, mind already spinning. "What do they need?" she asked, and for a moment, the sight of her, the kindness of her, was almost too much for Colt to bear.

"God, I'm crazy about you," he said.

121

A smile flickered through her eyes. "Or just crazy. How bad's the horse?"

"She thinks she can save her, but they're a ways out. South of the old Schneiderman place."

"Rugged country."

"Too rough for a trailer."

"But we can get horses in there." She strode toward the little foyer. "Haul them as far as we can, ride the rest of the way."

"Hear that?" Colt asked. Balancing the phone between his shoulder and his ear, he slipped an arm into his jacket sleeve as he headed for the door.

"You got a mount for me?" Hunter asked.

Colt grinned. "You want one that's not going to kill you?"

"It'd be my preference."

"I'll see what I can do," Colt said and pulled Casie in for a quick, hard kiss.

"You," he said, "are one in a million."

"You bet your boots," she agreed. "Hook up the trailer. I'll saddle the horses."

Chapter 13

An hour later they were making their way through the brush, calling out to locate Sydney. It seemed like an eternity before they got a response.

"I'm here," she yelled. It wasn't until that moment that Hunt caught sight of her braced against the head of a downed mustang. Beneath her, the animal thrashed. He swore in silence.

"Holy Hannah!" Casie's voice was breathy.

"I thought I told you to stay clear," Hunt growled.

"You brought a wire cutter?" Sydney's voice was rough.

Casie and Colt exchanged glances, but Hunter kept his attention locked on the pair on the ground.

"Listen, Sydney . . ." He gritted his teeth and pulled his gaze from the animal's mangled legs with an effort. "We're going to have to—"

"No!" Her voice was as hard as granite. "We're not putting her down."

"We don't want her to suffer." Sympathy was clear in Colt's tone. "Not any more than she already has." He shifted in his saddle. "I brought a rifle."

The horse thrashed again. Sydney's patrician features, just visible past a mess of tangled hair, were as pale as the snow lashed away by the animal's frantic hooves. Her hands were scraped raw, her cheeks smeared with blood, but whether it was hers or the horse's was impossible to tell.

"Are you going to help me?" Her words were barely discernible through her clenched teeth. "Or do I have to do it myself?"

"Her legs—" Casie began, but Sydney interrupted.

"Her legs are fine. They're fine."

Silence echoed in the little copse. Hunt's voice barely disturbed it.

"I'll cut her loose," he said.

"You can't," Colt argued, but Hunter was already handing Angel's reins off to Casie. Ty Roberts's gray mare, wise with age and experience, shook her head and backed cautiously away.

"Halter her first." Sydney's rasped words stopped him dead in his tracks.

"What?"

"I'm taking her home."

"You gotta be kidding," Hunter said.

Behind him, Colt exhaled heavily. "Maybe we can get her loose, Syd. Maybe we can manage that much, but we can't—"

"*I* can!" she snarled and fought to hold the animal steady through her angry words. She lowered her voice. "She won't survive on her own."

"I don't think—" Colt began, but Hunter interrupted.

"We didn't bring a halter." He glanced back. Tied to Colt's saddle was a thirty-foot lariat. "But we got a rope."

"Okay. I'll move back a little," Sydney said. "You get it around her neck."

Colt shook his head, loosed his lasso, and swung from the saddle. "I'll do it." He handed the reins to his fiancée. "You okay with all of them?"

She nodded brusquely. All three of their mounts had been cagey on the ride out. Spring could bring out the crazy in the most even-tempered animal.

"All right," Colt said. "That'll leave Hunt free to do the cutting."

Hunter pulled a pair of nippers from his saddlebags and stepped forward. The injured horse snorted, blowing brown grasses from beneath its barely visible nostrils.

Colt slipped the end of the rope through the leather-wrapped honda and moved cautiously around the far side of the downed animal. It would be idiotic to try to stand between its head and thrashing forelegs. But this whole thing was one short step up from suicide.

Sydney's gaze met Hunt's. Even her teeth were

bloodied. He clenched his own in reflexive empathy.

"I'll shift back a little," she told Colt. "When she lifts her head, you slip the rope underneath her neck."

It was a terrible plan. Foolish and deluded and possibly deadly, but it was the only one they had.

Sydney exhaled shakily and rose. Frantic to be free, the horse jerked up her head, allowing Colt to lunge forward and shove the rope under her neck. But the tiny reprieve had given the animal leverage. She thrashed more wildly, trying to rise. Her left fore caught Sydney's right knee. She gasped in pain.

There was nothing Hunter could do but throw himself down beside her. The horse struggled again, striking his head, his ankle, but she lay flat finally, limbs thrashing weakly.

"You two okay?" Colt's voice was raspy. Hunter nodded, ignoring the blood that dripped from his lip.

"Just get it done," he ordered and tossed the nippers aside.

Colt slid the end of the lariat back through the honda and snugged the loop up around the mare's neck. Dropping the rope, he retrieved Hunter's wire cutters and eased around the horse's tail to untangle the mess of wires, pushing some aside, snipping others. More than one was embedded in the animal's meaty gaskin muscle. Hunter felt his stomach quiver at the sight, but at least he was blocking Sydney's view. Still, it seemed like forever before Colt moved on to the horse's forelegs, clipping wires, tossing away snippets, crooning encouragement and curses under his breath.

"You're sure this is what you want?" Hunter asked and turned toward Sydney. Just inches away, she looked exhausted and tortured. A two-inch scratch marred her left cheek, a bruise colored her brow, but it was her eyes that caught him in a death grip. Agony and fear and hope shone there in equal measures.

She nodded.

"All right then." He breathed the words. There was a high likelihood that this was a mistake. Heartache, and lots of it, lived down this path. He turned his head toward Colt. "You done?"

The cowboy rose to his feet with a nod. "Give me a minute to grab my lasso and mount up. I'll snub her to Evie's saddle horn and hope like hell she won't make a fuss."

It was a pipe dream and Hunter knew it. This horse was trouble on the hoof. A mustang, by the looks of her, born in the wild, untouched by man. Holy hell. He was as crazy as Sydney was.

Scooting forward, Colt grabbed the end of the lariat, stretched it out as far as he could, then went to fetch the palomino from Casie. The mare stepped dutifully toward the downed animal, uncertainty in every twitching muscle.

"Yeah, I know," he soothed. "You'd have to be a damned moron not to be scared."

The mare blew gustily through nostrils wide with worry. It wasn't natural for a horse to be stretched out on the ground while in the presence of strangers. It wasn't normal. It wasn't right. They were prey animals, ready to flee at a moment's notice, to bolt just as Evie wanted to do right now, but she stood her ground as Colt retrieved the tail of his lasso and mounted the mare. Fewer than ten feet from the ragged hooves of the mustang, he dallied up to the saddle horn and prayed the four strands of Mexican maguey would stand the test.

"Okay." He breathed the word softly. "I'm dallied up. When I count to three, you two get the hell off her head and as far away as you can scramble."

"What if she can't get her feet under her?" Sydney's question was barely audible, but Hunter heard her.

"Listen." He caught her gaze with his own. "You're not going to help her up. You got that?"

"We can't just—"

"You get yourself out of the way," he ordered.

Her eyes screamed mutiny. He dug deep for patience.

"This here is a thousand pounds of crazy," he

said. "If she gets up while you're in the vicinity, you're dead."

"You don't—"

"Sydney!" He gritted her name as the mare struggled beneath them again. "If this horse kicks you in the head, there won't be anybody to take care of her while we're at your funeral."

For a moment he was sure she would argue, but finally she nodded.

"All right," Hunter said. "We're ready when you are."

If ever there was a time to curse this was it, he thought, as Colt began the count.

"Three!" he said.

Hunter scrambled away, but Sydney's legs, numb from an hour of immobilized fear, failed her. She fell. Hunter grabbed her coat and dragged her into the brush just as the mustang lurched to her feet. Panicked by the constraints, she reared, but her hind legs gave out. She toppled onto her side. Beneath Colt, the palomino stood firm as the mustang lurched up again, fighting for freedom. But suddenly the injured animal lunged forward. Evie leaped out of the way, nearly unseating her rider in the process.

The dun hit the end of the rope and swung toward them, neck squeezed tight by the lariat, eyes popping with pain and terror, bloody legs spread wide.

"Mount up," Colt ordered.

The mustang fought again, twisting wildly at the end of the rope. Sydney's face was pale.

"You ride the old gray," Hunt said.

"I don't ride," Sydney said.

"You don't have to worry. She'll be—" Hunt began, but just then the mustang threw herself sideways, staggered, and almost fell.

Sydney limped over to stand behind her.

"You tug her along toward the farm as best you can," she said, gaze on Colt. "I'll crowd her up from behind if needed."

Hunt gritted his teeth at her stubbornness, but mounted the gray himself. He wasn't even going to think about trying to get the beast into the barn. Or what kind of condition that barn was in.

The trip to Gray Horse Hill was like a circuitous journey through hell. The mustang's struggles became increasingly weaker until, barely able to walk, she wheezed like an asthmatic, ragged hooves dragging. A trail of blood and staggering hoof prints followed behind.

"What do we do with her when we get there?" Colt asked.

Sydney glanced at him. Mud blanketed the front of her borrowed coat. One pant leg had been half ripped away. She was no longer trying to disguise her exhaustion.

"Maybe we could get her into the trailer. Take her to the Lazy," Casie said, but Hunter laughed. Both women turned toward him, expressions suggesting he might have lost his mind. He didn't bother to mention that they had obviously gone down that road before him.

"We'll put her in my barn," Sydney said. Hunt couldn't help but notice that she didn't look at the animal when she spoke.

"You got a stall that'll hold her?" Colt asked.

Hunter shook his head. He wasn't sure that barn would hold a *dead* horse.

They struggled on. But eventually, they were trudging up the final hill, dragging the mustang through the first broken-down gate and into a dilapidated four-rail pen.

Hunter expected the animal to fight to the death before entering the barn. But maybe death was closer than he realized, because she barely balked as they entered the building. A trio of feral cats scattered as she staggered wearily into the wide, dusty aisle. Stalls lined both sides. Some of them were missing doors. All of them were missing boards.

"Any way to close up the barn?" Colt asked.

Sydney shook her head. "I don't think so. The third stall on the right might hold her, though."

Until she died of tetanus, gangrene, or blood loss, Hunter thought, but he kept the gloomy prospect to himself.

"Maybe Evie and I can pull her into the stall," Colt suggested, but Casie argued immediately.

"You'll all get hurt that way."

Hunter nodded agreement. "Just get her up even with the doorway, then block the far exit and set her loose."

"What?" Casie and Sydney spoke in unison.

Hunter gave them a ghost of a smile. "Maybe you could block that route back there in case she gets past me."

Colt did as he was told, dragging the tortured mustang along until she stood braced against the rope in the middle of the aisle.

"Okay," Hunter said.

Colt backed Evie up, gaining a little slack, then, flipping the rope from the saddle horn, tossed the lariat to the ground. Catching a whiff of freedom, the mustang spun shakily toward the door, but Hunter caught her by the nose as she charged past and wrestled her into the stall.

Hooves slammed wildly against plywood. Grunts and rasps and squeals echoed through the barn. Sydney stumbled toward the enclosure.

"Easy, little sister." Hunt kept his voice as steady as the earth beneath their feet, as quiet and slow as if he wasn't locked in a cage with a crazed animal five times his size. "All is well."

"Let him out," Sydney ordered, but Hunter spoke before Colt could comply.

"I'll stay here for a minute, make sure she doesn't escape while you get her feed and water."

"Do you have a bucket?" Casie's voice sounded tight.

"I'll get one," Sydney said and hurried away, too exhausted to hide her limp.

"Did we bring any hay along?" Colt asked.

"Some," Casie said and pivoted her bay toward the big open doors. She returned in a matter of minutes, carrying the fodder toward the mustang's stall.

Colt eased the door open. Hunter's eyes met Casie's.

"True friends are not easy to come by," he said.

"What?"

He nodded toward Sydney, just struggling down the hill with a bucket sloshing water onto her tattered pant legs. "She is lucky to count you as hers."

"I hardly know her," Casie argued, but he had already turned back to the mustang, voice as soothing as a lullaby.

Chapter 14

"Want some coffee?" Hunter asked.

"Always." Colt's voice was emphatic.

"Please." Casie's was appreciative.

The four of them stood inside Gray Horse Hill's kitchen. Everything in Sydney ached to apologize for their grotesque surroundings: the peeling wallpaper, the scarred floor, the plywood propped on sawhorses that acted as a substitute for a table.

"I'll get it," she said instead, but Redhawk blocked her way.

"You will sit," he ordered.

Embarrassment flooded her, almost edging out the weighty fatigue and throbbing pain caused by the ordeal just past. She could feel her guests' attention like a spotlight against her neck.

"Now," Redhawk insisted and she sat, despite his presumptuous tone, perching on a five-gallon bucket of joint compound in the middle of the room.

Still, she struggled for normalcy. "Please . . ." She made a regal motion with her hand, indicating the piano bench she had found in the hayloft, the ancient rocking chair Hunter had carried up from the basement. "Have a seat." Her visitors did as requested. Casie looked as if she was trying hard to make this surreal experience appear normal. Colt merely looked amused. Sydney linked her fingers loosely in her lap and raised her chin a bit. "So . . . do you think she's wild?"

The kitchen, decorated with one perfectly aligned towel and three impossibly red apples, went silent.

"I mean . . ." She refrained from clearing her throat. Sydney Wellesley had been entertaining dignitaries and celebrities since she was old enough to tie her own Hush Puppies. But the circumstances were a little different now. She didn't bother to glance at the urine-yellow oven or the drooping cabinet doors. "Obviously, she's *wild*." Casie had called a veterinarian while they were still in the barn, so there was nothing to do but wait . . . and feel this itchy discomfort like a burr against her skin.

Colt glanced at Redhawk, who gazed back before retrieving two cups from the overhead cabinet. She wasn't entirely sure, but she thought they might be questioning her sanity.

"I simply mean . . ." She tried again. "Do you think she was *born* wild? Or is it more likely that she's feral? An escaped saddle horse, perhaps?"

"Could be," Colt said, Indian-dark eyes narrowed as he considered. "But she's got some strange markings. What do you think, Redhawk? Is she Hunkpapa?"

He lifted heavy shoulders noncommittally, pulled a sleeve of crackers from the cupboard, and handed it to Sydney.

"I don't want—" she began, but he spoke before she could finish the sentence.

"Eat," he ordered.

She pursed her lips and considered mutiny, but fishing a cracker from the plastic seemed easier. She held it loosely in her hand. "Could she be a mustang?"

"Well, she's stubborn." Hunter scowled. "Makes me think she might have some English blood."

Colt chuckled. "Could be she's Scotch-Irish," he said and tilted his head surreptitiously toward Casie Carmichael.

"You're hilarious," his fiancée said.

"And one heck of a bronc rider," Colt added. His gaze was warm with humor and adoration. "But I think I'll let Hunt break out the dun."

Lifting the kettle he'd placed on the burner, Redhawk poured coffee, as fragrant as rose petals, into the mismatched cups. "Turns out I'm not bronc-busting material."

Colt grinned as he took the mug Hunter offered. "Guess you did kind of prove that at the Stampede."

Sydney raised a single brow. "You were in the rodeo, too?"

"Longest three seconds of my life," Hunter admitted.

"Redhawk's a little big for riding saddle broncs," Colt said.

Sydney sat very still, back straight. "I would have thought size would be advantageous in that particular sport," she said. Her fingertips ached. Glancing down, she saw that three nails had been torn to the quick.

"You hoping to pass out?" Redhawk asked.

Sydney looked up, prepared to give him a haughty stare, but her head swam at the simple motion and her hands felt unsteady. Biting back a sharp retort, she nibbled at the cracker.

Redhawk scowled while Colt, eyes bright, expression unreadable, explained. "The longer your legs, the more leverage the animal can get on you. Those limbs start swinging, it's hard to stop. But steer wrestling . . ." He turned toward Redhawk again, shook his head once. "That'd be a good event for you."

"When I'm in a hurry to break my nose again, I'll remember that," he said and handed Casie a cup of coffee before easing his hips against the counter behind him.

Sydney stared at him. Coffee, he very well knew, was as addictive as opium for her, and though they only had the two mugs, she'd be willing to drink it straight from the pot; Emily Post, after all, was unlikely to show up for luncheon. But Redhawk simply tilted his head toward the crackers again. She took another grudging bite.

Colt was eyeing them with unabashed curiosity. But Casie broke the silence.

"So you're not planning to return to LA?"

Redhawk shrugged.

Sydney scowled. "You lived in Los Angeles?"

"He moved down there to live the high life after—" Colt began, but Hunter interrupted.

"I realized I wasn't going to make my fortune in rodeo."

Colt watched him in silence.

"And what about you?" Casie asked, turning toward Sydney. "Have you decided to stay, too?"

"Not indefinitely, of course," she said and smiled as though the idea was ludicrous, as if she had a choice in the matter. "But I thought it might be . . ." She had hung Hunter's jacket in the hallway only to discover that two of the buttons on her blouse had gone AWOL. She couldn't help but realize how ridiculous she must seem sitting straight as a pin with her hair looking as if she'd lost an argument with a lightning bolt. ". . . amusing to spend a few months here." If one found frostbite amusing. Or poverty.

"Well . . . Dad has some real fond memories of this place," Colt said and glanced around the kitchen as if he weren't sitting in the middle of purgatory. "It'll be good to see Gray Horse get a facelift."

"Perhaps just a chemical peel," Sydney said and was met with blank stares.

The silence was beginning to burn when Hunter spoke to Colt again. "You want to see what we've done so far?"

"Sure," Colt said, and setting his coffee down on the pseudo-table, stood. Their footsteps tapped away.

Silence stole in. Sydney tightened her grip on the crackers and refrained from making a lunge for the abandoned coffee. "Thank you," she said finally.

138

"For what?" Casie's tone sounded honestly confused.

"For coming out. For helping with the horse. For risking your lives."

"Well, we could hardly leave you out there alone," Casie said.

Actually, that was exactly what she could have done, Sydney thought, and wondered how she would have reacted in the same situation. But she had more pressing things to worry about. "Do you think she'll make it?"

A muscle twitched in the other woman's cheek. "Maybe if we can . . ." She paused, exhaled, tightened her fingers around the warmth of the mug she held in both hands. "It looks bad."

Sydney glanced away. "You think I'm naïve to try. A city girl, too pampered to know better."

Casie watched her, taking in her marred skin, scattered hair, and ruined blouse. "Too *kind* to know better," she corrected softly.

Sydney laughed. The sound was rough, sliding toward hysteria if she wasn't careful. "You don't know me at all."

"Maybe *you* don't."

Their gazes met, clashed, softened.

"Vet's here," Casie said at the sound of a vehicle pulling up outside. She rose to her feet. Sydney stood, too, winced, and levered herself upright. For a moment a dozen ridiculous excuses trembled on her lips, but none of them seemed worth the effort, not here, not now. "Please don't pity me," she said and made her way toward the door. Once outside, however, she stopped short. The man who dismounted from the four-wheel drive was small, bent, and as old as black pepper. She glanced toward the passenger side, hoping perhaps for some young behemoth with a full head of hair and popping biceps. Foiled again.

Beside her, Casie chuckled. "He survived Pearl Harbor. He'll make it through this," she said and trotted down the sloping plywood.

"Plus he's the only vet currently available in a fifty-mile radius," Colt added and rambled after her.

"Thanks for coming, Doc," Casie called.

"So you found yourself a mustang?" The old man's voice was coarse but steady in the evening stillness. Dusk had settled in.

"We're not sure what she is," Casie said and shifted to widen the circle. "Sydney Wellesley, this is Doc Miller, best castrator in the tricounty area."

God save them, Sydney thought. But his handshake was strong, his eyes sharp as whispered secrets.

"You the one bought this place, Cindy?" he asked.

She didn't bother to correct the name. "Yes, sir."

He nodded briskly at the old house. "We used to have us some swell parties here." A quixotic blend of happiness and sorrow shone on his face, but in a moment it was gone, replaced by firm stoicism and old-world practicality. "Well . . ." He turned, strides short but quick as he headed toward the barn. "Let's get at it."

Sydney had to hustle to keep up.

The fact that two lightbulbs still worked in the high rafters of the ancient barn was nothing short of a miracle. Still, they did little to dissipate the falling darkness.

The Lazy's saddle horses had been tied close by in the hopes that their presence would calm the injured animal. And from between the mismatched boards, the dun looked almost tranquil . . . until she sensed their arrival. Then she tossed her tangled forelock and shuffled feet bloodied from a dozen awful wounds.

Steadying himself on the crisscrossed lumber that covered the front of the stall, Doc peered through the chinks at the animal inside. When he turned back his brows were low, his eyes squinted. "Been a while since I worked any miracles."

"I know her injuries look severe." Sydney realized with some surprise that she'd been holding her breath. She clasped her hands now, tattered nails clawing into scraped skin. "But she's a fighter. If you had seen how difficult it was to get her here, you'd realize she's not ready to give up. She wants . . ." She glanced through the boards, saw the tensed muscles, the jutting ribs, and felt the mare's pain like a knife in her own aching flesh. "She wants very badly to live."

The old man simply glared at her from beneath hoarfrost brows.

Sydney straightened her spine and raised her chin. "I don't know what your usual fee is, but I assure you—"

Doc flapped a gnarled hand as if shooing flies and glanced at Redhawk. "You a linebacker?"

"Not recently." The Hunkpapa's voice was low and steady.

Doc eyed him up, taking his time at his chest and arms. "Professional wrestler?"

"It's been a few years."

"You ever work with horses?"

"Used to do some relay racing."

"Indian relay?" Casie asked, tone bright with interest. "Really?"

Her fiancé raised his brows.

"It was a while back," Redhawk admitted.

"Mugger or rider or what?" Casie asked.

Something sparked in Colt Dickenson's eyes. Jealousy, maybe. "Racing's like patty-cake compared to bronc riding, you know."

Casie ignored him.

Hunter snorted. "Done some of everything," he said.

The old man nodded. "All right, then, if you see that beast coming toward me . . ." He nodded toward the mustang. "You divert him. You hear?"

It was Hunter's turn to nod.

Doc scanned the faces of the foursome around him. "Anybody who's scared of blood, his own or that horse's, should hightail it now." No one vacated the premises, though honest to God, Sydney considered it. "Okie dokie." He heaved a sigh. "We ain't gonna try nothin' heroic. No way we're gettin' an IV in right off the bat. So I'll just give him something in the muscle to take off the edge. But we're still gonna have to catch the bugger, and when I say 'we' I mean you all." He lowered his bristly brows and glared at Colt. "How's that leg you busted a couple years back?"

The cowboy's lips twisted into a sly grin. "If I say it hurts like a bear-cat, can I sit this one out?"

"Not unless you wanna be called a sissy in front of your girl there. Seems to me it ain't too late for her to run off with a fella could maybe bench-press you and that horse together," Doc said and nodded toward Hunter.

"Guess I'm in then."

"Good decision," the old man said. "Okay. We're gonna have to get a halter on him."

"We don't have a halter," Sydney said. "And it's . . . it's a mare."

"What?" He tilted his grizzled head at her.

"Courage . . ." She said the name softly to see how it felt on her tongue. It seemed right, good, strong . . . maybe even hopeful. "She's a mare."

"He's a mess is what he is." Doc Miller had never gotten the gender of a patient right in his fifty odd years of practice and he wasn't about to start now. "What the devil are you doing with a horse if you don't even have a halter?"

She had no answer to that. What the devil was she doing with a horse at all? She had sworn off the equine species.

"You got any in your trailer?" Doc asked.

Casie shook her head. "We were in a rush. Just put the horses in there loose."

"The mare shook off the loop," Colt said. "But I can get her lassoed again."

"Then what?" Doc asked.

"Then I can maybe ear her down," Hunter suggested.

"No!" Sydney's stomach lurched. She'd seen the practice done on spaghetti westerns. A cowboy would immobilize a rank horse by cranking on its ear.

Every eye turned toward her.

"I don't want to hurt her," she said. The words sounded silly even to herself. The mare was in far too much pain to worry about a twisted ear. But it was too late to retract her concerns.

"Listen, Cindy," Doc said, tone no-nonsense, gaze direct. "We'll be lucky if that beast don't kill each and every one of us before keeling over himself. But we gotta either treat 'im or put 'im out of his misery."

Sydney tightened her fingers around themselves. "We're not putting her down."

The barn went silent. A glimmer shone in the old man's eyes. He nodded once. Maybe in approval. Maybe to say she was city-slicker crazy. "All right. Well, we ain't gonna get much done if he tears us limb from limb before we even get our sleeves rolled up."

Her knuckles hurt where she squeezed them. "Okay." She exhaled carefully. "Do what you have to."

The old man turned toward the others. "You folks got to hold him still."

"No room for all of us." Hunter's voice was barely a rumble.

"What's that?"

"The more people we've got in there, the more's going to get trampled."

"The Hunkpapa makes a fine point," Colt said. "I should probably stay out of it. Maybe go fix us a little snack. You got any brownie mix, Syd?"

Doc snorted. "You always was a dang comedian. Amazing your mama didn't knock you on the head and throw you out with the bathwater. But the big Indian's right."

No one mentioned the less-than-PC terminology. Perhaps when one was leaning heavily toward the hundred-year mark, such things didn't matter. Doc curled knobby fingers around the scarred stall boards and glanced inside.

Courage snorted and jittered, hooves scraping nervously against the far wall. The saddle horses twitched empathetically.

Doc's brows were low above seen-it-all eyes. "You two boys'll have to handle that big devil yourselves."

Colt stroked a hand down Evie's golden neck. "Well, if I'm not whipping up a batch of brownies, we might as well get at it. Listen, Case, why don't you and Sydney take the horses back to the Lazy."

"Now?" Casie asked.

"They'll just get riled up with all this going on. You might as well—" Colt began, but Sydney interrupted.

"You're not going to get rid of me so you can put her down."

"I didn't say anything about that," Colt said, but there was a hint of guilt in his tone.

"And you're not going to," Sydney cautioned.

He blew out a breath, looking uncomfortable with being the voice of reason. "Things could go south pretty quick."

"Then I guess I'd better be here to push them north again."

Colt shook his head and Redhawk glowered, but no more was said on the subject.

"All right then, let's get 'er done," Doc said and motioned toward the stall door.

Chapter 15

Sydney watched as Colt recoiled his lariat. She clenched her fists as he and Hunter stepped inside the stall, and held her breath as Doc closed the door behind them.

One moment the barn was as silent as death and the next it sounded as if a bomb had been detonated. Something crashed. Someone gasped. A thousand pounds of wild struck the wall. The timbers shivered under the impact. Snorts and orders and curses sizzled in the air.

"Okay." It might have been Colt who wheezed out the single word or the sound might have been caused by a gusty flutter of wind. Whatever the case, the threesome in the aisle remained immobile.

"You got 'im?" Doc called.

Agonized, Sydney tried to peer past the old man's whipcord form, but only a scant section of one blood-smeared wall could be seen in the dim light.

"I think so," Colt rasped.

"Sooner's better than later." Even Redhawk's voice sounded strained. "Let's—"

A crash interrupted his dialogue. There was a grunt, a curse.

"Don't let him—"

"Hey!"

Able to wait no longer, Sydney squeezed past Doc and lunged inside. The mare was staggering backward. Hunter had one hand behind the animal's ears, one clasped over her nose. Colt was braced against the lariat, holding tight with leather-gloved hands. Both men were wide-eyed as they stumbled after the flailing mare, but adrenaline or something like it pitched Sydney into the fray. Grabbing the dun's left ear, she bent it double and squeezed tight. The animal went momentarily still, subdued by that odd black magic older than time.

"Okay! Hold 'im! Hold 'im!" Doc ordered and lurched forward, syringe at the ready. Raising his hand, he prepared to plunge the needle into the animal's hindquarters. But Courage twisted and reared, slamming into the old man. The syringe leaped from his hand. Doc was spun away and thrown against the wall. Casie torpedoed inside, prepared to drag him to safety, but he shook her off. "The syringe! Get the syringe."

Squinting into the gloom, Casie snatched up the sedative. As the others wrestled the frantic animal to a standstill, Doc urged her on. "In the haunches. Now! While you got the chance."

For a moment the mare stood immobile, and in that instant, Casie shoved the needle into the animal's muscle.

Courage leaped, dragging her handlers across the stall, then reared, shaking Redhawk loose and tossing Sydney to the ground. For a moment Colt dangled from his lariat like stubborn autumn fruit, but then he was down. He hit his knees and scrambled for safety just as the others did the same.

For one frantic moment there was a jam of bodies in the doorway, but finally they burst through and slammed the door shut behind them.

Colt shoved the latch home, pressed his back to the timbers, and panted.

"Whew!" His eyes were alight, his grin full bore. "Some fun, huh!"

So he was crazy, Sydney thought dazedly. Sure, made sense. All the good ones were. She turned woodenly toward Casie, sick to her stomach, nerves cranked tight. "Did you get it in?"

"Yeah." The woman's hands were shaking like wind socks, a strange juxtaposition against her fiancé's apparent delight. But maybe it was to be expected for a rough-stock cowboy to get a punch of pleasure out of an adrenaline rush. "I think so. I just . . ." She shook her head and glanced at Hunter, drawing Sydney's gaze with hers. His big body looked absolutely relaxed, his face all but expressionless. She blinked. "Are you okay?"

"Ai," he said.

Colt snorted as he shifted away from the stall

door. "This life-and-death stuff isn't boring you, is it, big guy?"

"You're sure you got it in?" Sydney asked.

Casie nodded. "I just hope I didn't get it too deep or . . ."

"It's okay," Doc said. "You done your best. All of you. Is everybody all right?"

They glanced at one another. There was a rip in Redhawk's flannel shirt, showing an inch of pale thermal underneath. It took Sydney a moment to realize the soft cotton was edged in blood. The others seemed to notice the injury at the same time.

"You all right, Hunt?"

The Indian glanced quizzically at Colt, noticed the direction of his gaze with mild surprise, and shifted his attention to the tear in his shirt. His nod was casual. "Just a scratch." He tipped his head toward the stall. "How long before she goes down?"

Doc shook his head. "Won't go down. Don't think so, anyway. Just gave him some Torb and a little Dormosedan. He'll stay on his feet, but it should slow him down considerable."

Inside the stall, the mare tossed her dreadlocked mane and pawed frantically.

"I hope," the old man added.

"Then how long do we have?" Sydney's words sounded squeezed tight.

"Once it takes effect?" Doc's scraggly brows

drew together over periwinkle eyes. "Impossible to say for sure, but we ain't gonna want to dilly-dally."

"What do we need to get started?"

"Hot water. I don't have none in my truck."

"I'll get that," Sydney said.

"You boys . . ." Doc spoke to the men as if they were barely out of swaddling. "Come fetch supplies with me. Case, you watch the horse. Yell soon as you see his nose drop to his knees." He stormed away, old joints swinging like pendulums as he strode past the saddle horses.

In a matter of minutes, they were all reassembled in the dusty aisle.

"We ready?" If the old man was nervous, he didn't show it.

Hunter went in first. Courage raised her head and shuffled sideways, but her movements were slow, her eyes dull.

"Good. That's just dandy," Doc said and sidled inside, but Sydney couldn't help noticing he was using Redhawk's body as a buffer. Proof, perhaps, of the old man's intellect. "Loop the lariat around his nose. Hold this, Case." He shoved a plastic bag of fluids into her hands. "Cindy . . ." He nodded sharply in Sydney's direction. It seemed too late to correct him. "You bring that tray there."

Her hands shook a little as she lifted the cooler containing bottles and syringes and needles.

Even drugged, the horse seemed bigger than life, but finally they had a makeshift bridle twisted over her nose and had backed her against the wall.

"Hold his head up," Doc ordered. "Turn him a little. Jumping jehosaphat, there ain't no light in here at all." He jabbed his thumb against the animal's neck, eased a needle in, and tugged at the plunger. Nothing happened. "Where's that blasted . . ." His voice trailed off as he tried another site. "Darn veins are drier than cockleburs. Can't even . . ." he began, but finally blood flowed into the tube. He shook his head at the sight of it. "Thick as molasses and near as dark." Twisting off the syringe, he stabbed the conduit from the IV bag onto the needle. "All right, Case, hold it up." He nudged her hand. "Way up. We wanna get him as juiced up as possible in the time we got. Colt, rig up something in the middle of the ceiling to hang that from. Redhawk, hold him tight. I'm going to start him on antibiotics. Hang it all, it's darker than hell in here."

"I could bring my car in," Sydney said. "Shine the headlights through the door."

"Do what you gotta do. Then start cleaning up them legs. Can't do nothing till we know what we've got."

Running to her rented BMW, Sydney crammed herself inside and roared toward the barn. In a minute she was bumping down the aisle. The saddle horses pricked up their ears at her arrival. The bay stallion jittered, but Evie and Angel remained as they were, watching while Sydney poked the right fender into the stall. Inside, the mare's eyes went wide. She raised her head with a jerk, but remained otherwise unmoving, tattered legs braced wide.

Sydney pulled her attention from those bloody limbs, jerked out of the car, and hurried around the bumper.

"Out of the light now! Get out of the way." Doc shooed her aside. "Better. Okay. Get to scrubbing. Don't worry 'bout being gentle. Too late for that," he said and turned back to the others, giving orders like a major general. But Sydney heard no more. In the Bimmer's harsh lights, the animal's injuries were fully exposed. She stood, bucket in one hand, rag in the other, staring at the swollen, bloody mess that had once been a leg. The hide had been stripped from the cannon bone. Flesh puckered around the coronary band, and the proud gaskin muscle that should have sent the animal flying across the plains was shredded like confetti.

"This ain't no time for daydreaming! Get it done or get out of my way," the old man snapped, and Sydney reached out, wet rag trembling.

Chapter 16

"Thank you." Sydney pushed out the words with an effort. It was past midnight and Doc had departed, along with the crew from the Lazy. Fatigue gnawed at her, weakening her legs, slowing her movements. But the man on the far side of the kitchen barely acknowledged her sparse appreciation.

"Eat," Redhawk said and shoved that damned sleeve of crackers back into her hand.

Instead, she paced, knees threatening to drop her face-first onto that god-awful linoleum. "I should check on her," she said and turned to charge out the door, but Hunter caught her by an arm and reeled her back.

"She's a thing of the wild, woman. Let her be."

"Let her be?" She stiffened her shoulders and tilted her head at him, taking some comfort in the habitual hauteur, though truth to tell, it took all her self-control to keep from slapping his hand away like a distraught toddler. Odd. So odd. She had never been the emotional sort. There were, in fact, a number of individuals back east who would attest to the fact that she had no emotions whatsoever. "Perhaps it would surprise you to know that she would have died out there. Would have expired from dehydration or starvation or . . ." She took a moment to breathe, nowhere near understanding her own internal turmoil. Animals, after all, died every day. Hell, she *ate* animals. But perhaps the fact that she didn't have to witness their deaths made all the difference. She didn't have to see the fear, the determination, the hope, dwindling like daylight in their mercurial eyes. Or maybe her reactions were even more elemental than that. Maybe she herself felt trapped, tangled, hopeless. "Wild animal attacks . . ." The image of predators circling while the mare lay unable to protect herself made her stomach twist. "She'd probably already be dead if . . ." She paused, took a calming breath, and remembered whom she was talking to. Remembered Hunter Redhawk charging into the fray for no good reason. "If you hadn't . . ." She cleared her throat and drew her shoulders back another half an inch. Pride, that painful, sharp-edged arrogance, still clung to her like a second skin. But some things couldn't be denied no matter how difficult it was to force out the truth. "If you hadn't risked your life to save her."

His eyes shone in the single overhead light as if he were amused but hadn't mentioned the fact to his face. His expression remained absolutely impassive, full mouth soft and unbowed. She pulled her gaze from those lips, letting her attention skim lower. His neck was corded with muscle, his shoulders endless, his shirt . . .

She scowled at the forgotten rent in the flannel. "You're injured."

He shrugged, movement dismissive as he placed an onion on the cutting board. The skin was as red as a pomegranate. "Eat, before you pass out."

She ignored him. It wasn't a simple task, but she had learned to focus from a man with a German accent and a riding crop. "How badly?"

"A scratch."

She huffed an exhalation of disbelief. "Let me see it," she ordered, but he neither acquiesced nor refused. Instead, he watched her with dead-steady eyes as he rinsed the blade of his bone-handled knife.

"If you eat I shall disrobe."

"Disrobe!" She actually flinched, jerked as if struck. "I'm not asking for a lap dance!"

"Ahh." He lifted one shoulder a quarter of an inch as if in apology. "My mistake."

"Yes, it *is* your . . ." She paused. Was there laughter in his eyes? Was he teasing her? She pursed her lips. There was nothing in the world she hated more than being teased. Unless it was being laughed at. Or patronized. Or pitied. "Remove your shirt."

"Eat your crackers."

She lifted the offensive package in one tight fist. "Why are you so insistent about these things?"

"We're out of escargot."

She huffed, glanced away, then looked at him again. Was it her imagination, or did his face seem a little pale above his scruffy beard? "Fine." She scowled. "How many would you like me to eat?"

"Five for each article of clothing."

"I only want you to take off your shirt."

His shoulders twitched. "Your loss."

She rolled her eyes and made some kind of a noise. It couldn't have been a snort. Wellesleys did not, under threat of death, snort. Opening the plastic sleeve, she removed a cracker and took the first bite. He watched, then turned toward the refrigerator. Removing a large glass jar, he poured milk into a coffee cup and set it beside her elbow.

She raised her brows at it. "Where did that come from?"

"Emily brought it."

"Emily from the Lazy?"

"Ai."

"Why?"

"In exchange for pictures," he said.

"I beg your pardon?"

"She is an excellent photographer. I think she wishes to take pictures of the mare."

"Courage? Why?"

"She cares. I believe she will be around quite often. Perhaps the boy, too."

"What boy? Ty?"

He shrugged, nodded toward the milk. "Drink it."

"It tastes funny." She took another cracker and wondered when she had become a five-year-old.

"Do you want me to start with my socks?" he asked and fiddled with the stove. It hissed, crackled, and spit forth a ring of blue flame. Though honest to God, she had no idea when he had repaired it.

She scowled at his back. It was the approximate width of the plywood they used as a table. "I thought the Indian was too proud to cheat."

"My mother was German," he said and nodded toward the milk.

German. Really? She took a sip. It wasn't too bad. Maybe she would get used to it, she thought, and finishing her fifth cracker, brushed off her hands and pushed the coffee cup aside. "Let's get this done."

"I'll take care of it," he assured her.

"You'll take off your shirt," she ordered and stepped forward. Temper flaring, she tugged his hem toward his chest. "Or I'll . . ." A two-inch crescent of incised flesh brushed her knuckles. Blood smeared liberally across her hand. She jerked back.

"You should sit," he suggested.

"I don't have to," she said, but the words sounded a little garbled.

"Sit!" he ordered, and taking her arm, eased her onto the piano bench.

She sat, not because he'd made her but because it was the practical thing to do. Swooning like a punch-drunk pugilist would be more theatrical than sensible to her way of thinking.

"You have to see a doctor," she said.

But he shook his head and moved toward the refrigerator again. It was as old as Medusa and just as ugly. He drew out a carton of eggs, cracked six into a chipped bowl he had gotten from who knows where, and mixed them with the tarnished tines of an ancient fork they'd picked up at the Re Uzit Shop in Custer. Turning his back, he added a number of ingredients she didn't know he had purchased.

"Hunter . . ." She said his name softly. He glanced over his shoulder at her. In the five days since their acquaintance, she had rarely used his given name. The look in his eyes made her stomach clench. Or maybe it was just the smell of bacon sizzling in the pan. It smelled astonishingly good. And she never ate bacon.

"Please . . ."

She wondered how often she had said that word in her lifetime. It felt foreign and out of place. "You have to have that looked at."

"You looked," he said, and removing the bacon, added the onions he had diced moments before. "It did little good."

"I'm not a doctor."

He stirred the onions, broke up the fried bacon. "That is why I let you look."

"Why don't you like doctors?"

His shoulders had stiffened, she noticed, his tone hardened, though his hands never ceased to stir and chop and fiddle. "They don't need me to stroke their egos or pad their bank accounts."

"Oh." The truth struck her suddenly. He was concerned about money. Just because he had helped her buy building supplies hardly meant he was wealthy. But . . . wouldn't insurance cover this sort of eventuality? It was embarrassing to admit, even to herself, how little she knew of life. Oh, she could canter a perfect pirouette or entertain a hundred A-list guests for a six-course dinner. But she'd never in her life filled out an insurance form or fed a baby or bought tires for her car. "I can . . . I can loan you the money, if that's the problem."

He dumped the contents of the bowl into the pan and glanced at her from the corner of his eye. "I wasn't aware that you had money to waste."

"I didn't plan to waste it."

He turned fully toward her, letting his hips rest against the stove behind him for a moment. "You cannot afford to repair your own home."

"It's not as if a quick trip to the emergency room is going to cost ten thousand dollars." She blinked, feeling foolish and a little sick. "Is it?"

"Not if I don't go," he said and returned to his cooking.

She scowled, certain his logic was full of holes. But before she could point them out, he had taken a lone spoon from a drawer, cut his concoction in two, and shoved a half-moon shape onto a chipped plate before placing it on the plywood in front of her.

"*Bon appétit.*"

She breathed it in, olfactory glands humming with the scent of cheddar and bacon. "You made me an omelet?"

He shrugged and tapped it toward her. "I am out of pemmican. And Emily brought eggs when she came for pictures of Courage."

She ignored most of his verbiage and focused on the meal. "You can cook?" Even to her own ears, her tone sounded blatantly offended at this unknown expertise, and for a moment she was half afraid she'd cry. What the devil was wrong with her? It wasn't as if she was completely without skills. She could . . . What? she wondered dismally. What could she do?

"Eat it," he ordered, but she shook her head.

"*You* eat it." Her voice had gone from insulted to petulant in the blink of an eye.

He gritted his teeth in irritation and for one

wild second a surge of fear rushed her. What did she really know about this man? Who was he? Why did he refuse to see a doctor? Maybe it wasn't for financial reasons at all. After all, he *did* have skills. Skills that could surely earn him a decent living. So maybe . . . Breath clogged in her throat. Was he a criminal? Was that why he was alone and homeless and reticent?

She drew a careful breath. "Are you wanted?" Her words were very quiet, but he heard them. Their gazes met with a soft clash.

"Not by many," he said and turned back to the stove.

"What does that mean?"

He angled toward her and folded his arms across his chest. His rucked-up sleeves displayed broad bone and corded muscle. Black hair was sprinkled lightly across dark skin. It looked hopelessly touchable. Which was ridiculous. She didn't like burly men. In fact, she wasn't sure she liked men at all.

"Eat," he ordered.

She was tempted. The bacon smelled like heaven, though it was common knowledge that nitrates came straight from the devil. Father had never eaten bacon a day in his life. Grandmother only ate chicken breast, carefully trimmed and spritzed with lemon juice. "I'll make you a trade," she said.

He stared at her in that quiet way he had.

"I'll eat if you go to the doctor."

"No." There wasn't a moment's pause before his refusal.

"Then I'm not going to—"

"But if you eat, I'll let you tend my wound."

She shook her head and knew she was weak because the truth was, she didn't want to. Not anymore. She had imagined his injury to be a scratch. An inconsequential nick that could be mended with a dab of iodine and an adhesive bandage. "Perhaps you've mistaken me for someone with skills, Redhawk."

His brows lifted a little. "I saw you with the horse."

She winced at the memory of the gore that filled the bucket she'd used to scrub the mare's legs.

"You have the touch."

She remembered words to the contrary. From her father, from her riding instructors. "That's not what I've been told."

He held her gaze, steady and soft, like a swallow in his hand. " 'All mankind was blessed with speech. Fool and scholar alike. But wonder I if jaded sage be gifted as awestruck tyke.' "

She raised her brows at him, mind riffling through a hundred memorized poems. "Yeats?"

"Ty Roberts."

She made a face. "Angel's owner?"

He nodded once.

"The boy's a poet?"

He shrugged. "Sometimes people are not what they seem."

"Are we talking about you?"

Another shrug. "Perhaps we speak of *you*."

She held his gaze for a second before looking away. "What you see is what you get."

"And what do I see?"

"A spoiled little rich girl with no patience for foolishness."

He narrowed his eyes and shook his head once, but didn't call her a liar outright. "To my way of thinking it would be foolish to pass out from hunger."

"It just so happens I don't think it would be all that brilliant if you dropped dead on my ugly linoleum."

They remained as they were. At a standoff. Staring at each other.

She was the first to break. "You'll let me bandage that if I eat?"

"Ai."

"Was that the German or the Indian talking?"

"This once they are in agreement."

"Then you have a bargain," she said and, turning fully toward her meal, tasted the first bite. The tang of melted cheddar struck her first. But it was the blend of farm-fresh egg and smoky bacon that made her taste buds sing. She chewed slowly, trying to quiet the symphony before she spoke. "Where did you learn to cook?"

164

Lifting the frying pan, he steadied it against his chest. The blackened cast iron against soft flannel made a homey picture, and did earthy things to her equilibrium.

"Mom took a job off the rez to help pay the bills," he said. "It was learn to cook or starve."

So he had been alone, too, she thought, and though she fought the warm feelings that bloomed like spring wildflowers, she couldn't stop the question. "And your father?"

"Could scorch water." He took his first bite. "And frequently did."

"So he was present?"

He gave her a quizzical look.

"I'm sorry. I shouldn't . . ." She paused, wondered if she had apologized more in the past three weeks than ever in her life, and continued. "This is . . ." She shook her head at the simple concoction and brushed back her wayward hair. "You shouldn't be able to fix a furnace *and* cook. It disrupts the natural balance of things."

He watched her in silence, meal momentarily forgotten in the pan.

"It's simply . . ." She cleared her throat. When had she become a throat clearer? Next thing she knew she'd be picking her nose and belching the alphabet. "I'm sure the reservation isn't like it's portrayed by Hollywood."

"How is that?"

She exhaled, considered softening her words,

but decided on truthfulness. "Poverty, abandonment, rampant abuse."

He took a bite of his omelet. She watched it travel to his mouth. His teeth looked primal white against his beard. White but not perfectly straight. Not like hers, which had been cranked into rigid uniformity by an orthodontist with no facial wrinkles whatsoever. She refrained from adding "lack of dental care" to her list of reservation curses.

"You forgot alcoholism and suicide," he said.

"I wasn't judging," she told him and found, to her surprise, that it was true. He had pitched battle for a horse others would have sneered at. Herself included. She felt strangely humbled, patently ashamed.

"I had three brothers."

She caught her breath at his words. In the past he had not exactly been one to ramble on about his childhood.

"None of them were blood."

She waited for more, but he ate in silence.

"Abandonment," he said finally. A muscle flexed in his jaw. "There are times when Hollywood hits the mark dead-on."

She tried to read the nuances and ventured a guess. "Your mother took them in?"

"Our father did not object." His lips twitched a little and his eyes flashed, as if he remembered something that almost amused him. "Not aloud, at least. He believed that courage was not proved by idiocy."

She drank some milk and waited for an explanation.

"She was known on the rez as the Hun. Some called her other things, but none to her face and not within my father's hearing." He smiled, just a glimmer of joy in the spark of his eyes, in the twist of his lips. "She could be . . ." He paused, carefully considering. "Bossy."

There was something in his voice, something almost unfathomable, a kindness, a melancholy, an admiration so deep it all but hummed in him.

"So you inherited your size from her."

"Don't forget the beard."

She raised her brows at him and wondered if she dared disparage his mother with a question regarding hirsutism, but it seemed that even he wasn't brave enough to slander the woman who had raised him.

"From her people," he corrected.

"And her impetuous personality?" she asked.

"The Hunkpapa have a saying."

She waited and ate while she did so. There seemed little point in trying to rush him.

"If the rain is coming, you will know it when your head is wet."

She considered that as she chewed. "Patience is a virtue?"

He shrugged, took the last bite of his meal,

and settled the pan on the counter beside him.

"My people have a saying also," she admitted. "It's 'Why are you standing in the rain, you moron?'"

The laughter seemed to be startled from him, prompting her own unwilling grin. She set her fork carefully on the edge of her regrettably empty plate and let his rumble of humor stir up an odd wash of contentment.

"The duchess made a joke," he said.

She returned his shrug, casual and slow.

"Clearly indicating she needs more sleep."

"Is that the Hessian speaking?" she asked.

He raised a brow.

"Trying to welsh on our bargain?"

"My injury will heal of its own accord."

She shook her head and forced herself to stand. "Take off your shirt."

He scowled at her. If he was trying to be intimidating, he was devastatingly good at it.

"I thought your people honored their bargains."

"Some were known to rape and pillage."

"Which side?"

"Both."

"Take it off," she ordered.

His glare deepened, but finally he reached down, grasped the hems of his shirts, and dragged them over his head.

Sydney drew breath slowly through her nose and didn't even consider passing out . . . until she saw his chest.

Chapter 17

He was built like the hero of the torrid romance novel he had purchased for her. Justin Stearns. Not that Sydney had any interest in the book, but it would have been rude not to read the back . . . and the first few chapters. Justin was what less sophisticated women might have called a hunk, but so far the writing was not atrocious and the terms *thrusting* and *heaving* were kept to a minimum.

As for Hunter Redhawk . . . Sydney felt her breath lock up tight in her throat. His arms were wide, corded with strength, and dark in color while his chest . . . Good gracious, it was packed with enough muscle to shift a freight train. A tattoo of a teddy bear was inked directly over his heart. Sydney pulled her gaze from the sight with an effort. She felt a little light-headed, but was certain it had nothing whatsoever to do with his pectorals.

"Winnie the Pooh?" she asked and tried to sound cosmopolitan, or at least lucid.

His eyes were as steady as stone. "Eeyore was too depressing."

She nodded as if his answer made a world of

sense and dragged her gaze lower, but those regions were no less disturbing. Iron-tight abs bunched like rolling hills above the belt of his buff denim jeans.

She cleared her throat, steeled herself, and punched her gaze toward the wound. The laceration was two inches long, crescent shaped, and ugly. It wept blood and serum and looked like nothing so much as a gory, winking eye. "Your mother's influence again?" she asked, and ripping a dish towel down the middle, doused half with hot water from the kitchen tap.

He raised a brow.

"All the muscle," she explained and dabbed carefully at the wound.

"Some called my father 'Fescue.'"

She dabbed some more and thought about the word. "Tall plant? Not much . . . bulk?"

"Ai."

She smiled a little, imagining his parents. "Am I hurting you?"

He glanced down at her from his towering height. "By your tickling ministrations or the suggestion that I am as delicate as a rose petal?"

"I don't want to get your trousers wet."

"Is that a duchess's way of saying you wish for me to take off my pants?"

"No! No," she said, then calmed her voice and smoothed her expression. She sounded like a prepubescent virgin. She wasn't a virgin. Hardly that. She'd had sex . . . several times. Though none of them came to mind at the moment. Not while in the presence of this rough-hewn warrior god. "I just meant . . ." She refused to glance up, though he might be taunting her again. And honest to God, if he was, he should be horse-whipped, as Megan O'Rourke, fiery temptress extraordinaire, had threatened to do to Justin on page 128. "Here." She shoved the second half of the towel into his hand. "Just . . . hold this over your . . ." She waved vaguely toward his lower half and wondered as neutrally as possible if it was as large as his upper. But she slammed the door on that line of thinking and dabbed more forcefully at the wound. "How did this happen?"

"A nail."

"A . . . what? There's a protruding nail in Courage's stall?"

He caught her eye, raised his brows. "In the aisle. I must have been in a hurry when I exited."

"Oh." She forced herself to relax. The mare's immediate environment was critical, but the remainder of the barn could wait.

"What of *your* mother?" he asked.

She scowled as she squatted before him again. The idea did not escape her that their positions might be misconstrued as sexual. "This should be stitched."

"Did she teach you to sew?"

She almost laughed at the idea. Tales of her

mother, while sparse, were always peppered with the message that she was the epitome of well-bred womanhood. A lady of wealth and quality to the very core of her being. "She died. Almost twenty years ago now, but I doubt she was the kind to mend breeches and darn socks."

"Or to cook."

Sydney wasn't sure what his tone implied. "She was a dancer. Prima ballerina for the American Ballet Theatre."

"A difficult act to follow."

"I had no reason to try."

He tilted his head in question, but she ignored his obvious misgivings.

"I never even mastered the waltz."

"So you did not feel you were living in her shadow?"

She pursed her lips, ignored the implications. "This is going to take a long time to heal if left untreated."

"Sometimes it helps to discuss it."

She glanced up, realized his meaning, and huffed a laugh. "I'm not talking about myself."

He managed to look mildly surprised. "Who then?"

"You! Your injury. I don't even have any ointment."

"I keep some in my truck."

She rose to her feet, thigh twinging aggressively. "Why didn't you tell me that sooner?"

"You did not ask."

"Well . . ." She flapped a jittery hand at him. "Go get it."

"Perhaps you, too, have some Hessian blood," he said and left the room.

Sydney rinsed the rag and fumed silently until he returned a minute later.

"I'm not—" she began, but somehow lost her breath. It wasn't that he was breathtaking . . . exactly. It was just that he was so . . . large and hard and . . .

Hunter raised his brows and glanced down, but his fly wasn't open and she'd already seen his wound. So . . . her gaze seemed to be fixed on his chest. Hmmmf, he thought, and set the jar of ointment on the counter.

The snick of noise seemed to wrench her from her trance.

"—bossy," she said, completing the sentence she'd begun long seconds before. "I'm not bossy."

He narrowed his eyes, held his smile in reserve, and nodded. "Okay."

"I'm just . . ." She looked flustered and pink-cheeked. The effect made her seem softer, sweeter, and . . . God help him . . . as young as a spring lamb. "What's that?" she asked and motioned toward the jar that had once held spare buttons. Before that it had contained his mother's homemade applesauce. Mavis Lindeman Redhawk knew how to pinch a penny. But with five hungry men in the house, she had also learned to break up fights and patch scrapes while simultaneously issuing threats and encouragement.

"Anti-inflammatory ointment?" Even to his own ears, his words sounded more like a question than a statement.

Her brows drew together like a swallow's dark wings. "In an unmarked glass jar?"

"Some of the ingredients are not currently approved by the FDA." It was a conundrum that still vexed him. But he had worked through this kind of problem before. Doing manual labor for minimum wage was all well and good, but he had discovered his entrepreneurial side some years ago.

She picked up the jar. "Is it . . ." She paused, as if searching for a PC term that eluded her.

"An old Indian remedy," he said.

Her frown was dark. "Are you lying to me?"

"The Hunkpapa does not fabricate the truth."

"How about that German guy?"

"He lies like a cream-fed cat."

She pursed her lips at him before turning her disapproval on the jar. "What's in it?"

"Purple coneflower, cohosh." He shrugged, skipping most of the components. "Juniper extract."

He could tell by her expression that she wasn't

prepared to believe him, but that was just as well.

"Does it work?" she asked.

He tilted his head as if uncertain, but the latest experiments had been encouraging. Despite a dozen problems with the concoction in the past, recent recipes had considerably shortened healing time. "I'll let you know in a few days."

"You actually want me to apply it to your wound."

"I believe it was your idea to treat it in the first place." He raised his brows. "Or were you just hoping for that lap dance after all?"

That blush again, as bright as poppy petals. "How much do I use?"

For a moment he was a little too intrigued with that blush to answer, but he let her slip the hook once again. "We'll begin sparingly, then wrap it."

"What?" She was now scowling and blushing. He had no idea why that would make him want to kiss her. She wasn't the kissable sort. She was more the sort one would fan with a palm leaf. Or kiss, *then* fan with a palm leaf. He handed her a rolled-up cotton bandage.

"I don't have the adhesive type." It was a falsehood. Despite the relatively limited space in his truck, he kept a fairly comprehensive first aid kit, but adhesive bandages took almost no time to apply.

"You had a track bandage in your vehicle?"

He raised a brow at her.

She lifted the white wrap. "They're used on horses, aren't they?"

"So you *are* an equestrienne."

Her gaze met his, then skidded away. "Father owned a racehorse for a time. Bandages like these were used to prevent injuries."

He watched her, but she didn't look up again. Her mink-dark hair had long ago escaped its habitual bun. Some would call it messy. Other deluded individuals might refer to it as sexy as hell.

"So your interest in horses was through the track?"

She pulled apart the bandage's Velcro. "He also owned several polo ponies."

Perhaps she wasn't lying exactly, he thought. But she certainly wasn't telling the truth. He could see it in the tight set of her lips, the downward shift of her eyes. It was dangerously intriguing.

"So you learned to ride while swinging a mallet and counting chukkers?" he asked.

She glanced up, expression strangely peeved. "Is there a subject about which you are unfamiliar?"

Why would he find her irritation endearing? Was there something inherently wrong with him or something innately fascinating about her? "My knowledge of Sydney Wellesley is limited."

She shrugged, unscrewed the jar of ointment,

and dipped her fingers inside. They were slim and tapered, and when she reached out to graze his skin, he exhaled carefully, keeping himself steady. It wasn't as if he'd never been touched by a beautiful woman. So perhaps it was the fact that he couldn't remember the last time that made the situation intoxicating.

"I've never played polo," she admitted.

He lifted his gaze from her fingers to her face. Best not to dwell on the capabilities of those delicate digits. "Well, then, consider me fully informed."

She smiled, and for reasons he dared not consider, he felt his heart jolt as if touched by an electric shock.

Their gazes met. The jolt sizzled.

She shifted her attention back to the bandage. "Father didn't think I was . . ."

He watched her, waiting. The silence marched away, but he was comfortable with the quiet. She, however, didn't seem entirely comfortable with anything.

"He didn't think it was something that would interest me," she said.

"Wouldn't that have been your decision?"

She shrugged. The movement looked stiff. "He's my father, and therefore deserving of my respect."

She said the words by rote, as if she had heard them a thousand times. Had memorized them like classic poetry.

"We respected our parents," he said gently. "Didn't mean we wouldn't question their every decision." He grinned at the wash of soft memories. "Or put spiders in the sugar jar. Dad was fond of sugar. But not so crazy about daddy longlegs." He chuckled and realized she was watching him as if he had lost his mind. "Come on. Tell the truth. You must have played a couple practical jokes on your old man."

She shook her head.

"Not even one?"

She pursed her wild-cherry lips. Sometimes, he realized, there was more to be learned from a glance or a gesture than from a thousand words. And her body spoke of a disappointment so long accepted, she was no longer aware of its existence.

"What of you, Hunter Redhawk? You learned to ride while still in diapers, I suppose." She was intentionally evading the subject, but he let her do so without complaint.

"Hollywood wisdom again?" he asked.

She sent him a slanted glance. "You mentioned something regarding a race."

He liked to hear her talk. Liked the neat cadence of her words, as if each one was a pearl carefully cultured.

The silence was lengthening. He glanced down, realized she was watching him. "Indian relay," he said. "Also known as suicide by horse."

"Are you planning to explain that or will you continue to play the stoic warrior?"

Sassy. Sometimes the sass just slipped through the chinks in her polished façade like water through a dam.

"It is a relay race," he said. "Involving four men and three horses."

"Some might call that sexist."

He watched her in silence.

"Women aren't allowed?"

"It is ridden without a saddle."

"A feat that surely no woman could master." Annoyance was sharp in her tone. Or maybe it was pride.

Interesting, he thought, and managed not to laugh. "I imagined you with a top hat and flat saddle rather than bareback."

"Strange, bareback is exactly how I imagine . . ." She stopped herself, looking appalled.

"You imagine me?" All humor had escaped from his tone. His voice was no more than a low rumble.

But she ignored the question. Fastening the bandage with the Velcro, she bumbled to her feet. "Done," she said, and turning with more speed than grace, fled back to the barn.

Chapter 18

It was a long night. And cold.

Sydney stood in the barn's dimly lit aisle. Up above, in the tilting loft covered with moldy hay, a paunchy marmalade cat watched her with unblinking eyes.

Sydney pulled her gaze from it and peered into the stall. Inside, Courage stood absolutely still, head drooping, thick forelock scattered over eyes drugged to dullness. Or maybe it was the pain that caused her lifeless demeanor. Then again, perhaps it was the fact that she was starving.

Every wisp of hay they had piled near the front of the stall remained. As did the water.

Doc Miller had assured them the long-lasting antibiotics should fight the infection, but what of dehydration? Of course, they had administered large doses of fluids, but perhaps the mare's kidneys were already shutting down. And what if, despite the less-than-sterile conditions, they were not able to fight off septicity? Were they condemning the mare to starvation? And if she did finally begin to eat, would she walk again or had her tendons been too badly damaged to allow her anything but the most limited mobility?

Sydney's thigh throbbed as she pressed closer to the stall and curled her fingers around the chill metal bars that made up the top half of the door. The mare shifted her weight and turned her head. Their gazes met and held. The wide brown eyes blinked, filled with wisdom and pain and a thousand worries.

"Don't give up," Sydney whispered. "Don't you dare give up." But Courage turned away, letting her muzzle drop back toward the floor.

Four hours later, Sydney inched her legs over the edge of the ugly mattress. Outside, the sun had risen in a cotton candy sky. The earthy scent of coffee was already seeping into her bedroom. Pinning back her hair, she noticed the garments folded and left near her door: much-abused blue jeans and a kelly-green sweatshirt. The words *University of North Dakota Fighting Sioux* were emblazoned above and below a Native American's dramatic profile. There were distinct similarities between the portrait and the man who had left the garments in her bedroom. Scowling, Sydney stripped off the clothes she'd worn to bed and pulled on the jeans. They were baggy at best. But the sweatshirt was kitten soft and comfortably roomy. She tugged the sleeves halfway up her forearms and headed downstairs.

Once again Redhawk stood in front of the

stove. He turned toward her and froze, spatula lifted nearly to his chest.

"What?" Sydney asked and raised a hand defensively to her throat.

He shook his head and managed a shrug. "You look good."

She laughed. "You need to get out more."

He turned back toward the stove with a snort. "Want some coffee?"

"As soon as I get back in."

He glanced back over his shoulder, eyes suddenly solemn in his chiseled warrior face. "There is no need to rush out."

"What?" The single word rasped like sandpaper against her throat. "Why? What happened?"

"I just returned from the barn."

"And?" She took a staggering step toward him and refrained from shaking him until the words fell out.

"She still lives. If what she does is living."

Sydney drew a careful breath and let her shoulders drop a quarter of an inch. "You disapprove of my bringing her here."

He handed her a mug. The ceramic was chipped, the color faded, but the aroma was as bright as spring flowers. "I did not say so."

"You don't say anything."

His lips lifted a little. "Her will is strong, but her body . . ." He shrugged.

Sydney wrapped her fingers around the warmth

and allowed herself a sip. A soft wave of cautious comfort washed in. Redhawk had a number of shortcomings, but he could brew a tantalizing cup of coffee. She sipped again and found that for the life of her she couldn't seem to recall what those shortcomings were. Fatigue, it seemed, was taking a toll on her memory.

"We have no syrup." His hands looked large and dark against the stainless-steel spatula. He flipped a pancake with casual grace.

She took another sip. "I don't eat breakfast."

"This is dinner."

"It's not even seven o'clock in the morning."

"Early dinner. Sit," he said and pointed to the piano bench with the flat end of the utensil.

"Mr. Redhawk . . ." she began, using her more-regal-than-thou voice. "While I appreciate everything you've done here at Gray Horse—"

"I ordered hay."

She scowled at the back of his neck.

"From whom?"

"Farmer I know. Should arrive this morning. Straw, too."

She longed to fidget, but couldn't allow such a blatant lack of control. "Thank you."

He nodded and set a plate in front of her.

"I don't eat pancakes."

"These are flapjacks."

"I don't eat—"

"She will die," he said.

She jerked her gaze to his.

"The horse," he said. "If you are too weak, too stubborn . . . too foolish to care for yourself, she will die. Is this what you want?"

What she wanted was to be left alone. To feel sorry for herself. But instead, she ate the flapjacks. Because he stood between her and the door. Because he watched her until she did. Because the horse needed her. And maybe, a little bit, because they tasted fantastic. In fact, she ate them all, shoved the plate away, and somewhere in the back of her stubborn mind kind of wished she wasn't too proud to ask for more.

He sipped his coffee and watched her with one brawny shoulder propped casually against the wall.

"Are you happy now?" she asked.

"Euphoric."

He barely looked conscious, like a sleepy bear just out of hibernation. He'd changed his shirt, hiding all that lovely muscle behind tan, narrow-ribbed corduroy.

She tightened her grip on the coffee mug and pushed her gaze back to his face.

"How are you?" she asked.

"Besides ungodly strong?"

His expression was as solemn as a dirge. She resisted the urge to laugh. "Your wound," she said. "How is it?"

"It is healing well."

"It must hurt."

"I am also extremely brave."

She did laugh now, but sobered in a moment. "Does the ointment help?"

"Ai."

She let one finger tap the rim of her mug. "We'll have to change Courage's bandages soon."

He nodded.

"The ointment . . . would it help her?"

"Tonk swears by it for his ponies."

She studied him through narrowed eyes and took a sip of coffee. "Tonk?"

"My youngest and most . . ." He shook his head as if trying to think of a suitable description. But he gave up in a moment. "My youngest brother."

"The one with the relay horses?"

"Ai."

"He thinks the ointment helps them?"

"If you listen to him, he will have you believing it can bring back the dead."

She waited a heartbeat before she spoke again. "Can we try it on Courage?"

For a moment she was certain he was about to warn her regarding the mare's prognosis, but finally he nodded.

She felt her muscles relax a smidgeon and took another sip of coffee. Silence stretched comfortably between them. Ideas, already rooted, bloomed silently in an imagination made fertile by the untamed country around her. Wild horses raced through her mind, manes flying, hooves pounding, but she corralled them in a moment and turned resolutely toward practicality. "Could you . . . if I bought the necessary lumber . . . could you build a jump course?" Victoria, bless her heart, had come through with the loan.

He narrowed his eyes against the steam of his own coffee as he raised the mug to his lips. Sensuously full beneath his proud, bowed nose, they curled at the corners, spewing up a half dozen unwelcome fantasies.

Sydney cleared her throat and wondered rather dismally if she sounded like a hillbilly with a phlegm problem. "I have this land . . ." She shrugged, trying to look casual. Or at least less desperate. "Hills, streams, prairie. Why not allow others to use it?"

"For?"

"The barn where I rode . . ." She gritted her teeth, resolved not to clear her throat again. "Yes, I rode," she said. He didn't interrupt. "Dressage. I was a dressage rider. But I didn't wear a top hat . . ." She tapped one rogue finger twice against the warm ceramic cup. ". . . all the time." Shadbelly coats and flat hats were reserved for the discipline's most prestigious competitions. Dressage riders were not, after all, barbarians. "Steeple Veil hosted several members of the Olympic eventing team."

He said nothing.

"Are you familiar with the sport?"

"A three-pronged event, isn't it? Dressage, stadium jumping, and outdoor . . ." He shook his head.

"Cross country. Jumping on an outdoor course. It's not my field of expertise." Her thigh throbbed at the magnitude of that understatement. "But I could train the dressage riders and hire someone to help with the other disciplines." She paused, calming herself. "The next summer Olympics will be held in less than sixteen months."

He made no comment.

"I believe it's my duty as an American citizen to assist our team in bringing home the gold." She resisted the burning need to squirm like a mouse in a hawk's talons.

"So they would train here for free?"

She kept her gaze steady on him. "I suspect if we made a modest profit, it wouldn't be the end of the world as we know it."

"We?"

And now they came to the marrow of the matter. "I thought perhaps you would be interested in taking a share of the profits."

"If I do the work."

"I would work, too."

He watched her. Not long ago, he would have laughed at the notion, but he had learned much about her since then. Much, and nothing.

"What about funds?" he asked.

"Funds?" She smoothed a finger over the chip in her mug.

"Money," he explained.

"As I've said before, there will be plenty of that soon enough."

"It has been my experience that where money is concerned, there is rarely plenty and never soon enough."

She forced a laugh. The look he gave her was something between astonishment and trepidation. She wouldn't try that laugh again. "What would you estimate the cost to be?"

"For an Olympic-caliber jump course?"

"Yes."

"Perhaps I have given you the wrong impression of my knowledge."

"You don't know everything?"

"No."

"You're right, you've misled me," she said and smiled when he frowned at her. "If I draw out a course, could you give me an estimate?"

"While replacing your windows, nursing the mustang, and rebuilding your porch?"

"Don't forget about cooking." Her tone was comically hopeful.

He raised one brow.

"The pancakes were quite . . . ." She searched for a moderate adjective and came up empty. "Perfect," she said.

She saw the surprise caused by her honesty and almost laughed.

"Well," he said finally. "I have always been comfortable with tradition."

"Which means?"

"The white slave owner." He finished his coffee, set the cup beside the sink, and turned to leave. "The downtrodden Indian."

She watched him depart . . . his endless shoulders, his tight buttocks, his loose-limbed swagger. *Downtrodden.* She snorted and tried her best not to think in terms of thrusting and heaving.

Good heavens, he was practically a god.

Chapter 19

"Two hundred thousand should cover it."

Mr. Anderson's statement was punctuated by the sound of Hunter's steady hammering, but he was pretty sure he had heard the other man correctly.

"Two hundred thousand," Sydney said. The words sounded a little breathless.

"Yes, ma'am."

"Dollars."

"Or thereabouts."

"For a barn."

He nodded. Lean as a white oak rail, the man had his designer jeans hitched low on practically nonexistent hips. His hair was coifed in a swanky do Hunter had seen on a hundred well-dressed hipsters in LA. "All new construction," he said and flashed a flawless smile. "Raw materials don't come free, you know."

"I see."

Where was she going to get two hundred thousand dollars? Hunter wondered. She couldn't even afford a decent mattress. He glanced up from the nail he was pounding. In the last three days, spring had come in earnest. Fresh-melted snow hustled along every gully, singing its way toward unseen oceans. A meadowlark, raucous with joy, sang from a rotting post near a just-budding white willow.

But the rest of Gray Horse Hill didn't look quite so fresh. The house was largely unfinished and the wooden barn yawned like an open crypt. Everything needed painting and renovating and redoing. Speaking of which . . .

"We're going to need more lumber," he said and abandoned his job to take the few steps that separated them.

Sydney turned at the sound of his voice. "I beg your pardon?"

"Found more dry rot around the windows."

"Hello," Anderson said and shifted his well-shod feet. "You must be . . . *Mr.* Wellesley?"

"No," Sydney said.

Was her answer a little quick? Hunt wondered and refrained from scowling.

"This is Mr. Redhawk, my . . ." She paused momentarily, making him rethink the wisdom of that scowl. ". . . employee."

"Well, aren't you the lucky dog," Anderson said and turned toward Hunter. "My boss weighs in at about three hundred and fifty pounds. 'Bout half of that is body hair." He flashed a mouth full of pearly whites and thrust out his hand. "I'm Anderson. Moses. But they call me Moss."

"Hunter." They shook while Hunt reminded himself there was no reason in the world he should want to crush the other's palm. It only took a moment for him to force his glower away from the contractor and back toward Sydney. "Maybe you could make a trip later this morning."

"Hey." Anderson spoke again. "Aren't you Verdell's brother?"

Redhawk turned back toward him. "One of them."

"Yeah. You're the guy who moved off to LA after—"

"You're thinking of Jesse."

"What?"

"My other brother. Jesse."

"Really? I thought sure it was—"

"He's still in Burbank."

191

"No kidding. Well . . . This is a nice place, too. You planning to keep your horses here?"

Hunter scowled.

"I saw you racing at the fairgrounds once." Anderson shook his head. "That was some crazy stunt."

"The horses belong to my family," Hunter said.

"Were all those boys your brothers then?"

"Ai."

"So your other brother . . . what's his name?"

Hunter waited several beats before speaking. "Tonkiaisha-wien."

"Yeah." Anderson shook his head, but didn't chance the pronunciation. "He's out of treatment?"

There was no reason in the world he should be irritated by this little bastard, Hunter realized. Still, he kind of wished he had another shot at that handshake. "Was there a purpose for your visit?" he asked instead.

Anderson grinned. "Oh, yeah. I came by to give Miss Wellesley an estimate for a brand-new steel barn."

"Steel?" Hunter asked.

Sydney raised a brow at his tone.

"Sure," Anderson said, unleashing the full force of that ungodly white smile again. Hunter refrained from shielding his eyes. "Unless you can talk your brother into lending you a couple mil, you can't afford to build them like they used to. Well . . ." He reached for Sydney's hand, held it a fraction of a second too long. "Give me a call if there's anything I can do for you." He raised his brows a quarter of an inch. "Anything at all," he added, and turning, sauntered toward his spanking-new four-wheel drive.

Sydney broke the silence. "If I had known you were a celebrity, I would have put out the fine china. How good were you at this relay-race thing?"

"We won some," Hunter rumbled and tilted his head toward the truck that zipped onto the road and roared up the hill. "Where'd you find *him?*"

She canted her head a little, questioning his unspoken sentiment. "On the Internet. Why?"

He lifted one shoulder. "No reason. Just making conversation."

She snorted. He had no idea why. It wasn't as if he was a deaf mute. Or that he had clocked the guy with an uppercut to the jaw or something. No. If he was going to take a swing, and of course there was no reason in the world for such theatrics, he would have planted one in Mr. Anderson's well-dressed gut. He looked a little soft in the middle.

Sydney was still watching him with a bemused expression. It looked patently out of place on her elegant features.

"What's wrong with the old barn?" Hunter asked.

Her lips turned up a little, making her face look

quizzical and young. Such New York sleek features, he thought, shouldn't have lips that were candy-apple bright and strawberry plump. "Besides the fact that it would make better matchsticks than shelter?"

He pulled his gaze from her mouth, pushed it toward the barn. "That building was constructed by men who created things through hard work and ingenuity. Who took pride in craftsmanship . . . not by some fly-by-night dandy with pearly teeth and truck payments."

Her eyes widened. The expression was tantamount to a shout in a woman as reserved as Sydney Wellesley. "Dandy?"

He felt a muscle tic in his jaw. "The point is, that barn has stood against the elements for a hundred years and would last another hundred if repaired."

"As impressive as that fact may be, I begin to suspect that you don't fully understand the kind of clientele I'm looking for, Mr. Redhawk."

"Maybe *you* don't." His tone sounded just a tad more childish than he had planned.

She folded her hands demurely in front of her body. She was, once again, dressed in perfectly tailored slacks and a button-down shirt. He missed the oversized sweatshirt and bare feet and couldn't help but wonder if she had donned those clothes for the well-groomed Mr. Anderson. "Enlighten me then," she said.

"If they have the best riding facilities in the country out east, why would anyone bother to come here?" he asked.

"Maybe their current stable is too costly or they're disillusioned with their trainers. Or perhaps they simply want something new. Something fresh."

"Or something old. Something solid."

"These are internationally acclaimed horses," she said. "World-class riders."

"Who can have spit-polished grooms and climate-controlled barns any day of the week. Why not promise them something different? A piece of history. An opportunity to get their hands dirty, to learn from the ground up."

She scowled at him, then turned her glower on the barn. It was a good-sized structure. Twenty by thirty meters at least. The roof had sustained some damage over the years and much of the interior would have to be gutted, but the overhead beams were as big around as a man's waist.

"I'll admit this isn't exactly my forte," she said. "But unless I miss my guess, it would cost nearly as much to restore as to build new."

"Unless you take the environmental degradation into account."

"I'm afraid I need to consider the degradation of my finances first and—" she began, but stopped at the sound of an engine.

Glancing to the left, she watched as a red Chevy truck turned into the drive and bumped through potholes and puddles toward the house. Mud was splattered liberally over its aging bumpers. It pulled to a halt not twenty feet from them, then rumbled hungrily for an instant before the driver cut the engine.

In a moment she stepped out from behind the wheel. "Hi." The speaker was a woman in her early twenties with bright eyes, a round face, and a swishy sundress that showed well-toned arms and brown legs.

"I'm looking for Sydney Wellesley . . ." The newcomer let the statement hang in the air like a question and glanced from one to the other as if either of them might be the person for which she searched.

Uncertainty and suspicion were written in equal measures on Sydney's face. Hunter raised his brows at the continued silence, bumping her back into action.

"I am she," Sydney said finally.

"Oh . . ." Their guest took the single step forward to shake hands. Her hair was long, dark, and curled in trendy spirals that fell softly against her sunny summer dress. "It's nice to meet you. I'm Bravura Lambert." When she turned to greet him as well, her handshake was firm and brisk. "But most people call me Vura." She stepped back, gaze steady.

"Is there something with which I can help you, Ms. Lambert?"

Hunter heard cautious reserve return to Sydney's voice as he watched her erect a barrier as unimpeachable as the ancestral fortress in which she had surely been raised.

"Oh . . ." Vura rocked back on her heels when she laughed. She had a girl-next-door kind of face, pretty, but not so stunning as to scramble a man's brains. The way she stood suggested she was comfortable with her body and with her skills. The weathered pickup truck she drove said much more. "I'm sorry. I guess you're not a mind reader. I'm looking for work. I was told you might be hiring."

Surprise shone on Sydney's face. "Oh. Well, I'm sorry, but—" she began.

"What kind of work?" Hunter asked and, pulling his gaze from the vehicle behind her, ignored the annoyed expression Sydney flicked in his direction.

Vura shrugged. "They say hunger makes us flexible . . . so . . ." She chuckled again. "I can do back bends."

There was something about the woman's easy laughter that seemed to increase Sydney's tension exponentially.

"Unless you're a roofer, I'm afraid we can't use you," Sydney said.

"Well . . ." The girl glanced at the house with a

critical eye. "What is that? A 9/12 pitch?"

"About that," Hunter said, "but we're considering patching up the barn right now."

"Yeah? Well, good for you," she said and turned toward the other building with an admiring gaze. "What a beauty."

Sydney looked at her disbelievingly.

"Wouldn't it be great if we could use all-dowel construction to restore it? Maybe have a cedar shake roof and double Dutch doors. We could add dormers in the loft. Get some natural light in there and . . ." Her eyes widened in excitement. "What about cupolas? We might be able to find a couple lying around that were from similar old barns. Lots of them have been dismantled and . . ." She paused, jerked her attention back to Sydney, and laughed at herself. "I'm sorry. Dad always says I can get more excited about power tools than most girls get about diamonds."

"How long have you been in construction?" Hunter asked.

"You're a carpenter?" Sydney said the words like another might ask if she was visiting from Mars.

"The only kid of a contract builder. To hear Dad talk, you'd think I was born with a hammer in my hand."

"My sympathy to your mother," Hunter said and she laughed again. It was a good sound, round, full bodied, and wholehearted. "You do interior work?"

She nodded. "Drywall, trim, framework. I'll even pour a little concrete if I have to."

"Well . . ." If Sydney's back got any stiffer it would crack right in two, Hunter thought, and worked hard to contain his chuckle. Not that he had been jealous about Mr. Mossy Anderson, but it never hurt to even the score a little. "That's very . . . impressive, Ms. . . ."

"Mrs." The correction came quickly, followed by another laugh. "I've been married nearly four years now," she said, but there was a jitteriness to the words.

"Mrs. Lambert," Sydney corrected, "I'm afraid—"

"I'm a hard worker." The smile had slipped a little. She hoisted it back up. "And conscientious." She sent one quick glance at her truck.

"I'm certain that's true, but—" Sydney began.

"Do you paint?" Redhawk asked.

"Like Michaelangelo."

"How about stripping old flooring? You do that?"

"I just finished Meryl Baker's living room. Harp's older sister. You know her? Lives over by Pringle. Prettiest black walnut flooring you'll ever see. I can get references, if you like."

"I'm afraid we just don't need—" Sydney began.

199

"—references," Hunt finished.

Sydney snapped her scowl on him, but he was undeterred.

"Can you start Monday morning?"

The girl's eyes shone. With gratitude, relief, or hope, he wasn't sure. "I'm an early riser," she said.

He nodded and turned away. "Bring your own tools."

By the time Sydney caught up with him, she had worked up a full head of steam. "Perhaps you could inform me about what you think you're doing." Apparently, a full head of steam still required perfect diction.

He shrugged and picked up a battered bushel basket he'd found hidden in the dried buffalo grass near the creek. "She needs work."

"I have to assume there are others in the great state of South Dakota who are also looking for employment. Do you plan to hire them all?"

"I'll leave that up to you."

"Up to me? Really? Just because I own the property, I hardly think—"

"I noticed that," he said and pressed past her. She followed him like a hound on a hot scent. Beside the silo, he knelt to pull dead foliage away from the tiny spears of hope just peeking through the damp soil. They were as red as autumn apples.

"What are you doing?"

It seemed obvious. But he could play along. "Weeding."

"I'm fully aware of that, Mr. Redhawk. But what are you weeding?"

"I suppose you don't know how to make rhubarb pie."

She remained silent.

He glanced up. "You do know what pie is, don't you?"

"You are a very amusing man."

"I'm working on my stand-up routine," he said and went back to the task at hand.

"I can't afford to hire every drifter who comes along."

"You can afford *her*."

"Because she needs a job or because she has big, heaving breasts?"

He wouldn't have been more surprised if she had sprouted a tail and a fiery pitchfork. In fact . . . he thought, but stopped that uncharitable line of thought in its tracks.

"Because she has a kid," he said, and rising to his feet, left her to stew in her own well-bred juices.

Chapter 20

"How long will you continue on this path?" Hunter asked.

"As long as it takes," Sydney said and didn't glance up at the man who controlled the mustang with a long-handled twitch attached to the mare's upper lip. Neither did Sydney straighten, though she had finished applying Hunt's homemade ointment and re-bandaging the dun's legs. In fact, she wasn't entirely certain she *could* straighten. Once again, she had spent most of the night in the barn, with the previous hours being consumed by backbreaking labor and heart-wrenching worry.

Courage stood with her legs braced wide and her head drooping toward the floor. How much of that lethargy was caused by the sedative necessary to keep her quiet and how much was dictated by her deteriorating health? Sydney wasn't entirely sure she wanted to know the answer; despite the fact that the mare's injuries seemed to be healing, she looked as if she had already begun the long slide toward death. Beneath her scraggly, clay-colored coat, her ribs looked as sharp as knives, her eyes as dull as dust. Guilt blended with the sorrow and anxiety already awash in Sydney's system. The toxic mix made her tone strident. "I suppose the Indian way is to let her die."

"If she does not eat soon, she will have little choice in the matter."

Sydney's stomach twisted and her thigh throbbed as she rose to her full height. "If we eliminate the sedatives, she'll reinjure herself."

"Perhaps."

"And how would we change her bandages? Give her the necessary injections? The chances of infection are astronomical."

"You are right. It would be easier if she were dead."

Sydney gritted her teeth and faced him dead-on. "You're—" she began, but footsteps distracted her.

"Hey." Vura Lambert strode into the barn. Her smile was bright, her blue jeans worn, her hands covered in scarred leather gloves that were snugged in at the wrists by beaded strips of rawhide. "I knocked at the house. Nobody answered. So I thought . . ." She shrugged, making her dark ponytail bounce. "It's Monday morning," she said, as if they might have forgotten. Which actually was a possibility. The days ran together like river water out here in the long quiet of the hills.

Sydney said nothing. Hunter nodded.

"Have you eaten?" His voice was little more

than a rough murmur in the soft morning light.

"Yes. Thanks. But listen . . ." She shuffled her feet, which were laced into chunky leather boots. "I don't want to cause . . ."

"Mama?"

Sydney snapped her gaze toward the door, where a tiny person was even now shuffling down the aisle toward them. Dressed in purple-footed pajamas bright enough to make you squint, she came rubbing her eyes and dragging a tattered something behind her. It looked a little like a one-eared rat.

"Hey, Lily Belle," Vura said, and after one quick, apologetic glance at Sydney, turned to scoop up her daughter. "I asked you to stay in the truck, remember?"

"But I want to see the cows." There was the faintest lisp in her voice. Her eyes were magic-fairy bright.

"There aren't any cows, baby." Vura shot the other adults a look rife with regret. Sydney merely stared. She was no expert at this work scenario thing, but she suspected it was some-what unconventional to bring a midget to your place of employment. "And right now . . ."

"But it's a barn. And barns is the houses of cows. Our book said so. Remember? The black and—oh!" Her eyes were wide and forest green beneath a frazzled cap of runaway hair as she peered between the bars of the stall. "Horse!"

"Yes." Vura's cheeks, usually a soft sienna hue, were brushed with pink. "There's a horse, but right now I have to talk to these nice people."

"Horse. Horse. Horse," the child chanted, and wriggled like an inchworm in her mother's arms.

Sydney stared, dumbstruck. If she had acted in such a manner, she wouldn't have left her suite for a month. Wellesleys did not cause scenes. They might topple governments or sell century-old businesses piecemeal, but they would do so discreetly.

"I'm sorry," Vura said, daughter still writhing in her arms. "Can she see the horse? Just for a minute?"

Sydney scowled. Some might find it strange, but children had not generally been a part of the fabric of her childhood. Well-paid nannies had been her companions while experienced tutors had taken the place of overworked public teachers. "I wish she could," Sydney lied, "but I'm afraid—"

"As is the horse," Hunter said and approached mother and daughter on silent feet. "But if you are quiet . . ." He caught the child's gaze in his own. Hers went round as cat eyes. "Like the night owl, you may see her."

Her tiny body stilled.

"Can you do that?" he asked.

She nodded once, then, leaning sideways, she reached out for him.

For a moment, Sydney thought he would back away, felt it in his body language, in the stillness in the air. But after a second, he lifted her from her mother's arms and turned, expressionless, as he trod across the dusty aisle to the stall.

"Ohhhh . . ." The lisping voice was little more than a whisper of sound. Behind Hunter's broad neck, her tiny fingers tightened and loosened in his collar-length hair. They stood in silence, watching, until finally Hunter drew back and returned to her mother. "Mama." She was still whispering.

"Yes, baby?" Vura's voice was almost as soft.

"There's a horse in there."

"Is she pretty?"

"She's the most beautiful thing in all the world."

Sydney winced. The horse was ugly, drugged, wasting away to nothing, and probably dying.

"Is she?"

"Can I ride her?" Lily asked.

"No, honey." Vura didn't look at them when she answered. "She needs her rest."

"When she wakes up? Can I ride her then?" She turned her gaze to Hunter before her mother could answer. Her kitten-soft cheek was inches from his. "Do you know how to ride a horse?"

"Ai."

"Will you teach me?"

His body was stiff as if he longed to run, but he

held steady, eyes somber as stones on her hopeful face. "That is not for me to decide."

She blinked. "Mama?"

"I'm sure Mr. Redhawk has important things he needs to see to."

The girl scowled, feathery brows lowering. "Like Daddy?"

"Yes." Vura's face tightened almost imperceptibly. "Like Daddy."

The baby's expression had gone somber, too. Reaching out, she cupped Hunter's hirsute cheeks in her tiny hands. "I likes you anyway," she whispered. "Even if your face is scratchy and you have more important things to do than to teach me to ride horse."

The barn went deadly silent.

Hunter shifted his gaze toward Vura, who opened her mouth, apology ready on her lips.

"I will teach you," he said, and abruptly handing the child to her mother, left the building.

Sydney watched him go. Silence echoed like thunder in his wake.

"I'm sorry." Vura turned back to her, expression worried. "My babysitter canceled at the last minute, and I didn't want to be late for work so I . . ." She faltered for a second. "So I had to bring her."

Sydney tugged her stunned gaze from Hunter's retreating back. The woman still intended to work today? With a child? Was she serious?

"She won't be any trouble."

It was a lie if Sydney had ever heard one. And she had; David Albrook had been a virtuoso. But good manners kept her silent. Or maybe it was the memory of Redhawk's broken expression that kept her from stating the obvious.

"And she's smart. She reads already and she's great at math," Vura babbled. "So she can help out. Plus she's brave. Can climb anything. But she won't!" she rushed to add. "If I tell her not to, she won't. She minds very well . . . usually. Sometimes. I mean—"

"Can you pull up fence?" Sydney asked, effectively stopping the nervous chatter.

"What?"

"I know it's beneath your abilities," Sydney said and clasped her hands loosely in front of her body. "But I don't want another situation like that one." She nodded toward the stall.

Vura's dark brows lowered. "What happened there?"

"Barbwire."

"So you want to dispose of the old fencing." She was all business suddenly, though her body kept up a steady bounce and the child hummed to the stuffed rat she held tight to her cheek. "How much land are we talking?"

"Almost a thousand acres."

"Any idea how many miles of old wire there is?"

"Not really."

"You don't have a plat map that would tell where the fence lines ran, I suppose."

"No. But I'll need new fences."

"And the barbwire is probably half buried by now."

"Some places, anyway."

"How about the new fencing? Are we talking post and rail, twisted galvanized, electric?"

Sydney laughed, feeling foolish and oddly self-conscious. Despite spending most of her life in the equestrian world, it seemed she knew next to nothing about the practical end of things. "I guess I don't have a lot of answers for you."

Vura shrugged, ponytail bouncing. "Hey, no problem. You'll have plenty of time to consider what you want while I rip out the old stuff."

Though she tried, Sydney couldn't quite stop the spritz of admiration that coursed through her. "You weren't overstating when you said you were flexible."

The younger woman laughed. "Did I tell you I didn't have any brothers?"

"And your mother didn't object to your doing manual labor?"

Vura's gaze caught Sydney's. "Mom died," she said. "Shortly after I was born."

"Oh." Sydney cleared her throat, felt a tug of unwanted camaraderie. "I'm sorry."

Vura quit bouncing. "What about you?"

"I beg your pardon?"

The woman had gone very still. The child continued to hum. "Do your parents live around here?"

"My mother is also deceased."

"Oh?" Was she holding her breath? "How old were you when you lost her?"

Sydney felt a need to turn the topic aside, but Vura was watching her with such avid eyes. Even the child had gone quiet, all but one hand, which loosened and tightened restlessly in her mother's chunky ponytail. Sydney tapped her thigh with a restive finger and felt another unacceptable thread stretch between them. "I was four years of age at the time."

"Just about Lily's age."

Sydney remembered being small, staring at the endless black. Black hose. Black pants. Black hats. All backdropped by their ancestral mausoleum. "Well . . . I'll show you where I found . . ." Sydney began, but Vura stopped her.

"How did it happen?"

"I beg your pardon?"

"Your mother." She began swaying slightly, an unconscious rhythm perhaps meant to soothe. "How did she die?"

It was none of her business. None at all, Sydney thought, but she answered nonetheless. "There was a car accident."

"Do you remember her?"

"Just a little. Tiny pieces. Like snapshots. Her voice . . ." Or she thought she remembered . . . singing, low and sweet, as she was rocked to sleep in her perfect taffeta room. "Her scent. She always smelled of roses."

"Prairie roses."

"What?"

Vura laughed, seeming to bump herself back to the present . . . to her own life. "I just . . . I love prairie roses. Have you ever seen them? They grow wild in the ditches around here. In the pastures. They're considered a weed, but they're so pretty. Maybe we should plant some around the house."

Sydney tilted her head. "I don't believe you'll have time for that sort of thing."

There was a momentary delay, then laughter. "Of course. You're right. What am I thinking? You're not paying me to plant flowers. You're paying me to . . ." She tilted her head quizzically. "What are you paying me to do exactly?"

"Everything," Sydney said. "Come on. I'll show you where to start with the fences."

"We might as well take my truck," Vura said, and opening the door of her Chevy, let Lily climb into her car seat in back. Sydney eased into the passenger side. The cab smelled vaguely of tobacco.

"I'm sorry," Vura said and snapped the ashtray closed before turning the key. "Dane . . ." There

211

was a wealth of feeling in the single name. "He's trying to quit."

"Take a left here," Sydney said and pointed to the gravel road that wound east into the hills. "Dane's your husband?"

"Yeah." Vura cranked the steering wheel. Behind them, Lily was chattering to the items she pulled out of a much-abused backpack. "Lil's father. He's working up in Williston."

"Where?"

"Williston, North Dakota. Pours cement for Barnett Petroleum. Frackers. It's booming up there. He wanted to stay here, of course. It's really hard for him to be gone so much. Away from Lily. And me. But he lost his job at T and T and . . ." She shrugged, glanced out the side window, a soft frown creasing her brow. "Is this the fence line?"

"Yes." Sydney nodded. "It starts here, then runs west and north, I think."

"Well, we'll get rid of it. Lily and I." She said the words with a strange finality, then smiled. "Where should I put the posts?"

Posts. New fence lines. Steel barns. Drywall. Oak flooring. So many things she had never before considered. "I'm not sure."

"Well, you don't have to worry about it yet." She was already backing around to return to Gray Horse Hill. "We'll think about that when I have the first load."

212

The cab went silent except for Lily's humming.

"He'd be here if he could," Vura said softly.

Sydney glanced at her.

"Dane," she explained and managed a smile as she turned back toward the passenger seat. "He hates that man camp where he's living. I'll make sure you meet him when he's home next time."

"I'll look forward to it."

"You'll like him," Vura added, attention riveted on the bending road ahead. "Everyone likes Dane. He's a charmer. He wouldn't have left if he didn't have to."

In the backseat, Lily was singing a lisping version of "Old MacDonald" to her rat. Her mother watched her in the rearview mirror. Devotion as warm as sunlight shone on her face. "I mean . . ." Her words were little more than a whisper. "You'd have to be nuts to leave a great kid like Lily."

Sydney winced, though she didn't know why. It wasn't as if her own mother had left her on purpose. Still, the memory of her loss made her throat feel tight and her eyes sting.

"Right?" Vura asked and smiled, upbeat again.

"Absolutely," Sydney said and felt her heart break a little.

Chapter 21

In the end, Sydney spent the day with Lily and Vura. By seven p.m. she was quite certain she was going to die. By eight, she half hoped she would. She'd put in some long days with Redhawk, but given their size difference, her inability to keep up seemed reasonable. With Vura, who matched her in height, she couldn't find a justifiable reason to fall behind. And Vura was a virtual dynamo. She could, it seemed, pull out posts, roll up wires, and entertain a child while carrying on a conversation and fixing snacks from the passenger seat of her Chevy. She had, in fact, refused to return to the house for lunch. Instead, she and Lily had remained in the shade of the bluff not far from where Sydney had first found Courage.

Evening came and went, bringing blessed darkness and an end to the work day.

Redhawk didn't look up from the pan that sizzled with melting butter as Sydney pulled off the gloves he had loaned her. There was a hole in the leather of the left thumb. A blister had formed and broken hours ago. She glanced toward the stove, trying to judge his mood. It was a little like attempting to psychoanalyze a bear.

"It smells good in here," she said and felt the homey scents slide contentment through her system.

"Fry bread."

"I beg your pardon?" she said and washed up at the kitchen sink.

"Old Indian recipe." He nodded toward the table. It wasn't until that moment that she realized they had one. It was old and battered, with claw feet and rounded legs.

He didn't have to tell her to sit down this time. She sank onto the nearest cushion. As he opened the oven and gave something a poke, she slouched against the slats of the newly purchased chair and realized it had three mates. It was almost like sitting in a real kitchen. "You've been busy," she said.

"Windows came in. Had to go to town."

"Is that where you got the . . ." She studied the jumble of knives and forks he had tossed onto the table. As far as she could tell, they were like snowflakes. No two alike. "Silverware?"

"Went back to Re Uzit," he said. "Bought the plates, too."

She glanced at the two that had been set out. They were matching and only one was chipped. It was a good day. "Aren't you a little Suzy Homemaker?"

"Martha Stewart."

"My mistake." She straightened a little. If her nanny saw her slouching, she would have to recite Keats. If Grandmother saw, her penance would be more severe. Coleridge might be involved. She suppressed a shudder and turned her mind aside. "Vura's a good worker."

He nodded. "Mother lions," he said, and removing a formerly unknown casserole dish from the oven, turned toward the table.

Sydney raised her eyes . . . and gasped at the sight of his face.

He watched her, expression impassive. "I also bought a razor."

She stared at him, tried to speak, then shook her head once and tried again. "Why?"

"You preferred the beard?"

Was he joking? The beard had been as ugly as sin. While his face . . . Well, she wouldn't call him handsome, exactly. But rugged might work. Or chiseled. Or *gorgeous!* His jaw was square and lean, his skin the color of the bluffs outside her bedroom window.

He raised his brows at her.

She exhaled carefully, eased back into her chair. "Not necessarily." She shrugged, going for casual. It had always been clear that he wasn't deformed. He hadn't been hideous. On the other hand, he hadn't been Adonis, either. Not before now. "No, you look . . ." This didn't change anything, she assured herself. She wasn't shallow.

Rigid, maybe. Arrogant. Unskilled. Mean. Condescending. But not shallow. "Clean."

"Clean?"

She cleared her throat. "Nice."

His lips, unimpeded by that god-awful beard, lifted a little. "You look nice, too."

She breathed a laugh, smoothed her hair behind her ears. "I look a fright." It was, perhaps, the first time in her life that she had ever disparaged her physical appearance. Looks were unimportant in the Wellesley family. Grooming, however, was tantamount to godliness.

He watched her with bright-agate eyes. "Relaxed," he said and removed the milk from the refrigerator.

"Is relaxation synonymous with exhaustion?"

"Frequently," he said and set the milk beside the casserole on the table.

She shifted her shoulders a little. Pain skittered across her back. "What is that?" she asked and nodded toward their meal. It wasn't easy to resist making a face, but the entrée didn't look like anything she had ever seen before. Perhaps that was because she'd never been employed in a kennel. Or employed at all, come to that.

"Lefties," he said and turned back toward the stove.

"Lefties?" She was hungry. Ravenous, actually, but she had always been a picky eater. It was one of the few faults about which her grandmother had not complained. If she didn't wish to eat what had been prepared, that was acceptable. But there would be no substitutes, no additions. Nothing at all, in fact, until the next scheduled meal. Treats were for poodles and those who cleaned their fingernails with toothpicks.

"Five men in the family," he reminded her and slid a piece of fry bread onto her plate. It looked, she thought, like a mistake, but smelled a little like heaven. "Mom never wasted the leftovers."

"Ahhh." She had heard of leftovers. Had never seen any, but had heard of them. She hadn't been allowed in the kitchen. "Hence it is made of . . ." She paused, wondering how hungry she would be by morning.

"In this instance?" He shrugged. "Beef, corn . . . potato chips."

"You're joking," she said.

He gave her a look.

"As it turns out, I'm not as hungry as I thought I was."

He took a seat across the table from her. "I would have been happy to trade in a brother or two for you."

She watched as he dished the mush onto his plate.

"More for me," he added and reached across the table toward her plate. "You don't want the fry bread, either?"

It was more difficult than she would have

expected to keep from stabbing him in the hand with her fork. Despite his newfound Adonis status, she would fight him for that misshapen bread. "Yes," she said.

"Yes?" His hand was still poised to seize.

"I want it." She cleared her throat, found the verbal cadence her grandmother would have approved of, and tried again. "I would like to taste your fry bread."

He shrugged and pushed the butter toward her. It still resided in its paper wrapper. Apparently, Re Uzit had been short on butter dishes. Or perhaps Martha Stewart didn't endorse them. Either way, Sydney had been taught early on to eschew animal fats. She shook her head and cut into the bread, knife and fork in hand.

He watched her from beneath raised brows.

Sydney glanced up. "Is something amiss?"

The corner of his mouth twitched.

"No," he said, but his lips curved again. "It's just that fry bread's not usually eaten like Cordon bleu."

She considered a snide remark, but her salivary glands were acting up. So instead, she picked up her fried dough with both hands and lifted it to her mouth.

He watched her chew and swallow before taking another bite. She was, he thought, the only woman he had ever known who could look elegant in an oversized flannel shirt and enough mud to plant corn. She sat very straight and chewed slowly. She might also be the only woman who didn't like his fry bread, which was strange. It was his mother's recipe, after all; the lard made all the difference.

"It is better with butter," he said and felt like an idiot. What did he care if she liked his meal? He wasn't a smitten bridegroom, breathlessly waiting to see if he'd pleased his new wife.

"Really?" She set the bread carefully back on her plate, then stared at it as if it were a strange new breed of cat that might leap for her throat at any given second. "I don't actually think it could be."

So she liked it? A splash of pleasure washed through him, but it was strange how her pleased face and her angry face were nearly identical. What was her sex face like? he wondered and drowned the question with a quaff of raw Lazy Windmill milk.

"Better with butter," he added again, "and lefties." He took a bite of hotdish. It wasn't as good as Mavis Lindeman Redhawk's. But what was?

She was staring at the casserole. Reaching out, he tapped the serving spoon toward her with the tines of his fork. After a long, calculated moment, she scooped up a minuscule portion and sampled a kernel-sized bite.

Good lord, she wouldn't have lasted an hour at the Redhawk table. He watched her nibble off another crumb of fry bread, chew thoroughly, and wash it down with the coffee he'd put by her plate before her arrival.

"Your mother taught you to cook?" she asked.

He shrugged, finished off his bread, and reached for another piece. "Her and the Casa de Hambre."

"Excuse me?" She sequestered off another morsel of lefties with a single tine of her fork. Honest to God, he had seen ants eat more.

"Little café in Tampico." *Café* was actually a pretty fancy term for an establishment like the Hambre. But they'd been happy to have him and he had needed the money. People should, he thought and liberally applied butter to his bread. People should need a reason to work.

"You were a cook?"

The surprise in her voice made him chuckle a little. "Not apparent by my meal, I take it?"

"No. I didn't mean that. It's quite good."

"Careful."

She glanced at him, brows raised.

"You're making me blush," he said and she laughed.

The sound was silvery soft, like rainwater against parched earth.

They stared at each other for several breathless heartbeats, but she finally broke free and shifted her gaze back to her meal.

"Could you teach me to make it?"

"Lefties?"

"Yes," she said and took a second helping. The portion was almost big enough for an anorexic prairie dog.

"Can you dump ingredients into a pan?"

She scowled. "I'm honestly not sure."

He didn't bother to suppress his chuckle. "I can teach you," he said.

Their gazes caught. Something sizzled along his nerve endings. Too much sun probably. He pulled his attention back to his plate and picked up his coffee cup. He hadn't purchased more mugs. They had two. How many did one kitchen need?

"When were you in Tampico?" she asked.

He shrugged, allowed himself to look at her again. "Long time ago."

"How old *are* you?" she asked.

"Why do you wish to know?" He wasn't sure if he should be embarrassed by his reluctance to tell her.

"Idle curiosity." Her eyes crinkled a little, apparently amused by that same reluctance. "Why don't you want to tell me?"

"I hate to risk the cat."

"The . . . ahh," she said. "The one that curiosity killed."

He gave her a head tilt and hooked an elbow over the back of his chair.

"Okay, then how old were you when you worked in Tampico?"

He thought a moment, then, "Fourteen."

Her dark, neatly groomed brows shot toward her hairline. "You were gainfully employed when you were fourteen?"

"Gainfully may be an overstatement."

"Is that even legal?"

He shrugged. "Easier than picking coffee beans. But it does not teach you how to choose the perfect cherry." He glanced wistfully into his cup. "Juan could brew coffee so poetically rich, it would make you cry."

She stared at him. "You're making this up."

He returned her attention, felt his stomach flip at the sight of her avid eyes, and carefully ignored the sensation. "So you are happy with Vura?"

"Vura . . ." She scowled a little. "Do you know her from somewhere?"

"She came here last Friday. Did you forget?"

She almost smirked. "I meant before that."

"No." He stood and returned to the urine-yellow counter. It was a wonder of Red Sea proportions, he thought, that any right-thinking person would make such an ugly laminate. "I did not."

"Then how did you know about Lily?"

He turned to settle his hips against that laminate. "Bravura did not seem like the type to read *Buffalo Knees* to herself."

223

Sydney's brows twitched in question.

"The book on her dash," he explained. It had been one of Sara's favorites, but he tucked away the emotions that accompanied those memories.

"And you were certain she didn't have a niece or a younger sister?"

"She needed a job." He didn't admit that he had recognized the desperation in the woman's eyes. Had felt that same gnawing anxiety himself on more than one occasion before he'd forged his own path. "You are happy with her work. Where is the problem?"

"There's no problem. I just . . . Why would you promise to teach Lily to ride?"

He shifted. Why indeed? "You learned to ride as a child, did you not?"

"Yes, but . . ."

"Is she any less valuable because she does not have a wealthy father?"

She pursed her lips. "That's not what we're talking about."

"What are we talking about, Sydney?"

She was quiet for a moment. "Courage is going to die." She said the words softly, then cleared her throat. "You know that as well as I."

He felt her sorrow, her fear, her inexplicable guilt. "And yet you sit by her stall through the dark of night."

She watched him, breath held as if wondering how he knew.

"The front door shrieks like a mountain lion in the small hours of the morning."

She looked down at her plate. She had finished off her morsel. "My point is, Courage will never be able to be ridden."

"It would be kinder to be rid of her now, then," he said. "If you are so certain she'll not survive. Better now than after she suffers more. And after Lily becomes attached to her."

"Lily's got a mother." The words seemed to leave Sydney's mouth without her permission. She pursed her lips as if wishing she could pull them back.

"And you didn't." It wasn't as if he had forgotten. But perhaps he hadn't realized how much it still mattered.

"I just meant Vura will be able to comfort her if . . . when . . ." She let the sentence fall flat.

"How did she die?"

She squirmed the tiniest bit, then stilled as if even that much fidgeting was a weakness not to be borne. "It was a long time ago."

"And still it hurts."

"It's not as if I was raised by coyotes." She laughed, jiggled her fork, then stopped abruptly, setting it carefully beside her plate. "I had excellent care."

Excellent care. God save the children, he thought. "Your father must have spoiled you."

"Yes," she said and didn't raise her eyes to his. "Of course."

A lie, he thought. He could spot them as well as he could tell them and wished he hadn't asked. He wasn't the nurturing type. Hadn't he proven that a hundred times?

"And what about you?" She shifted the conversation to him. It was an obvious ploy, but he was happy to let her do it.

"Cake and ice cream every day of my life," he said.

She smiled at her plate, then lifted her gaze to his, eyes bright. "Really. What's it like?"

"Life on the reservation?"

"Life with a . . ." She paused. She was going to say mother. He could feel it in the velvet softness of her voice and felt his heart crack around the edges.

"Life with the Hun?"

"The Hun. Yes," she said and almost smiled.

"She was funny, unless you made her angry. Then—" He shook his head.

Her eyes were wide. "Did she strike you?"

He watched her, wondering. "Mother Redhawk was more diabolical than that."

She remained silent.

He shifted his hips against the counter. "It was my job to feed the pigs."

"You had pigs?"

"We had everything. Horses, rabbits, ducks.

But the pigs . . ." He shook his head. "I am here to tell you that their legendary stench is not exaggerated. I hated feeding them. One night me and the boys went fishing." He shrugged. "A friend of ours, Smokey, found a twelve-pack of Buds. Probably his father's. We emptied that thing in ten minutes, tops. By the time I got home I had forgotten pigs even existed." He chuckled. Good lord, his mother was a piece of work. "But it came back to me in the morning."

She waited, as if it were a life-or-death story.

"She put them in our bedroom," he said.

"You shared a room?"

He hadn't thought that would be the surprising part of this particular tale. "With Tonk . . ." He shook his head, remembering. "He'd talk our ears off six days out of seven, but he didn't say a word. Not till morning."

"When there were pigs in your room."

"Piglets. Nine of them. There was . . ." He paused. He wasn't a swearing man, but the word *excrement* seemed wrong for the porcine species. "Feces everywhere. The walls, the blankets. My ears."

"You're making this up," she said.

He chuckled, suddenly glad he wasn't. "My imagination's not that distorted."

Her lips curved. "She sounds like fun."

"That's not exactly the word I would have used at the time. But I never neglected to feed the pigs again. Some days I still wake up in a panic, worried I've forgotten them."

She laughed a little. He took a sip of coffee and pretended the sound didn't make him want to weep.

"What about you?" He let the silence lie for a moment. "Tell me about your dad."

"Father?"

"Was he fun?"

"Sure." Another lie. She wouldn't have gotten away with anything in the Redhawk family. "But he was gone a lot. On business. He made certain I was in excellent hands, however."

"He didn't remarry?"

"No." She stared at her fork as if longing to fiddle with it again. But her control was absolute. "Mother was . . . extraordinary. Irreplaceable."

"How so?"

She shrugged, the slightest lift of trim, sharp-bladed shoulders. "Sophisticated. Intelligent. Talented. She was a ballerina when they met. With all the poise and class that implies. I've tried not to disappoint him."

"Disappoint him?"

She laughed at herself. "I didn't mean it like that. I had a privileged childhood. The best of care at home and at school."

"Which was where?"

"I was tutored until twelve, after which I moved into the Ashville Academy." She put her hands carefully in her lap. "It's what Mother would have wanted."

He actually winced. The thought of her alone, motherless . . .

"Sydney," he said and took a step toward her, though honestly he had no idea what he intended, but it was a moot point for she rose abruptly to her feet.

"I'm going to check on Courage," she said, and pressing past him, hurried outside.

Chapter 22

"Does he drink?" Doc Miller's voice was gruff as he gazed into the mustang's stall. Courage moved restlessly against the far wall. They had discontinued her sedatives almost forty-eight hours before.

"Some." Sydney stood as straight as a cadet, voice steady, expression composed. Only the quick tap of her index finger against her thigh told the truth of her emotional state.

Hunter had to resist pulling her into his arms, cradling her against his heart like a wounded child. And what the hell was that about?

"Eat?" the old man asked.

"No." It had taken her a moment to force out the word. "Or very little."

Outside, the rain pattered like a paradiddle against the barn's ancient roof.

Doc turned toward her, expression hard. "But you want me to continue treating him."

She entwined her fingers, held them loosely in front of her. If she were any more controlled, she would come complete with an instruction book and a set of marionette strings. "If it's a question of money . . ." she began, but the old vet glared her down.

"It's a question of morals," he said and shambled sideways along the stall front for a better view. The mustang, made nervous by his nearness, snorted and twitched. "And maybe of being killed, while we're at it."

"That's just it, though," Sydney said, voice suddenly animated. "She's a fighter. A warrior. Shouldn't we fight for her . . . with her?"

Doc Miller glared for a second, then turned toward Hunter. "You ready for this?"

Hunt glanced inside. The horse's eyes were rimmed in white, her ears laid back in tacit warning. "Hard thing to get ready for," he said.

"Boy's got a point. But at least she's got the halter on this time. Let's hope the line's still in her vein."

Hope was pretty much all they had. That, Hunter's brute strength, and Sydney's newfound inability to give up.

Forty-five minutes later the bandages had been

changed and the necessary drugs administered.

Sydney and Doc scrambled out of the stall while Hunter remained, still holding the halter and the twitch in his bear-like grip.

"You clear?" he asked and glanced toward the door they had shut but not latched behind them.

"Let 'im go," Doc called.

Hunter untwisted the twitch and turned the mare loose. She rose on her hind legs like a geyser. He scrambled backward, but not fast enough. Crashing into the wall behind her, Courage fell, then struggled to rise, legs scrambling with Hunter's in the process. Half crawling, half sprinting, he spurted into the aisle, breath coming hard.

Sydney slammed the door behind him. "Are you okay?" Her face was white with worry. If she wasn't always as pale as a snowflake, he might have been flattered by her concern.

"Ai," he said and failed to notice the pair behind Sydney until Lily spoke.

"Can we ride her now?"

They turned as a unit. Vura stood behind them, holding her wide-eyed daughter by one hand.

Doc snorted, then raised a hand. "I gotta go. Call me if you got any questions."

"Thank you," Sydney said, but Hunter was already hurrying toward the newcomers. "You must not go near that horse, Lily."

"But you said—"

"I said we would ride. But not that one. That one cannot be ridden."

"Even by you?"

"Even by God Himself."

"Why?"

He shook his head, straining to find an answer. "She needs to rest."

A hoof slammed against the wall, causing the barn to vibrate around them.

The little girl's expression was dubious. "She doesn't sound real tired."

Good point, Hunter thought. In fact, she sounded like she was going to tear the building down around their heads.

"She's sick, Lily," he said. "You must leave her be."

The girl's eyes were as green and round as marbles. "What's wrong with her?"

"She hurt her legs."

"What part of her legs?" There was a singsong melody to her new-morning voice. "Is it her hocks?"

He glanced at Vura.

"She's been studying horses," her mother said.

"They have lots of joints in their legs. Especially their hind legs," she lisped. "The coffin, the pastern, the fetlock, the hock, the stifle, the hip, and the sacro . . . the sacro . . ."

"Iliac," Vura finished for her.

"The sacro lilac," she said and lifted her arms toward Hunter.

He told himself to turn away, but her eyes were wide with wonder, bright with concern. Reaching down, he lifted her into his arms. She snuggled against his chest, ripping his heart on contact.

"The hock is the largest," she said.

He nodded, ignored the sting in his eyes, the tightness of his throat. "Which is the smallest?"

"I don't know that," she admitted solemnly. "But I bets my book says. It's in our truck."

They left the barn together, Lily perched on his arm like a songbird, twittering away as he walked.

"She seems very intelligent," Sydney said and tried to put the trauma of the morning behind her.

"Yes." Vura's smile lacked a bit of its usual effervescence. She turned toward Courage, as if forcing her thoughts in another direction. "What are her chances?"

"I beg your pardon?"

"The horse." She nodded toward the stall. "Will you ever be able to ride her?"

The question almost made Sydney laugh . . . or cry. "No."

"But she'll survive."

Sydney inhaled carefully, exhaled slowly. "Probably not."

"I'm sorry," Vura said. Her brow rumpled with compassion.

Sydney shook her head. "She's just a stray that . . ." She couldn't complete the sentence and cleared her throat instead. Outside the wind was driving the rain from the northwest. "It doesn't look like we'll be pulling up fence."

"Or roofing."

They stood side by side, watching the elements beat the earth. "Guess it's inside work then."

They hurried toward the house together. Neither spoke. Hunter was at the stove already. Lily sat on the counter, hefty book opened across legs clothed in purple tights and frilly skirt. She didn't so much as glance up when they walked in. A tiny dent of concentration was creased between her feathery eyebrows.

"And they have two hundred and five bones. Thirty-four of them are in their heads. It seems like one big bone. Or maybe two. But it's not. It's thirty-four. Their backs are like ours, but different. Because they have a tail and we don't."

"Lily honey," Vura said, "why don't you play hopscotch in the basement for a while?" She had chalked the boxes onto the crumbling concrete days before.

"There are three bones just in their feet."

"Lily Belle," Vura said, and lifting her daughter from the counter, caught her gaze from inches away. "Go play."

"I'm telling Hunk about the bones—"

"Hunt."

"What?"

"His name is Hunter. Or Hunt."

Lily nodded emphatically. "Hunk. I was explaining to him about a horse's bones."

Vura sighed. "I know, but you can do that later."

"But I still haven't told him about the ribs. There are thirty-six of them, but some of them aren't—"

"Lily . . ." Her mother's voice held a soft warning.

The child's brows lowered slightly, her lips puckered, but she nodded. Vura set her down. She trotted away, stopped at the door, little skirt hiked up over plum-bright leggings. "Some of them are real and some of them are false." She shrugged. "Even though they're all real," she explained, and turning away, disappeared into the adjoining room.

The kitchen fell into silence.

"I bet it'll be a relief to get rid of this counter." Vura's tone was forcefully cheery.

Hunter ignored both the tone and question. "Has she been diagnosed?"

Sydney frowned. Silence beat a quick tattoo through the room.

Vura inhaled quietly. "My father is very bright. And busy. Always has to be doing something with his mind, something with his hands. And I thought . . ." She shrugged, then glanced toward the door through which her daughter had disappeared. "I just thought she took after him."

"She probably does," Hunter said. "Asperger's

235

wasn't diagnosed much until fairly recently."

Sydney glanced from one to the other, feeling like an idiot. "She has Asperger's syndrome?"

"She's extremely high-functioning." Vura's words were quick. "You don't need to worry. She won't cause any trouble. In fact, she's very helpful. Always wants to—"

"It will be fine," Hunter said.

Vura's words slipped to a halt. She shifted her gaze to Sydney's. "There's no one in the area who specializes in kids with her condition, but I'll find another day-care provider if that's what you want."

Sydney waited a beat, certain Hunter would jump in, would assure them both that day care wasn't necessary. That Lily could spend every waking minute with them until hell froze over. She glanced at him. He stood silent, watching her. Their gazes met. Was he holding his breath, she wondered, waiting for her to disappoint him? Or was he hoping, instead, that she would do the right thing? The kind thing. This once.

"No." Her answer was slow. She filled her lungs and held the air in her chest, wondering what had become of the woman she used to be. "As long as we can keep her safe, she can stay."

The world seemed to be frozen for a moment, but Vura broke the silence. "Okay, then. Okay." She nodded, eyes unusually bright. "Well, I'd better get to work," she said and turned rapidly away.

"How about some breakfast first?" Sydney asked.

"I don't want to put you out." Her words were barely audible from behind.

Sydney laughed. "Not me. I couldn't poach an egg to save my soul. Redhawk's the cook."

"Oh? Well . . . I don't want to put him out, either," she said and hurried into the elements to retrieve her tools.

The remainder of the day was spent inside. Hunter sanded the parlor's hardwood floor while Vura hung the upstairs doors, and Sydney returned the freshly stained knotty pine trim to its rightful windows. She could, she discovered, hit the tiny finishing nails on the head two times out of ten.

The rain stopped just before dusk. Sunlight slanted through the clouds in rainbow hues, painting the earth in Genesis colors. Sydney settled back on her heels and let the green of the landscape ease her tension. Still, it felt as if her arms had been used in a game of tug-of-war. She sighed and raised the hammer one more time.

"If you make supper, I'll finish up here."

Sydney glanced up. Redhawk filled the doorway, big shoulders, narrow hips, powerful thighs. She kept her gaze resolutely on his face. "This may be hard to believe," she said, "but my aptitude for carpentry is somewhat superior to my skills as chef."

His lips curved with humor. "How are you as sous chef?"

"Lily?" Vura's voice rang through the house.

No one answered.

"Hey, Hunt, can you send Lil up with my thermos, please?"

Redhawk's brows dipped dramatically toward his dark-agate eyes. "Lily's not here."

"What?" Vura's footsteps were tapping down the stairs in a matter of seconds. "She made paper boats. I told her she could sail them in the kitchen sink if she got your permission."

"I haven't seen her for most of an hour," Hunter said. Sydney shook her head in tacit agreement.

"That girl . . ." Perhaps Vura was trying to keep her tone light, but it already sounded worried. She turned and headed toward the door. "She must have gone back to the truck for her giddyup bag."

Hunter followed her outside, but Lily was nowhere in sight. Vura was already slamming the Chevy's passenger door and glancing toward the creek.

Swollen from spring rains and still-melting snows, it hustled along, as cold and swift as death.

Vura ran in that direction even as Hunter jolted toward the barn. Sydney hurried after him. There were a hundred places a child could get hurt in there. The stairs were broken, the floorboards rotten. She rushed inside, but he held up a warning hand.

Little Lily was slumped against Courage's stall, brightly clad legs curled beneath her. The *Encyclopedia of Horses* was perched against her knees, but her head was drooping sideways, and her downy lashes were soft against her apple-dumpling cheeks.

Hunter exhaled shakily, then strode across the dirt floor to lift the tiny figure into his arms. She stirred, kaleidoscope eyes blinking. "Eight bones just in one knee," she lisped and drowsily slipped her arms around his neck. "That's . . ." She paused, fairy-bright face scrunched in thought. "Sixteen in both."

"Lily, you can't—" he began, but stopped when his voice betrayed him and simply tightened his arms around her.

"Are you okay, Hunk?"

He was already striding outside. "Your mother was worried," he told her.

"I had to tell Courage about her bones," she said and twirled her fingers in his hair. "She's very brave. That's what *courage* means. Brave. She was hurt real bad and now she's alone, but she doesn't whine. Mama says no one likes a whiner." She was fully awake, from sleep to chatter in nine seconds flat.

Retrieving her fallen book, Sydney followed them from the barn.

"Horses are . . ." Lily was babbling like a brook, gaze set somewhere in the middle distance. ". . . gregors . . . gregurans . . . greg . . ."

"Gregarious?" Hunter guessed.

She nodded emphatically, little chin bobbing. "Gregarious. That means they don't like to be alone. So I thought—"

"Lily!" Vura's voice cracked like a whip as she ran toward them. "Lily, where were you?"

"Courage is lonely."

"Were you in the barn?"

"She shouldn't be alone," Lily said.

"I told you not to go outside!" Vura's words were a jumble of anger. Of worry and fear and heart-stopping relief. "I told you—"

"She is safe," Hunter intoned.

Vura glanced at him and paused, a dozen rampant emotions flashing through her eyes.

"Be grateful," he added, and delivering the child to her mother's arms, he slipped into his truck and drove away.

Chapter 23

Sydney sat alone in the kitchen. The Genesis moment experienced earlier in the evening had passed. Another storm was blowing in. Or maybe it was a continuation of the weather that had haunted them most of the day. Rain pattered the new windows, rattled the doors. The ancient house groaned like a banshee. But Redhawk's absence didn't make it more frightening. He'd been gone since handing Lily back to her mother, but that was fine. Still, she couldn't help wondering where he was. Not because she missed him or because the lightning that forked across the blue-velvet sky brought painful memories, memories that eased into the past when he was near. She *didn't* miss him. But it was impossible to pretend that she didn't pine for his cooking.

Sighing, she heated up a can of soup. She would never quite understand how she managed to scald the bottom without warming up the entirety of it. Disgruntled and exhausted, she trudged up the stairs, stripped down to the silky long underwear she had been wise enough to bring on what she had once thought would be a vacation, and fell into bed.

But at midnight she was still awake. She lay in the darkness, surrounded by a half-dozen tools Vura had left behind, and remembered things that should not be remembered. The giggle from the tack room. The heat that rushed to her cheeks. The tremor in her hands. The hard beat of her heart as she swung her leg over Eternal Flame's bright-penny hindquarters. The roar of righteous anger as they soared. Then pain. Deep, throbbing pain almost unrealized as she watched the light die in the gelding's trusting eyes.

Sydney sat up abruptly, heart fisting in her chest. She'd been a fool, and in retrospect could barely remember why she had ever wanted David Albrook in her life. Was it to prove she was not unlovable or was it simply to stem the loneliness? Whatever the answer, she'd made a grave mistake; he hadn't been worth the life of the brave, honest jumper that had died. That had been destroyed. Because of her.

Her throat felt tight. She barely noticed the headlights that swept across the water-stained wall of her bedroom. Pain drummed softly in her thigh as she pushed to her feet and made her way to the window.

Moonlight fought through the Gothic-purple clouds, illuminating the truck and trailer that eased to a halt in front of the barn.

Curiosity was her first emotion. Panic was the second. It struck her like a blow.

"No!" she rasped, and grabbing the nearest tool, raced down the stairs.

The gravel was cold and sharp against her bare feet, but in a matter of seconds she was beside the pickup truck, heart pounding like hoofbeats.

The driver's door opened. A shadow stepped out.

"Just stay where you are!" Her voice sounded guttural.

Face hidden beneath the brim of a dark hat, the man stopped and raised his hands.

"What's going on?" Hunter's voice was low and quiet as he exited the passenger side and rounded the front bumper, but it did nothing to dull the alarms that rang like sirens in Sydney's brain.

"I could ask you the same thing," she said, and tightening her grip, raised the metal rod to shoulder height.

"And I could answer," he said, "if you'd put down that crowbar."

"You're not taking her!" She growled the words from between gritted teeth.

There was a moment of silence, then, "Taking—"

"It's not her fault she got tangled up." She loosened her fingers, tightened them again. "Not her fault she's confined to that stall. Or that Lily wandered in. Just a bunch of bad luck. And she's not going to take the blame for it."

"Sounds like an interesting story," the driver said, hands still raised. "I think I might enjoy it if you weren't threatening to crack me in the head with a demolition tool."

A sliver of reality slipped into Sydney's overheated mind. She scowled. "Colt?"

"Hey, Syd," Colt Dickenson said. "How's your mustang?"

She wasn't placated. "What are you doing here?"

His shrug almost went unseen. "Redhawk here said he needed some help with a horse."

"Well, Redhawk was wrong." For reasons she couldn't quite fathom, her knees felt wobbly. "Courage is doing just fine." Her throat felt tight, making the last word tremble slightly. "You're not going to take her."

"Okay."

She shuffled her feet, found a more comfortable stance. "And we're not putting her down."

"All right."

She blinked, wondering, guessing. The reason for this late-night visit seemed a little less obvious than it had a few minutes ago. "Or turning her loose?"

There was a moment of silence. "Good to know."

It wasn't until that second that something stirred inside the trailer. Sydney glanced hesitantly to the right, only to realize that two animals resided in the two-horse slant. Munching rhythmically, they gazed at her through the open slats. She stared at them for several seconds before shifting her attention back to Colt. "Who's that?"

"Guess the bay's name is Fandango. The chestnut's called Windwalker."

Sydney blinked, shifted. An icy pebble seemed to be determined to dig its way through the sole of her left foot. "Why are they in that trailer?"

"Hunt seemed to think your mustang could use some company."

Seconds ticked silently past.

"Oh," she said finally and felt her muscles whine as she lowered the iron rod. "That's fine then," she added, and turning on her heel, tried not to limp as she marched toward the house.

Behind her, Colt Dickenson exhaled carefully and lowered his hands. "She, ahhh . . . she do that often?"

Hunter watched her go, body straight as an arrow, shoulders drawn back like a bowstring. She was as haughty as a duchess and as rigid as a two-by-four, but damn . . . He felt a sliver of pride slice through to his soul. If the chips were down, he'd want her in his corner.

"Redhawk, you awake?"

Hunter dragged himself back to the moment, forced a shrug. "Guess she's attached to the horse."

"Attached?" Colt nodded. "All right. Anything else she's attached to that I should know about?"

Hunter narrowed his eyes and found Colt in the darkness. The man had been a flirt the day he'd popped out of his mama's womb. After that he'd been a player. "I think you know all you need to about her," he said and, opening the back of the trailer, he led the chestnut into the barn.

Chapter 24

Sydney had her back to Hunter when he entered the kitchen. It was still straight, still stiff, and she still smelled like peaches. What the devil was that about?

She had pulled one of his freshly laundered flannel shirts over the silky long johns in which she had accosted Colt. The hem reached almost to her knees, and though she had folded back the cuffs, the sleeves nearly swallowed her narrow, smooth-skinned hands.

He opened the fridge and glanced inside. Three cartons of Greek yogurt and a bag of romaine lettuce gave him the stink eye. Sighing, he poured himself a glass of water from the cider bottle that resided there and sat down at the table to enjoy it.

"You bought horses?" she asked and turned from the window. Beneath her cool-water eyes, half-moons of lavender fatigue shadowed her face.

"Borrowed," he corrected.

"You borrowed horses?"

"Ai."

She clasped her hands loosely in front of her, a sign that her patience was already running short, and for some reason that always improved his mood.

"Why?" she asked.

He drank again, studied the glass, and fervently missed his drinking days. But he did not miss the headaches or the guilt that followed. "Why not?"

She waited. He wondered if she was silently counting to ten. That had been his mother's ploy. That and threatening him with additional visits from the porcine species.

"Because they're expensive and labor intensive," she said.

"I thought you might want to ride, get a better chance to see your property."

She stared at him. Her face looked exceedingly pale. And solemn. And beautiful in its tough fragility. "You ventured out in the middle of the night during a thunderstorm to find horses because you thought I might want to ride someday?" Her expression was haughty, but there was something in her eyes. Gratitude maybe.

And more. Could it be fear? And if so, what made her so scared? She didn't seem like a woman who should be frightened.

"Do you?" he asked.

"Do I what?"

"Want to ride someday."

"No."

"Why not?"

She drew a deep breath. "Horses are dangerous."

He laughed, watched her for a moment, then sobered finally. "Are you serious?"

"Of course I'm serious."

He shook his head. "That pair I just brought in are like kittens compared to the beast you've been keeping in the barn."

"But they don't . . ." She paused, shut up, shut down.

"Don't what?"

She pursed her lips and inhaled through her nose. For a moment he was certain she would remain silent, but finally she spoke. "They don't need me."

Their eyes met.

"And you need to be needed?"

"No. Of course not." She pulled her gaze away. "I wish I had never found her," she said and let one finger tap her flannel-clad thigh.

"Why not turn her loose then? Let her take her chances?"

She opened her mouth, then pursed her lips and

watched him in silence for a moment. "You're a fine one to talk."

"What does that mean?"

"You brought her companions."

He considered arguing, but he shrugged instead, sighed. "Lily was right."

"About?"

"Horses aren't meant to be alone."

She watched him, unblinking, straight and proud and hopelessly alluring with her brave stance and broken-doll eyes.

"Neither are you," he added.

She raised her brows at him. "I'm happy alone." She held his gaze. "Well . . ." She glanced away again. "Not . . . not ecstatic maybe, but Wellesleys are historically . . ." She huffed out a breath and pursed her wild-raspberry lips. "Why'd you bring the horses?"

Those lips, so incongruous with the rest of her perfectly sophisticated face, called to him, stirring his interest, bumping up his heart rate. It was as surprising as hell. Tonk had once said that if Hunter were any calmer, he would have no pulse at all.

"Why the horses?" she asked again.

"You do not think Courage should have companionship?"

"I don't believe that's why you did it. Or not the only reason, at least."

He stretched his legs out in front of him. He

felt tired and old and sore. "I doubt I need to inform you that you are welcome to your opinions."

"You did it for Lily," she said.

He turned the glass in his hand and said nothing. Memories could be sadistic little bastards.

"I wonder why." Her voice had gone soft. He stifled his wince. He was a fool for softness.

"I'm concerned about your liability coverage," he said.

She was quiet for a moment, as if trying to guess his meaning before giving up. "Has anyone ever told you that non sequiturs are the first sign of mental illness?"

Laughter rumbled quietly in his gut, tempering the mood.

Pulling out a chair, she eased into it. "I'd expound on the beauty of my liability, but I'm not entirely sure what that means . . . and I'm a little too tired to try to figure it out."

He watched her. She had loosed her hair from its habitual bondage. It lay in soft, dark waves against her shoulders and teased across her neat little breasts. "That may be my favorite thing about you," he said.

"That I'm tired?"

"That you work to exhaustion. That you go after what you want."

She stared at him. In the entirety of her life, no one had accused her of such a thing. But perhaps she had never known what she wanted. And maybe she still didn't. Except for Courage. She knew she wanted a safe place for Courage. And maybe, if she were honest, she wanted a refuge for other wild things, too. But Redhawk was still watching her, waiting for a response. "I don't know if I should be proud or insulted," she said.

"Maybe it's time to quit worrying about what you should be and just be it."

She drew her shoulder blades back a quarter of an inch. "Indian wisdom?" she asked.

"It is powerful medicine."

She felt her lips twitch a little, felt the muscles in her stomach uncoil a notch. "How did you know Lily had Asperger's?"

"It is a well-known syndrome."

She held his gaze. "And you discovered a cure while meditating in the foothills of the Himalayas at age two and a half?"

Humor shone in his eyes. They looked amber-bright tonight, flecked with dark umber and ancient wisdom. But she refused to be charmed. Instead, she raised one brow.

"I worked as a para in Tallahassee for a few months."

"How old *are* you?"

" 'Age is opportunity no less than youth itself, though in another dress.' "

She paused a second, thinking. "How do you know Longfellow?"

"You can read a lot of poetry in a hundred and fifty years."

She couldn't help but laugh. He chuckled in return. The soft noise made something bump a little in her chest. Looking down, she studied a chip in their old, newly purchased table and failed to stop the truth that formed on her lips. "I wonder sometimes if I've wasted my entire life."

The kitchen went silent.

"Far better," he said finally, "than wasting the lives of others."

She glanced up at him, but his face had gone stone cold. He was already rising to his feet.

"Oh no you don't," she said and rising, too, grabbed his arm. Feelings flared between them. Her breath stopped in her throat, but she pulled her hand away. "You can't just . . ." She glanced toward the window. Outside, the world lay in black-velvet silence. "You can't just throw me a crumb, then march off to sleep."

"I doubt I will sleep."

"What?" She blinked at him. "You don't sleep?"

"I've been known to . . . at times."

She linked her fingers in front of her. "I've often wondered how people can spend so much time in bed."

"An eternity," he admitted.

Their eyes met. She refused to shift hers away, though his gaze burned on contact.

"Would you have attacked me with the crowbar if I attempted to take Courage?" he asked.

"In a heartbeat. Why does Lily make you cry?" It was more honest than she had intended to be, but she was tired and the words were out. For several long seconds she thought he wouldn't respond. In fact, she could see the desire to turn away in the tension of his muscles, the striking planes of his face, but finally he spoke.

"There is a saying: In every girl there is a goddess."

"I don't believe my father heard that one."

His brows dipped as he searched for a question, but she spoke before he found it.

"Do you have a daughter?"

The pause was so long she was certain he hadn't heard her, but finally he spoke again. "I did."

His sadness lay between them like an open wound. "I'm sorry."

"Well . . ." He straightened to his full intimidating height, but she placed a hand on his arm again.

"How old was she?"

He met her eyes. "Some say it is helpful to speak of hardships. I have not found that to be true."

"I didn't even know you *could* speak."

He exhaled an almost laugh and she shook her head.

"Don't make me try to sleep again. Not yet."

He watched her for a long moment, then turned toward the cupboard and took out a bag. Setting the Doritos on the table, he sat again.

She folded her hands in her lap. "I tasted those once."

"Once?" he asked and uncoiled the twist tie.

"At Lindsay Haggle's house." She thought back. The memories felt ashy in her mouth. "Her father was an investment banker. Her mother was a psychologist. They were acceptable people . . . or so Grandmother thought. Until she learned that they served chips for luncheon."

"They should have been horsewhipped."

She let herself relax a little. "I never saw Lindsay and her improper nutritional habits again." She stared at the bag.

"Why not live dangerously?" he asked and turned the opening toward her.

"Tell me about your daughter."

His eyes hardened, but she couldn't face that ugly bedroom again. "Please," she added.

His exhalation was long and soft. "She was tall for her age," he said finally. "Slender as a willow switch." Another pause. His gaze looked far away, as if he were living in another reality. "Even when she was born, her hair was as black as a wild bay's mane. And when she laughed . . ." His lips lifted a little at the memory. "She laughed like my mother. With her entire being. Like there was nothing but joy in all the world."

"That's nice."

He shook his head. "It would have been easier if I could have doubted that she was mine."

She had no idea how to respond to that.

"But I did not doubt, and still I failed her," he said and left the room.

Chapter 25

Sydney exited the house at the rumble of an engine. It was 7:24 in the morning; Vura always arrived early.

But it was not her oversized Chevy that pulled into the drive. The man who stepped out of the aging jeep looked unfamiliar. He was already gazing up at Sydney's ancient barn when she approached him from behind.

"Can I help you?" she asked. He didn't turn toward her immediately.

"What a beauty she is," he said.

"I beg your pardon?"

He twisted toward her. His eyes were as black as obsidian, his long hair just as dark. "I said . . ." He paused, raised his brows when his gaze fell on her face, and flashed a brilliant, crooked smile. "What a work of art she is."

"The . . ." She leaned back a little and brought

her hand to her throat, though she didn't know why. "The barn?"

He chuckled. "That, too. You are Sydney."

"Yes, I—" she began, but he had already taken her palm between his own.

"De yani ju dat'sayah, Min'/dtoh ci we dom tawe'." His words, though incomprehensible, were a low, sensual chant.

Sydney stared at him. She knew she should tug her hand away, but for the life of her, she couldn't quite seem to manage it.

"Tell me," he said, gliding closer, "what brings a princess such as yourself into this harsh land?"

"I—" she began again, but a low voice interrupted the words she had yet to formulate in her mind.

"What the devil are you doing?"

She jerked at the sound of Hunter's voice, but her visitor didn't seem the least surprised. Instead, he tightened his grip on her fingers almost imperceptibly and raised his midnight eyes with slow mischief. "You did not say she held magic in her hand, Hunter Ray."

"Give the hand back," Hunter demanded.

The younger man laughed, kissed her knuckles with fervent warmth, and winked. "As you wish, brother."

"Brother?" The word came out as little more than a peep of sound. Sydney snapped her gaze from one man to the other, but their similarities did not reach past their Native American features.

The smile again, crooked with charm. He nodded once and stroked her hand before releasing it with a shallow bow. "Tonkiaishawien Kientuankeah Redhawk, at your humble service."

"What are you doing here, Tonk?" If Hunter was happy to see his kinsman, he was an excellent actor.

"I have taken time away from my muse to help you with—"

It was then that Vura pulled up beside Tonk's decrepit jeep. Stepping out, she loosed a lilac-clad Lily from her car seat, and settled the child onto one curvy hip before approaching them. Her signature strides were long and sure. Her ponytail bounced with every step, sassy as a teenager.

Tonk raised dark brows in undisguised interest. "A princess and an angel." The trio watched in silence for a moment as she approached. "There is much you haven't told me, brother." Turning, Tonk reached for Vura's free hand and kissed her knuckles. "I am Tonkiaishawien Kientuankeah Redhawk."

She scowled at him. "Hunt's brother?"

"Ai."

"Hff," she said and pulled her hand unceremoniously from his grasp before turning toward her employer. "When did you say those shingles will arrive?"

Sydney tried to shake herself back to reality. "Ahh, today, I think."

"Good. I should be ready for them this afternoon," she said, and taking Lily with her, turned to gather the tools she had left in the house.

Silence followed in her wake. Humor gleamed in Hunter's eyes. "Strike one." His words were barely audible.

"There are other players in the game," Tonk said and returned his gaze to Sydney. But she took a quick, involuntary step to the rear.

"Looks like you're mistaken," Hunter said, and taking his brother by the arm, steered him toward the barn. In a matter of minutes, they were examining its ancient roof.

Sydney shook her head, then wandered inside to feed the horses. Fandango whinnied. Windwalker pawed. Courage remained silent, but sidled a scant few inches closer to her door.

Hope bloomed softly in Sydney's soul.

"She has begun to eat."

She jumped at the sound of Hunter's voice, blinked back any unacceptable emotion, and glanced behind him. The doorway was empty. Turning toward their modest cache of hay, she gathered up two flakes and moved toward Fandango's stall. "You didn't tell me your brother was coming."

"I was uncertain of his plans." His expression was unreadable.

"You should take a day off. Spend some time together."

"He is busy."

"Doing what?"

"Removing shingles."

She stopped. Alfalfa stems poked at her wrists and belly. "You have him working?"

"He said he came to help."

"Well . . ." She waited as he stepped forward to open the stall door. She dropped the hay inside. "You could have at least offered him a cup of coffee first."

"He has drunk enough."

"What does that mean?"

Hunter scowled. "He is not as charming as you think."

"I didn't say he was charming."

He studied her in silence. Her cheeks felt warm, but the sun had finally shown its face. She was unaccustomed to the heat. Unacceptably flustered, she stroked a hand down the bay gelding's swayed back.

"How old is he?"

"Tonk?"

Irritation edged her jitters. "Fandango."

Hunter shrugged and moved in a little closer. "I wanted a sensible mount."

"Sensible?" She shook her head as the bay heaved a sigh and cocked an arthritic hip. "I'm not even sure he's conscious."

"Tell me, Sydney Wellesley, when did you become an expert on horses?"

Age five, she thought, but didn't voice the words.

Outside the barn, a door slammed. The noise was followed by the patter of lightning-quick feet, announcing Lily's exit from the house.

"I hope you don't plan to ride the wind on *him*," Sydney said, nodding toward the other horse.

"Sometimes the wind blows faster than others," Hunt replied and turned as the little dynamo burst into the barn.

"Is she healed yet?" Lily asked, eyes wide, legs slowing.

Inside the enclosed stall, Courage snorted a warning.

"Not yet, little Lilac," Hunter said. "But other horses have arrived."

"More horses?" Lily asked and held up her arms to him.

He lifted her against his chest with reverent slowness. His eyelids dropped a little, dipping heavy lashes toward high-boned cheeks, as if the weight of her against his heart was almost too much to bear.

"Are they sick, too?"

"They are not," Hunter said and nodded toward the bay as Vura drew near. "Is she allowed?"

"Like I could stop her," she said and laughed

as her daughter clasped excited hands in front of her mouth. In a moment the pair was inside the stall. Vura turned toward Sydney. "Did you know about Hunt's brother?"

"What?" Gathering more hay, Sydney moved toward Windwalker's stall. There was something about feeding time that helped her relax, that filled an unknown emptiness inside her.

"Tonkewheezie . . . or whatever his name is . . . what's he doing here?"

Sydney glanced over, baffled by the other woman's tone. Vura seemed the type who liked . . . and was liked . . . by everyone. "I guess he came to help out."

"With what?"

Sydney shrugged. "The barn roof?"

"Do you really think we need—"

"Mama!" Lily shot out of the stall like a missile. "Hunk says I can ride him."

"Hunt," Vura corrected.

"Can I?"

"If Hunter says it's okay."

He appeared behind her and nodded. "Come then, coneflower," he said, and slipping a halter behind the gelding's long ears, led him out of the stall. In a moment Lily was clinging to his mane, wide-eyed and speechless.

The women watched them make a slow passage down the driveway. "I've never seen her quiet this long," Sydney said.

Vura laughed. "I was the same way when I was little. Dumbstruck when there was a horse in the vicinity."

"You ride?"

"Sure. Well . . ." Her eyes were bright with unconcealed adoration as she watched her tiny daughter's progress. "Obviously, not like you, but—" She stopped abruptly.

"What?" Sydney asked and yanked her attention away from the trio on the driveway.

Vura laughed, shrugged. "You just look like you belong on a horse. Well . . . I'd better get to work. My boss is a slave driver," she said, and leaving her daughter in Redhawk's care, hurried off toward her truck.

The days that followed were filled with sawdust and hope and backbreaking labor. The fences went up. The kitchen counter came down. Hunter, Sydney thought, worked his brother like a slave, but Tonk didn't complain. No wages had been discussed, but he didn't seem to mind that, either. He spent endless hours on the barn roof before heading into town each evening. Sydney's suggestion that he save money by staying at Gray Horse Hill was met with a flat refusal. Tonkiaishawien, Hunter said, was not the kind of man who paid for hotel rooms.

She didn't know what that meant, and maybe she was too content to ask. Things were going well. Courage was growing stronger. She was putting on a little weight, and her eyes looked bright as baubles behind her tousled forelock. It was becoming nearly impossible to change her bandages without risking life and limb. Someday she would be free again, Sydney told herself, and imagined the mare galloping, unfettered and joyous, across the open plains, dark tail streaming behind her like a triumphant banner.

But in her mind's eye the mare was never alone. Hunter was right, Sydney thought, stomach twisting a little; few creatures were meant for solitude.

Spring headed toward summer. The Canadian geese returned in trails so long it seemed as if they had been hatched by the horizon. The temperature had tapped into the sixties and stayed there even into the evening hours.

Sydney and Vura were sweating in tandem as they strained to hold up the swinging end of the gate they were attempting to hang near the barn. Above them on the frightfully steep roof, Tonk was carefully replacing the barn's original shingles and adding new cedar as needed. He and Vura had fought like badgers over whether they should use the eighteen- or twenty-four-inch lengths.

"A little higher," Hunter said and fiddled with the hinges.

They lifted.

"Too high."

They adjusted.

"More to the left. Not that far."

"Holy—" Vura panted, but Hunter interrupted.

"Right there!" he ordered and finally the heavy tubing settled onto the hinges. They loosed their hold, letting it swing free.

"I was just about to come over and slap you upside the head," Vura said, and pulling off her gloves, flexed sore fingers. "But . . . Hey!" She paused, shaded her eyes against the setting sun, and watched as a white Silverado pulled into the drive. "Oh!" she breathed, and dropping her gloves, sprinted across the yard.

In a matter of seconds, a man was wrapping her in his arms. There was something about the sight of him swinging her in a circle that made Sydney's throat close up. Something about the sound of their laughter that made it impossible to look away.

"Who's that?" Tonk had appeared beside them near the gate. He could, it seemed, move just as silently as his brother. Maybe history insisted that they retain their stealth.

"It must be Dane, her husband," Sydney said. Since Vura's first-day explanation, she had barely mentioned the man. But apparently, their relationship was intact. Sydney managed to pull her gaze away. "Well, it's my night to cook. If you're partial to poor food, badly prepared and hideously served, you're welcome to join us," she said, but Tonk didn't seem to hear her.

"Looks kind of long in the tooth, doesn't he?" he said.

"None of your business," Hunter growled.

Tonk grinned and turned toward Sydney with a conspiratorial wink that lit his eyes and carved a dimple into his left cheek. "Guess those old codgers have to stick together."

"I've been wondering . . ." she said. "Just how old is—"

"Sydney. Hunt . . ." Vura and her visitor were already striding toward them. They had linked arms, and though the man's eyes were shadowed by a weathered baseball cap, his smile matched hers. His adoration was all but tangible. Sydney felt her stomach cramp and wondered what kind of person would feel uncomfortable at the sight of such happiness. She glanced toward the house, but she'd missed her opportunity to escape.

"I'd like you to meet my dad, Quinton Murrell," Vura said.

Surprise touched Sydney, but honestly, she wasn't sure if the truth magnified or diminished her jealousy. She hadn't heard from Leonard Wellesley in weeks.

"Dad, this is Hunter Redhawk." They shook hands.

"And his brother . . ." She gave her head a sassy tilt. "Tonkashaweenie."

265

Tonk's dark brows lowered. "Tonkiaishawien."

"Right," Vura said, tone crisp before she exhaled softly. "And this is Sydney Wellesley."

Quinton Murrell removed his cap. His salt-and-pepper hair was short and thick.

"Sydney." He said her name softly. His voice was deep and melodious, but it was his eyes that struck her, intense and solemn and kind. His handshake was firm but gentle.

"Hi," she said and felt strangely unnerved. "It's very nice to meet you, Mr. Murrell."

"You look like your mother."

She tugged her hand from his. "I beg your pardon?"

His expressive eyes cleared. He smiled. "I knew your parents," he explained.

Sydney blinked at him.

Vura laughed. "Dad knows everyone."

"You knew my mother?" Sydney asked.

"We met. Briefly," he added.

Overhead, a pair of swans trumpeted as they stretched their endless necks toward the north. The sound of their wings brushed the stillness.

"When I heard your name . . ." He examined her face as if searching for clues. But in a moment he shrugged and stepped back. "Wellesley. It rang a bell. Turns out I did some construction work for your father back in the nineties."

"Dad's the best master carpenter this side of the Mississippi," Vura said.

"But it's not," Sydney said.

"What?" Vura had paled a little.

"Virginia. It isn't on this side of the Mississippi," Sydney said.

Murrell smiled, but there was something in his eyes. A wistfulness maybe. "I spent a few years out east."

"Working for my father?"

"He wanted a studio built. It was a big project."

"Mother's dance studio." Sydney felt herself relax a little. What was she thinking? That the paparazzi had found her? That the press cared about a broken equestrienne with shattered Olympic dreams? Isolation was making her delusional.

"Can you join us for dinner?"

Hunter's question surprised her, then made her feel silly. There had been a time when she was a decent hostess.

"Yes, please," she said. "I confess to being the world's worst cook, but we would very much like to have you stay."

"That's kind of you," he said, "but I just wanted to drop in, see how my little girl was doing . . ." He watched Sydney for another long second, then pulled his gaze away. "And kiss my granddaughter. Where is she?" he asked and glanced around.

Vura rolled her eyes. "She's in the barn. She's *always* in the barn."

"Just like her mother was," Murrell said.

Vura laughed. "She sits by the stalls and reads to the horses. I'll get her."

"No, don't. I'd like to see her there," he said. They turned as a unit and entered the barn together, but the aisle was empty.

"Lily?" The panic came immediately to Vura's voice, but Hunter silenced her.

Premonition soured his gut. Stepping softly, he padded toward the mustang's stall and peered between the planks.

Courage tossed her head and backed into the corner. It wasn't until that moment that he caught a splash of purple, a tangle of tousled hair, just beside the door.

Breath held, he eased up the latch and stepped inside. The tiny, brightly dressed form was slumped against the boards, body bowed, hair flopped over her face, and for a second his heart stopped dead in his chest, but when he touched her, her eyes opened sleepily.

"Hunk," she lisped. Against the far wall, the mare huffed nervously.

"Hush now," he said and lifted the child into his arms. His heart hammered like a gong against her tidy framework of ribs. Backing out of the stall, he turned woodenly and handed her off to her mother. If he was lucky, she wouldn't feel the trembling in his arms, see the terror in his eyes.

"Lily!" Vura squeezed her tiny daughter to her chest. "What were you thinking? I told you never to go in there."

"She's lonely." Her voice was little more than a sigh as she rested her head against her mother's shoulder.

"She's not," Vura said. "She has the geldings now. You can visit either of them. But not Courage. You know that."

"The geldings have each other," she said, and lifting her head, saw their visitor for the first time. "Poppy!"

"Hello, little Lil," he said, and taking her in his arms, gratefully kissed her silky head.

It was the second familial meeting Sydney had to witness that day. She hoped it would be the last.

Chapter 26

"Add it slowly," Hunter said.

Sydney stared at the fresh cream. It was as thick as pease pudding. Emily had delivered it from the Lazy Windmill just that morning . . . which had been more than twelve hours ago. But they'd nearly completed one paddock. Vura had insisted on staying even later than usual to put in one more post. Tonk was leveling the sand hauled in for the dressage ring. Their inexplicable rivalry seemed to be increasing their productivity if not Sydney's calm. "I'm not really supposed to use all of this, am I?"

"Ai," Hunter said, hand never slowing as he chopped carrots on a scarred wooden board. "And keep stirring."

She shook her head, but did as ordered, maybe because her knowledge of cooking didn't extend beyond scalded soup or maybe because the broth was beginning to smell a little like a culinary fantasy.

"Is the wild rice ready?" he asked.

She lifted the cover from a battered pan, glanced at the unappetizing mush inside, and scowled. "Is it supposed to look like scrambled frog eyes?"

He shook his head and moved in beside her. Their elbows brushed. Lightning tingled discreetly up her arm, just a tiny piece of everyday magic. "May my Ojibwe brothers forgive your lack of understanding."

Just outside the window, a truck door slammed. Sydney glanced through the kitchen window. Lily had just scrambled into the backseat of her mother's Chevy. Vura was poised on the far side of her truck when Tonk reached her.

"Bravura," he said and she turned, striking him with her turquoise eyes. Sydney saw him grin as if he knew some secret jest. "Giving up kind of early tonight, aren't you?"

She shoved leather gloves into the back pocket of her jeans and didn't bother looking at him. "Some of us got here before noon."

Tonk had pulled up at 7:07, three minutes after Vura's arrival. "And some of us have reasons to stay in bed." He smirked and watched her stiffen as his barb struck home.

"Well, you'd better get back to her," she said and reached for the Chevy's door handle, "before she finds another client."

He grabbed her arm. "She's not a—" he began, but she snapped out of his grasp.

"Don't put your hands on me." She said the words through gritted teeth.

He raised his palms in surrender. "I'm sorry." The apology came immediately. "Listen, Bravura, I do not want to argue."

"I know what you want."

He paused a moment, then huffed a laugh. "You know very little."

"I know your type."

"My . . ." He shook his head, then stopped, as if willing himself to resist the argument. "I made something for you," he said and lifted the gift he held in his left hand.

She scowled at it. "What is it?"

"What does it look—" He refrained from grinding his teeth and found his old world cadence. "It is a sacred necklace, crafted of silver to cleanse your mind, acoma black jet to heal that which ails you and—"

"I thought you guys made license plates."

Frustration swamped him. "Just because your old man walked out on you doesn't—"

"You know nothing about the situation."

"And you know nothing about *me!*" He stabbed a thumb at his heart. "Doesn't stop you from being a . . ." His words stumbled to a halt.

She narrowed her eyes at him. "Say it! I dare you to say it."

They stared at each other, tension streaming like an electric current between them, but finally Tonk jerked away, dropped the necklace into the pocket of his jeans. "Never mind."

Watching from the kitchen window, Sydney exhaled and Hunter scowled as Vura jerked into her truck and sped toward the road.

Tonk was already out of sight.

"Will we be meeting your other brothers anytime soon?" Sydney asked and glanced toward Hunter.

He narrowed his eyes as he shifted his attention to her. "Why do you ask?"

"Don't get me wrong," she said, worried suddenly that she had offended him. "He's a great worker and he's good with the horses. It's just that . . ."

"Just that what?"

She straightened her back a little, a defensive pose she had adopted decades ago. "He seems to irritate Vura a little." And that had to bother Hunter. His feelings for the young mother and daughter were hardly a secret, but he didn't address that issue.

"What does he do for you?"

"What?"

"Tonk." He stood very still, shoulders rigid, muscles taut. "How do you feel about him?"

"Well . . ." She wished, quite fervently now, that she hadn't started down this particular path. "He's very nice. Really. And . . ." She searched for the right adjectives. "Skilled . . ." She turned with a jerk toward the stove, but his attention remained on her face. She could feel her cheeks warm under his perusal.

"You don't like him." You could have lined the drive with the gravel in his voice.

"I like him. I just—" she began, but the sound of his chuckle stopped her words.

"You don't like him." His grin was watermelon wide.

She glanced over her shoulder at him. "I don't understand you at all," she said, to which he laughed out loud. But at that second the front door opened and the subject of their discussion strode in.

"What's so funny?" Tonkiaishawien usually looked as if he was about to laugh or had just finished doing so, but that wasn't true at the moment.

"Nothing," Sydney said, cheeks burning hotter. "We were just—"

"She doesn't like you," Hunter informed him.

Tonk watched him a moment before shifting his gaze to Sydney. "That can't be true," he said.

"It's not!" Her denial was quick and emphatic. "I was just saying—"

"Everybody likes me." He scowled at the kitchen window. "*Almost* everybody."

"That's what I thought, too." Hunt laughed again.

"Some people want to punch me in the throat," Tonk added.

Hunter nodded and lifted one broad palm as if to say, "Well sure."

"But they *like* me."

Hunt shrugged, grinned, and returned to his carrots.

"Have you been talking to Bravura about me?" Tonk asked. His expression looked honestly confused, more than a little curious, and not the least bit miffed.

"No," Sydney said. "Of course not. And I *do* like you. I do! It's just that . . ."

The kitchen went quiet. Both men faced her.

Tonk raised one brow.

She tapped one restless finger against the

wooden spoon and looked from Hunter to his brother. "You're kind of a flirt."

There was another moment of silence before Hunt snorted.

"And?" Tonk asked.

"Well, I just . . ." She was starting to sputter a little. It wasn't like her at all. "I'm just not the type who—"

"You've got a thing for *him!*" Tonk said suddenly.

"What?" She stumbled backward a half step, already shaking her head.

But it was Tonk's turn to laugh. "And here I thought I had seen it all. You know he snores like a buzz saw, right?"

"No, I don't know . . ." She was sputtering in earnest now. "How would I know . . ."

"You haven't slept with him yet?" Tonk tilted his head at her. "Well, that explains part of it, I guess, but still . . . he's as charismatic as a rock. And he moves with the speed of a glacier. But . . . hey . . ." He shrugged. "They say it takes all kinds. I never believed them, but now . . ." He shook his head. "Oh . . ." He lifted his hand. "I made this for you."

She blinked foolishly at the object in his hand. "What is it?"

"It's a vase made with horsehair. It is called a memory vase." He looked a little peeved about it.

She shook her head, though honestly it was

beautiful beyond words. Squat at the bottom and lipped at the top, it looked like marbleized jade . . . deep green flecked with amber and crisscrossed was dark, jagged lines.

"It is Courage," Tonk said.

"What?" She raised her gaze from the vase to his eyes. All humor had fled from them.

"I gathered tail hairs from the mustang and fired them into the pot." He nodded. "Whatever the future, Courage will be with you."

Sydney reached for the vase. It felt smooth and cool against her fingertips. A trio of rough stones hung from a strip of rawhide knotted at the top. "You made this?"

"Ai."

"You're a . . ." She glanced at Hunter, but his eyes remained on his brother. "He's a potter?"

"Tonkiaishawien was gifted with art long before he was gifted with wisdom." Something echoed in Hunter's voice. It sounded a little like pride.

"You wondered how I was spending my nights," Tonk said. "Now you know."

Their gazes met. "Now I know," Hunter agreed.

Tonk nodded and turned away, but he stopped at the door and caught Sydney's eye. "Tell me when you tire of him," he said, and grinning, stepped outside.

She stared after him in silence.

"It needs a few more minutes," Hunter said.

Sydney blinked at the vase, lying like a treasured pearl in her hands. "What?"

"The rice," he said. "It needs a bit more time."

She nodded, turned toward him. "What was that about?"

Scooping the chopped vegetables into a pan, he set them to boil. A half-dozen rich aromas melded in a culinary symphony, but she scowled.

"Hunter?"

He was silent a moment, but finally he spoke. "Life on the rez . . . it is difficult enough with decent parents." He exhaled slowly, glanced at the pot nearest her. "Stir that."

Hugging the vase to her chest, she picked up the abandoned spoon. "His were indecent?"

"His were monsters." He glanced toward the door. "And the reason he drinks." His sigh was as heavy as silt. "But there is only so long you can lean on your excuses before you must carry your own weight and learn to stand tall." Lifting a frying pan, he began scrubbing it with a Brillo pad. Gray Horse Hill had never been blessed with a dishwasher. It was, in fact, lucky to have a sink.

Sydney set the vase on the counter, where it captured the harsh overhead light and transformed it into a moonlight luster.

"I'd like to do that," she said.

"Scrub pans?"

She breathed a laugh. "Carry my own weight."

"Looks like you're on your way."

"You think so?"

He nodded once.

She inhaled, filling her lungs. "You think riders will come here?"

"It is a good place."

"Yes, but I don't know if I can convince them of that . . . or instruct them if I do . . . or . . ." She exhaled, stirred vigorously. "Or if I'm even on the right course. I mean, Courage almost died. She still might," she added quickly, afraid of the black magic that surely accompanied an excess of optimism. "Or she may never run. And how many more are like her? Wild horses that need a hand, need a place?"

"What are you saying?"

"Just that . . ." She shook her head and laughed at herself. "I don't know."

"You want to save the wild horses?"

"No. Maybe. I don't know. But . . ." She exhaled slowly. "I used to feel like Lily does. You know? Thrilled to be in the presence of anything equine."

"You still do."

"I do?"

"You simply forgot."

"I forget about the object of my obsession?"

"Momentarily," he said.

"I didn't think that was possible."

"Now you do," he said and nodded toward the mixture she was stirring. "Taste it."

"What?" She watched him drizzle oil into the pan he had just washed.

"A good chef must taste his masterpieces."

"I'm not a good chef."

"And never will be if you do not taste." Taking a spoon from a nearby drawer, he dipped it into the kettle before lifting it to her mouth. Her wild-berry lips closed over the stainless steel. He pulled his hand away. Her tongue peeked out, coral against cool porcelain skin. Her broken-girl eyes found his. He leaned in, breathless, aching.

But kissing her would be wrong. Bad. So bad. She was young. And wounded. He was old. Well . . . not that old. But he was jaded. And he wasn't staying. And she should stay. Forever. She belonged here, whether she knew it or not, belonged in the rugged wild of the hills. And he belonged . . . He didn't know where he belonged. So kissing her was out of the question. But damn . . .

He managed to draw back a fraction of an inch. "What does it need?" His words sounded like they had been scraped from the bottom of his truck.

She blinked as if just awakening and cleared her throat. "I suppose it would be wrong to add bacon."

She probably wasn't nearly as adorable as she seemed, he told himself, and spoke again. "It is never wrong to add bacon," he said, and pulling himself away from her eyes, retrieved a paper-wrapped package of hickory-smoked meat from the bottom drawer of the fridge.

She fried it while he put pre-frozen dinner rolls in the oven. New scents melded with old as they danced through the rest of the preparations, arms brushing, fingers skimming, nerve endings singing.

They ate on chipped crockery and drank from mismatched cups. No five-star restaurant had ever delivered a better meal.

"My compliments," Hunter said and nodded toward the soup. Sydney felt a ridiculous flush of pleasure.

"Heart attack in a bowl," she said, but he shook his head.

"Happiness," he corrected. "Happiness in a bowl. Why did you forget how you felt?"

She took another sip of soup, considering. "About horses?"

"Ai."

She set her spoon aside, stomach cramping a little. "There are certain expectations when you're the daughter of a prima ballerina and a financial tycoon."

"You had no desire to become a dancer?"

She shook her head. "And even less aptitude. I wasn't particularly good at . . ." She paused, slipped her hands under the table. "Anything. But there was a pony down the road from us. He was a potbellied little skewball with one glass eye and a popped knee." She smiled at the memory. "I called him Sir Lancelot. I thought him the most glorious thing I had ever seen and imagined myself riding him. Racing like the wind, his mane flying in my face." She should stop talking, she thought, but failed to do so. "Excitement is frowned upon in the Wellesley family. So I played that down. I told Father riding would be good for my posture."

He watched her, waiting.

"I was never very strong. And I had a mild case of scoliosis. Some research suggested horseback riding could have a positive influence on spinal deformities, and Mrs. Dobbs"—she managed not to wince when she said the name—"thought the discipline might do me good."

"Mrs. Dobbs?"

"My . . ." *Nanny* didn't seem like quite the right word, but she had nothing else. "Nanny. She was . . ." She paused, exhaled softly.

"Terrifying?" he guessed, gaze steady on her.

"No. No. She was just firm and . . ." She huffed a little . . . at herself . . . at the world. "Yes, actually, terrifying is a pretty apt description. But she convinced Father to let me ride."

"So you trotted into the sunset on the pot-bellied little pinto with the popped knee?"

She had finished her soup. She took a sip of coffee. "I think you know better."

"Wellesleys only ride thoroughbreds?"

"We can ride warmbloods, too." She smiled again, almost laughing at herself. "If they're imported . . . and trained by someone related to a monarch. They don't have to be first-generation nobility," she assured him, but he didn't smile. She set down her coffee. "So I rode at world-renowned stables. It was still wonderful. The way the horse smells when he warms up. The satisfying finality when their hooves strike the earth." Feelings unfurled, half forgotten, but she shook them away, rose to her feet. "Well, my turn to clean—" she began, but he stood up beside her and took her hand.

She watched their fingers meet, brown against white, felt the warm sizzle of desire sear her and raised her eyes to his.

"Come," he said.

"Where?"

"To hear hooves strike the earth."

"What are you talking about?"

"The horses need exercise."

"We'll have a paddock done soon. We can turn them out then."

"Windwalker's stocking up," he said. "Bad for their legs to stand around so long. Fluids build up around their cannon bones. Makes it hard for them to—"

"I know what stocking up means!" she snapped, then cleared her throat and soothed her tone. "But . . . it's late."

He caught her gaze with eyes as dark as dreams. "What do you fear, Sydney Wellesley?"

"Me?" She lifted a shoulder, breathed a laugh. "Spiders. A stock-market crash. Global warming." Everything, she admitted silently.

"Come," he said and squeezed her hand. His fingers were warm and powerful and as gentle as a sonnet. There seemed nothing she could do but follow him.

Outside, the night air was cool and absolutely still. Above them, the sky was inky black, perforated by a billion winking stars. But fear was beginning to creep up her spine. A thousand things could go wrong with a horse in the best of circumstances. But Hunter was already leading Windwalker from his stall.

"Is he limping?" Sydney asked, studying his gait.

"He is well."

"You didn't even look."

"He is well."

"You can't know that."

"I can."

Fear crept toward panic. "This is ridiculous!"

"Perhaps."

"It's cold." The weeks had flown by. Nights were already cool, mornings crisp and clear.

"You'll warm up."

Her heart actually clutched in her chest.

"I . . . no!"

He glanced at her.

"It's . . ." She swallowed. "Slippery."

"The horse . . ." He glanced at the handsome chestnut. "He was meant to run, to fly through forest and field and never falter."

The fear was almost painful in its intensity, but maybe it was time to set it aside. To move on.

Courage nickered from her stall and limped closer. Sydney glanced over, throat tight, eyes tearing.

"Are you ready?" Hunter's voice was low and quiet.

She shook her head, barely able to manage that much. "I don't think I can do this."

"You will be surprised what you can do."

"Listen . . ." She straightened her back and tried to push down the fear, but it was as strong as a geyser, rising up in her throat. "The truth is . . . I was injured a few months ago."

"Ai," he said and motioned toward her.

She scowled at him.

"Come. You can tell me how it happened."

"I would rather not talk about it."

He shrugged. "Then we will ride in silence."

She shook her head and backed away a step. "I would like to." It was as blatant a lie as she had ever told. "But I'm not supposed—"

"Will you let the bastards win?"

"What bastards?"

His expression was somber, his eyes intense. "The ones who hurt you."

"Nobody hurt me."

"There is fear in your eyes."

"That's because . . ." She took a deep breath. "The truth is . . . my injury was incurred while riding." She cleared her throat. "I shattered my femur. Broke a vertebra."

"And no one helped you get back on the horse?"

"On the horse. No. In fact, the doctors—"

"Are often wrong. Come."

"Hunter—"

"I will not let you fall," he promised and raised his hand for hers.

She gritted her teeth, ready to resist, but he remained exactly as he was, waiting, watching, arm outstretched. She closed her eyes, felt her body tremble, and stepped forward. His fingers felt warm and strong beneath hers. She lifted her gaze. His eyes were steady on hers. "Windwalker will carry us both."

"Ride double?" She shook her head. "We'll never both fit in the saddle."

"Which is why we will ride bareback."

"What? No!"

"Sydney . . ." He tightened his fingers around hers. "One should not live in fear."

"Yes . . . well . . ." She sounded hysterical. Felt breathless. "It's not so great to die in the middle of the night because . . ." She flapped her trembling left hand at him. "Because some big Indian thinks he's indestructible."

His eyes glinted. Was he laughing at her? She caught her breath and lowered her brows. "Is there something amusing about this situation?"

"I do not think myself indestructible." He shrugged. "And I begin to believe you are not the wild child I once thought you to be if you think ten o'clock is the middle of the night."

She exhaled carefully. "As it turns out, I don't particularly wish to die at ten o'clock, either."

His lips turned up a little. "Come," he said and tugged her toward the chestnut. She could feel the warmth of the big animal's body, could smell his sweet equine scent. "Are you ready?"

"If I break my neck, I'm never going to forgive you."

"Very well. Can you mount alone?"

"I'm accustomed to having stirrups."

He shrugged.

"And a mounting block."

"Sorry."

"And a groom. In fact, two is my preference."

"Step into my hands," he said and cupped his palms.

"I can't. I can't do this."

His expression was kindly, his eyes steady.

"You, Sydney Wellesley, can do anything you wish."

She held his gaze for an endless moment, then swallowed once, exhaled shakily, and stepped into his hands. There was a moment's hesitation before he boosted her upward. She swung her right knee over the animal's back out of habit and self-defense. Windwalker took a step forward. She grappled for the reins, but Hunter was already swinging up behind her. She had no idea how he managed to do so without unseating her. His chest settled solidly against her back. His thighs cradled hers.

The intimacy of their positions almost made her forget her fear.

"Is that how you mount for the relay race?" Her fingers ached on the smooth leather reins.

"Ai. Are you impressed?"

"I might be if I'm still breathing an hour from now."

"It is good to have incentive to keep you alive. Let up on the reins a little."

"What?"

"The reins . . ." Reaching around her, he gently eased her fingers open. "Loosen up or we'll never leave the barn."

"I didn't say I wanted to."

"But you do," he said and nudged the gelding with his endless legs. The chestnut stepped forward.

Sydney's muscles coiled like springs.

"Relax."

"I am relaxed."

"I'd hate to see you when you're anxious."

"I guarantee it," she said and exhaled cautiously.

"All is well," he assured her, but just as they stepped over the threshold, Windwalker tripped.

Sydney grabbed for the mane, but in a second the horse had righted himself. Behind her, Hunter felt as solid as stone.

Embarrassment brushed her. There had been a time, years, in fact, when she had ridden with the same casual effortlessness he exhibited. "I'm sorry." She wasn't entirely sure why she was apolo- gizing. "It's just that . . . this isn't easy for me."

"I know."

"Have you ever been injured?" she asked and refused to look down, to watch the earth move beneath her dangling feet.

"By a horse?"

"Yes."

"I dislocated my shoulder coming out of a bucking chute in Boise."

She nodded and managed to breathe. "Anything else?"

"Tore the ligaments in my knee when one of Tonk's ponies went over backward."

She knew his words shouldn't help relieve her tension, but she felt her shoulders drop a little. "And?"

"Got a concussion jumping a log while riding bareback in the dark."

"I'm kind of sorry I asked."

He chuckled.

Silence settled in. Beneath them, Windwalker's strides felt smooth and cadenced.

"Have you forgiven him?" Hunter asked into the quiet.

"What?" She turned her head a little.

"Your father. It was he who made you believe you could only do those things that are easy, was it not?"

She rode in silence, back straight. "You don't know him," she said. Her voice was soft in the darkness as she defended him by habit alone.

"I know it was his job to keep you safe."

"What are you talking about?" She laughed. It sounded rough and out of place in the quiet darkness. "I was perfectly safe."

He tightened his arms around her. "You cannot feel safe without feeling loved."

"I felt . . ." She paused. "We lived in an excellent neighborhood. I had everything I could possibly want. Except bacon." She laughed. "An omission for which I am making up even now."

They rode in silence for a time. Fireflies blinked in the blue-velvet night.

"We often delude ourselves about what is important."

She watched the mercurial lights blink off and

on and felt the magic swell in her soul. "Who's we?"

"People. Men." There was impatience in his tone. Anger in the set of his shoulders, in the strength of his arms against hers. "I had things to do. Important things. And Nicole . . . my wife . . ." He said the name softly.

"She was an actress, a rising star, the *Times* called her. There was a party in Malibu." He was silent as he gazed into the darkness. "Everyone who was anyone would be there. It would have been inappropriate for our daughter to accompany her and of course I couldn't spare the time."

His pain was all but palpable, an almost visible force that punched through her back to the core of her being.

"She planned to drop Sara Bear off at a friend's house."

Sydney remembered the bear tattoo on his chest, felt his sorrow in the tightness of her throat.

"They were running late," he said. "In a hurry." He paused. "She did not stop at a traffic light. The police said she died instantly. Sara lived another forty-eight hours." Silence echoed around them. "The doctors said they did all they could."

She felt her stomach drop. Felt her hands tremble on the reins. There was little mystery about why he disliked hospitals. "I'm so sorry."

"Call your father." Their faces were inches apart. She met his gaze from a crooked angle.

"Why?"

"It is said that everyone deserves a second chance."

Light glistened on the smooth surface of Beaver Creek, casting diamonds up to a star-studded sky. "Do you believe that?"

"I would like to."

They fell quiet. Overhead, the silken clouds flowed like mystery ships past the somber moon. They'd made a loop through the pasture. Ahead, Gray Horse Hill lay like a sleeping dove, strangely restful against the ebony sky. A sanctuary of sorts. For her. For Courage. And maybe for Hunter Redhawk.

"Will you?" he asked.

"Will I what?"

"Call him." Exasperation edged his tone.

"I don't . . ." She exhaled, trying to expel the tension that cramped her muscles at the mere thought of such a conversation. "I don't know what to say."

"He is your father. The man who shared your yesterdays." His voice was heartbreakingly soft. "Who picked you up when you fell. Who held you when you cried."

"We *are* talking about Leonard Wellesley, right?" She tried to lift the mood, shift it toward something lighter, but he was unmoved.

"Everyone makes mistakes. It does not mean he doesn't love you, does not have regrets. Be honest with him. Tell him your worries. Your dreams."

"About making Gray Horse into an equestrian center?"

Somewhere in the distance a coyote yipped to the sky. A chorus of others joined in.

"Is that what you truly want?"

A herd of rough-coated horses, the antithesis of sleek Olympians, raced across the high plains of her mind. "It's not as if I have a lot of other marketable skills."

"You might be surprised."

"I could be a carpenter, I suppose," she said and winced as she remembered the latest hammer strike to her thumb. "Although I may never be as good as Vura."

"I'm not certain you would ever be as good as Lily."

She laughed and felt a bit of anxiety ease out of her shoulders. "You're making a difference for her," she said.

"For a short time, perhaps."

"Are headhunters hounding you to join their ranks every waking hour or something?"

He drew a breath, chest expanding against her shoulder blades. "It is hard to be so desired."

She smiled. The last of her tension slipped cautiously away.

Windwalker's footfalls sounded muffled against the packed clay of the barn aisle. Fandango cocked his head at them. From her stall, Courage nickered a low greeting.

Hunter slid to the ground and Sydney swung her leg over the gelding's croup. But suddenly her thigh cramped. She half fell, only to find herself caught against Hunter's powerful body.

She turned in his arms, feeling foolish. She was no romance-novel heroine. She lacked the courage. Not to mention the cleavage. And yet she felt breathless.

"Are you okay?" His voice rumbled gently in the center of her being. She could feel the heat from his body, the strength in his arms, the tenderness of his soul.

"Yes. Thank you. I'm fine. I can . . . I can stand alone."

Seconds ticked into silence, then, "It is time you realized this."

His hands felt broad and strong against her waist. His eyes met hers, almost smiling, almost sober. Somehow her fingers had come to rest against his chest. Beneath her palm she could feel the steady beat of his heart, above which he had inked a memory of the daughter for whom he still mourned.

She held her breath, knowing she should draw away, but he was leaning in, eyes intense, hard-packed body tempting. His lips touched hers.

She almost resisted. Almost. But he was everything she'd never wanted . . . until now.

His mouth moved against hers, stirring a thousand unknown feelings, a million sleepy desires.

She slid her hands around his granite waist. He pulled her closer, breathing hard. Their bodies pressed together, chests, hips, thighs. She didn't realize she was moving into him until his shoulders struck the wall behind him, but she barely noticed. Didn't care a whit; desire, too long banked, had grabbed hold of the reins. It roared through her like a wildfire, burning her up, consuming her. He kissed her neck, then stormed lower, blazing a trail. She curled her nails like talons against his skin and pulled him closer.

He trembled, froze, then drew back a fraction of an inch, but the knowledge of his desire made her tighten her grip. Her hands had become lost under his shirt, but the distance between their bodies was growing. Her fingernails dragged across his flesh. Some sort of pathetic whimper scraped her throat.

Still, he managed to escape, to capture her hands between his, to catch her gaze, hard and fast.

"Call your father," he ordered and left her alone in the darkness.

Chapter 27

"Father?" Sydney's voice sounded small and pitiful in the dimness of her newly spackled bedroom. She tightened her grip on the phone.

Outside her window, the sun had barely crested the burnt-gold bluffs on the eastern horizon. But the Wellesleys were early risers, and it was two hours later in Middleburg, Virginia.

"Sydney?" Was there relief mixed with the surprise in her father's tone?

"It's good to hear your voice," she said and realized with painful disbelief that it was true.

"How are you?"

"I'm well," she said and felt her face crack into a cautious smile. "Getting stronger."

There was a moment of silence. "Are you still in North Dakota?"

"*South* Dakota." She paused, already at a loss for words. "It's very pretty out here." And she was in love, she thought, but she dared not say it out loud, barely allowed herself to think it.

"It could be a nice enough place to vacation, I suppose." His voice had already chilled a little. She heard ice cubes tick against crystal. Some might say he liked his carrot juice at the same temperature as his interpersonal relationships. "But it's time for you to come home."

She didn't speak.

"Listen, Sydney . . ." He drank, chairman-of-the-board tone firmly in place. She imagined him in his charcoal suit and dove-gray tie, understated but perfectly tailored. Flamboyance was for those who had something to prove. "I know David made mistakes, but I think you still have a chance of patching things up with him."

She took a deep breath and held on to the warmth, real or imagined, that she had originally heard in his voice. He was, after all, her father. And he cared for her. She was certain of that.

"I'm sorry," she said. "David's a good person." It was nice to know she could still lie under pressure. "But we're not right for each other. I see that now. I see a lot of things more clearly now."

"Do you?"

"I'm riding again." Excitement soared through her, filling her, like wind in a sail. "Well . . . a little. And I . . . I found a horse."

"A horse?"

"She's amazing. So brave. So resilient."

The other end of the line was silent. Leonard Wellesley did not like horses. But he liked the thought of them, the old-world elegance, the ability to dabble where others could not. The plans, the schemes, the training schedules, the dreams of gold metals.

"Is it Pinault?" he asked finally. "Did you fly to Duindigt to see her?"

She shook her head at the absurdity of the thought. How would she afford a ticket to Holland? He had cut her financial strings. But she didn't mention that fact. Didn't want to strain the fragile peace that stretched between them. "No. Not a warmblood. She's a mustang."

The world went silent except for the hard thrum of her heart against her ribs.

"I beg your pardon."

"The horse, she's a mustang. I found her on my . . . on the land I bought. She was tangled in wire. I thought she wasn't going to survive, but she's a fighter. These wild horses, they're amazing, the foundation for most of our light horse breeds. But they're disappearing. Most of their natural habitat is gone and they're breeding with domesticated animals, losing their unique qualities, their hardiness."

"So this horse you've got . . ." His tone wasn't exactly encouraging. But it wasn't condemning, either. Hope sparked cautiously in Sydney's soul. "It's a mare?"

"Yes. I call her Courage. She's a dun. Black mane and tail. Striped legs. The perfect Spanish Mustang coloration. And I keep thinking . . ." She paused, fear flaring up again. "There are probably hundreds of others like her. Horses that have become separated from their herds, who have wandered onto private land where they'll be . . ." She paused, momentarily overcome by emotion. "There just isn't enough raw land for them anymore. And we owe the horse so much."

"How do you mean?"

"Well, you know . . ." Perhaps in her entire life she had never shared a longer conversation with her father. "They say that mankind's pathway to glory was paved with the bones of the horse."

"So that's what you've spent my hard-earned money on? Land for a bunch of rat-tailed horses?"

The sudden change in his tone shouldn't have surprised her. Perhaps it was her time in the Hills that had made her forget how fast he could turn. "No. I . . . No. Of course not."

"You're just like your mother."

"What?"

"Why, Sydney? Tell me why you insist on dragging the Wellesley name through the mire."

She actually felt herself wince and braced herself against the onslaught, but he wasn't through.

"Are you just trying to embarrass me, or is it David you're—"

"I'm building an elite equestrian center." The words flew from her like an arrow, striking out in self-defense.

The phone went silent for a moment.

"And how will you finance such an endeavor?"

"That's my concern." She didn't tell him about

the loan from Cousin Tori, didn't mention the fact that Hunter had paid for dozens of necessities out of pocket. He hadn't asked for a dime in return, had rarely even told her of his purchases. She would pay him back someday. Somehow. But she couldn't think of that now. "For Olympic-caliber riders," she added. Her voice sounded strangely robotic. "I'll have to hire someone to train for the cross-country portion, of course." Since she had always known she wasn't strong enough, wasn't good enough for that discipline. "But I'll teach the dressage riders myself."

"What makes you think you can attract top-tier equestrians to such an unlikely location?"

"I'm a Wellesley," she said and felt tears sting her eyes. "Blood always tells, doesn't it?"

Silence stretched between them. "Maybe I can put the word out. Pull some strings."

She glanced out the window. A hawk folded its wings and dropped from the sky, skewering a hapless rabbit that had wandered into the open.

"That would be good," she said and wondered vaguely whether she was the falcon or the hare.

"When do you project to be ready for clients?"

"The end of September."

"That's awfully late in the year," he said.

"But just six weeks from now, and it will still give us time to prepare for the Rolex."

He was silent for a moment. "Very well. I'll speak to the appropriate persons." He exhaled noisily. "We'll set a date for . . ." She could hear him tapping buttons, checking his online schedule. "The first Saturday in October. I will try to come prior to that to make certain you're on track, but you know what my calendar is like."

"Yes." He'd been in Zurich when she'd contracted the mumps, Shanghai when she'd ridden in her first competition.

"Very well then. Good-bye."

"Good-bye."

"Oh, and Sydney . . ." He paused as if uncertain where to go from there.

She held her breath, hoping. "Yes?"

"Don't disappoint me this time."

He hung up, but she remained as she was, phone to her ear, knees weak, pulse pounding solidly in her temples.

"Flapjacks or eggs and bacon?" Hunter's voice sounded from the hallway, an earthy counterpoint to the dove's morning coo.

Sydney glanced toward her unfinished door.

"Syd?" He rapped twice on the hardwood. "Are you up?"

She tried to articulate a response, but her mind was spinning.

"Sydney?" He opened her door. Their gazes met. "What's wrong?" He stepped inside, filling the room. But his nearness only made her weaker.

"Nothing," she said and backed away, out of reach. "Nothing's wrong."

Silence filled the space between them. His eyes were as solemn as stone.

"Let us eat then," he said finally. "You can tell me of this nothing."

"No." She cleared her throat and lowered her phone. "Thanks. I'm going to get to work," she said and escaped from his kindness.

The days sped by. The house was almost livable now. Well . . . livable, Sydney discovered, was a relative term. She had realized early on that there was no way her finances were going to stretch to refurbish the entire house. And she dared not allow Hunter to pay more. Her mind shied away from the thought of his generosity, his allure. They had barely touched since the kiss. Just the accidental brush of fingers, the unconscious clash of their gazes, was enough to stop the breath in her throat. But she had no time for that. The conversation with her father had set her course in stone. And that course was well on track. Gray Horse Hill was nearly ready to host its first students. To show the world what she could do if she set her mind to it.

True, the upper floor of the house was mostly untouched. In fact, the majority of the lower level remained equally dismal.

The old parlor where the students would converge, however, was almost complete. The rough fieldstone fireplace had been restored to its original rustic glory. The exterior walls had been re-daubed and the new windows were wide, granting a view of curling river and sweeping hills. Beyond the gravel road that wound like an amber ribbon toward the west, Fandango and Windwalker grazed on endless pasture. They only came up to the barn to be groomed and ridden. But those times had been precious, for with each careful ride, Sydney had found it possible to do a little more . . . to pick up a trot, to try a cautious canter, until her heart all but sang with hope.

Courage, however, remained inside. Sydney sighed as she peered through the iron bars of the mare's stall. The animal longed to be free. That much was made clear by the distant look in her farseeing eyes, the restless toss of her dread-locked mane. But she wasn't ready . . . or maybe it was Sydney who was unprepared for the change. There was no telling what would happen when she was turned loose. No guessing whether she would gallop or stumble and fall. Though they had bandaged and medicated and sutured and prayed, it still seemed they should have done more. Should *do* more. But was it fair to continue to keep the mare confined? She had not left the barn since they'd brought her there months before. Courage circled her stall now. They had moved her into one of the new enclosures just days before, allowing them to tear down the original and replace it with something befitting an Olympian. She stood now, head raised, tangled forelock all but obscuring her limpid eyes.

"She's something to see," Vura said, work boots ringing in the aisle.

Sydney didn't turn at the sound of the woman's voice. Strange how love for this feral animal swelled like a hot wave through her. Strange when she had never felt the same for any of the royally bred mounts she had ridden in competition. Not that it mattered. Her course was set, she reminded herself. "She is."

"It'll be interesting seeing her with the Olympic horses they bring in for training."

Sydney tightened her hands around the mustang's bars and felt a fresh squeeze of terror slide through her. She had sent out the invitations, made all the appropriate contacts, offered a free month of riding at "America's newest elite equine facility." But the responses had been slow in arriving. "You think they'll come?"

"They're not idiots, are they?"

Sydney turned toward her, entirely unsure how to answer that.

"I mean, they'd have to be, right? To turn down the chance to work with the great Sydney Wellesley."

They stared at each other. Vura grinned. "We were bound to check into your past eventually."

Sydney blinked.

Vura laughed. "Dressage rider extraordinaire.

Took second at the World Cup. I saw a video on YouTube." She shook her head, expression sobering. "You were riding a black horse."

"River Magic." He had a beautiful passage and performed lovely tempi changes, the skipping lead transfers so difficult to execute, but he had sustained a fracture to his left front cannon and the Olympic machine could not wait for him to recover. Sydney had moved on to a handsome sorrel with better bone.

"*Für Elise* was playing in the background." Vura swallowed, eyes bright as diamonds. "It was like a dance. Like a Viennese waltz. The most beautiful thing I ever saw in my life."

And yet they had discarded Magic for another, only to find that the sorrel didn't possess the temperament of a winner. Or maybe it was his rider who had been lacking. Insecurity swamped her. And where did that come from? Sydney Wellesley didn't doubt herself. Or did she do just that every day of her life? Did she doubt and cover it up with an aloof demeanor and chilly distances?

"Who wouldn't want to work with you?" Vura asked.

Sydney's mind churned, dredging up a dozen cool comebacks. But they would not be delivered. "Those who have met me?" she asked instead, but Vura shook her head.

"Then they're fools," she said. "And you don't

need them. Anyone who has seen your talent and your heart and your kindness . . ." She nodded. "They'll come."

Sydney searched for her old self, that crisp, polished woman who showed no doubts, no weaknesses to the world. But she seemed to have gone missing. "I believe you might actually be thinking of someone else," she said, and Vura laughed.

"Was your mother like that?"

"Like what?"

"Never satisfied with perfection?"

"I don't know." She shrugged, vaguely wondering how the conversation had turned in this unlikely direction.

"I read a review once that said she was her own worst critic."

"Sydney," Tonk said and stepped into the barn. "I am going to retire for the night. Unless you have objections."

"No. Of course not," she said. "Have a good evening."

"There is a spirited little redhead in Custer who will help me do just that," he said and grinned at her before turning toward Vura. "Or is there something else that should occupy my time?"

"I don't have any idea what you're talking about," she said and scowled.

He shrugged. "I thought, perhaps, you would like some assistance around the house since your beloved has been gone for so long a time."

"Well, you thought wrong." Her voice was cool.

He nodded. Irritation snapped in his eyes. "It must be difficult for him to stay away from his blushing bride."

Perhaps Vura caught his sarcasm; her tone chilled to glacial. "It is."

"Where did you say he was again?"

A muscle ticked in her dimpled cheek. "Williston."

"That's right, he is employed by one of those fracking companies that steals the earth's soul."

She opened her mouth as if to blast him, but Sydney interrupted. "You read Mother's reviews?"

Vura jerked her attention back to her employer. "Yes. Well . . . just one."

"Why?"

Vura's right knee jittered.

"Dad loved her . . . cabriole. Is that what it's called?"

Sydney scowled. "Your father saw her dance?"

"I guess so," she said and lifted her jacket from a pile of lumber near the door.

"When?" Sydney asked, but Vura was already backing away.

"You wouldn't think Dad would be into ballet, would you?" She shrugged, grinned. "But . . . people will surprise you. Well . . . I'll see you tomorrow."

"When did he see her?" Sydney asked,

following her out. "She'd quit dancing professionally by the time they built her studio."

"Listen . . . I'd love to stay and chat, but I've got to get going. Lily has an appointment with a specialist in Hot Springs," Vura said, and seeing her daughter playing in a pile of dirt near the silo, hustled her toward their truck. Once inside, she closed her eyes and gripped the steering wheel with white-knuckled fingers.

"What's wrong, Mama?" Lily asked.

"Nothing." Vura glanced into the rearview mirror and fixed on a smile. "Nothing's wrong, baby. Are you ready to go?" she asked, and cranking the engine, drove out of the yard.

"They're not staying for supper?" Hunter asked from behind.

Sydney watched the truck turn onto the gravel road. "Tonk, do you know what a cabriole is?"

Tonkiaishawien frowned after the speeding truck. "My hands were gifted with the ability to craft beauty. And though my brother, poor unfortunate, did not receive that talent, he did inherit the poor substitute of intelligence."

Sydney turned her gaze on Hunter. "Do *you* know?"

"I test better on a full stomach."

"I mean it," she said and kept her attention steady on his face.

"It's a piece of furniture," Hunter said. "Or a dance movement."

She scowled. "Would the average person know that?" she asked.

"I *am* the average person."

"No, you're not," she argued.

"I am about to depart," Tonk interrupted.

Her eyes were steady on Hunt's. She couldn't seem to pull them away.

"Try not to miss me over much," Tonk added.

How had Hunt's lips gotten so close?

"Oh, for Pete's sake!" Tonk said, and losing his carefully maintained verbal cadence, stomped toward his jeep.

Sydney pulled herself from Hunter's gaze and turned in a daze. "What's wrong with *him?*"

"So many things," Hunter said and exhaled, breaking the spell. "Come and eat."

She shook her head. "I want to see that combination jump you're working on."

"You don't trust me to get it right?"

She looked into his honest features and felt the truth strike her softly. "As it turns out . . ." She paused, surprised at the aching truth of it. "I do."

She shrugged, sending him a playful grin. "But I still want to see it."

"I'll saddle the horses."

"You don't have to do that. I can drive some of it. Walk the rest."

"It should be ridden," he said and turned away. "You're better on a horse. More grounded, more centered, whether you know it or not."

"Well, then . . ." She hurried after him, boots rapping quietly. "I'll tack up my own mount."

"I can manage two," he said.

But it didn't seem right, she thought, and wondered when that had happened. Someone else had saddled her horse since she'd stepped into her first stable. Saddled him up, cooled him off, and cleaned up afterward. But things had changed.

They were silent as they walked to the pasture. But it felt right, easy, quiet. Still, Vura's words nibbled at Sydney's peace of mind even as the horses trotted to the fence to greet them. Grain, they knew, waited in their stalls. Taking a halter from the fence where it hung, Sydney slipped it over Windwalker's ears, snapped it at the throatlatch.

"Does it seem strange to you that Vura's father knew my parents?" she asked.

Hunter turned away, strides long and smooth. He looked so right, perfectly in his element beside the bay. "I suppose it is good business for a carpenter to know many people."

"So you think it's just a coincidence?"

"What else would it be?"

She shrugged. "You don't think . . ." Her mind spun out of control. She reeled it back in. "It's just something Vura said. Several things, actually."

He waited in silence. Patience *was* *his* virtue.

Perhaps that was why Lily adored him. But maybe it was because of a thousand other reasons.

They secured their horses in the cross ties that spanned the native stone flooring. Hunter retrieved two dandy brushes from a room earmarked for tack. She stroked the long bristles down the chestnut's arched neck.

"She said her dad mentioned Mother's cabriole."

He shrugged. "Then either he admired her taste in furniture or saw her dance."

She gave him a smirk. "Do you think . . ." She paused, trying to clear her head. "Do you think he had a crush on her?"

Silence stretched comfortably between them. "Your mother . . ." he said finally. "Do you resemble her?"

She turned toward him, but he remained as he was, stroking the brush down the length of Fandango's cocked hip.

"I'm told I inherited her physical features."

He caught her with his gaze, real and powerful and warm. "Then my guess is yes, he was drawn to her." His matter-of-fact tone only made the compliment more meaningful.

"I didn't . . ." She cleared her throat and found she wasn't sure where to look. "Thank you. I wasn't fishing . . . I hope."

"Do you know how?"

"What?"

"There are trout in the river. Rainbow and cutthroat. We could make some poles."

"Interesting segue," she said, "but to answer your question, no." She set her brush aside. "Wellesleys don't fish."

"Too wild a pastime?" he asked and watched as she meticulously picked a knot from the gelding's tail.

She laughed at herself. "Maybe you were right."

He turned his attention from her. "Blue moons are known to occur."

"Maybe I *have* been trying to live up to Mother's reputation." She sighed. "But she was so perfect. Absolutely above reproach. Or . . ." She scowled. "That's how it always *seemed*. I used to assume that her death had blurred Father's memory somewhat. Even Winona Begay Wellesley couldn't be the epitome of woman-hood that he painted her to be. But I think . . ." She exhaled softly. "Maybe I tried to match her perfection anyway." She paused in her grooming. "He said I was just like her."

His eyes met hers. "It is time that he realized your value."

She felt flushed by the compliment, embarrassed by the truth. After endless debate, she was certain Leonard Wellesley had not said those words as praise. Instead, he had used them as if they were a weapon, a barbed taunt that drew blood.

"Yes, it's . . ." She paused. "Father can be rather distant at times."

"Distant?"

"Some might call him cold." She glanced away, unable to hold his eyes. "Like me."

"You think you are cold?"

"You don't?" She snapped her gaze back to him, stunned by the surprise in his tone, embarrassed by the hope in hers.

Their eyes met. "I am no expert on the matter," he said. "But I think my wounds suggest otherwise."

"Wounds?"

"There are still furrows down my back," he said.

"Oh! I—" Memories of that singular kiss rushed over her, washing a tidal wave of heat into her cheeks. "I'm sorry," she said, and swinging onto Windwalker's back, cantered out of the barn.

"I am not," Hunter said and grinned as he followed her.

Chapter 28

"That's it," Vura said and straightened to her full five-foot-three stature. "The one we've been looking for."

Hunter slid the final stall door closed and nodded. Outside, Sydney was fencing. Say what you would about royalty . . . some duchesses knew how to plant posts. "Just the latches left."

"And the grain bin and the wash stall and the flooring," Vura said and laughed. Lily's back was curved against the wall. They had found her in with Courage on a total of five occasions. Hunter had finally been forced to fit the stall with a combination lock.

"You did a good job on the windows in the loft," he said. The added light made the barn seem roomy and welcoming.

"Dad was a big help."

He nodded his agreement. Quinton Murrell did exceptional work. "So he knew Sydney's parents?"

"What?" She froze, right hand clamped hard around the bubble level she had lifted to check their work.

Hunter watched her nervous reactions. Vura

was always energetic. But nervous? No. "He built her dance studio?"

"Yeah. I guess. It wasn't like I was there."

"So you never discussed it? Didn't talk about her?"

"Her?"

"Sydney's mother."

"Why would we?" she asked and turned toward her daughter. "Let's get going, Lil."

The girl lifted her gamine face. Dirt was smudged across her nose. Only one pigtail had survived the day. "But I has to be here when Hunk turns Courage out."

"What?" Vura pivoted toward Hunter. "You're turning her loose?"

He shook his head. "Not today, Tulip."

She wrinkled her nose at him. "My name's not Tulip."

"Snapdragon," he corrected solemnly. "We will not turn her out unless you are here to give her your blessings."

"Do you promise?"

"You have my solemn vow."

"Mom says we can takes your word to the bank," Lily said and rose to her feet. Today even her shoes were purple. Or had been before she'd tromped through the puddles looking for tadpoles. Skipping over, she handed him her jacket. He squatted down and slipped the garment behind her back. She shoved her little arms

314

through, then turned to fold them around his neck so he could lift her against his chest and breathe in her little-girl innocence. She felt no more substantial than a butterfly against his heart.

"I can't decide if I should feel jealous or blessed," Vura said. He cleared his throat, making certain it wasn't clogged with emotion, but he didn't dare meet her eyes.

"About?"

"You and her." She shook her head, tugged the hood over her daughter's wild-wind hair. "She thinks you're Wyatt Earp, Iron Eyes Cody, and Batman all rolled into one," she said and started toward her truck.

He followed, but once they reached their destination, he realized he couldn't avoid Vura's gaze forever, tears or no tears.

"Thank you." The words sounded a little scratchier than he had intended.

"For what?" She stood with her hand on the door handle.

"For this." He tightened his grip on the little blossom that had bloomed in his heart.

Vura raised her brows at him.

"You wouldn't have to share," he said.

She searched his eyes. "Are you kidding me?"

It was a nice idea, but he couldn't have joked to save his life. "She is sunshine to the shadows. Rain to the desert of my soul."

Vura stared at him another moment, then

laughed, that deep saloon-girl chuckle she had. "Our very own cowboy poet," she said. "How'd we get so lucky?"

"The sentiment is mine," he admitted. "But the words are Tonkiaisawien's."

"Oh." She pursed her lips. "Well, they're still beautiful, and we're still lucky."

"I am the lucky one," he said, and leaning down, kissed her cheek.

From between two fresh-planted posts, Sydney heard Vura's laugh, saw the adoring gleam in Hunter's eyes, felt the kick in her gut as she remembered kissing him. Perhaps she had imagined that he had kissed her back. Perhaps she'd imagined a lot of things. Physical fatigue considerably improved her ability to fall asleep, but when she was awake thoughts of his dark workman's hands . . .

He turned toward her. For a second their gazes clashed, but she pivoted away and hurried into the cool silence of the barn. There were a thousand things to do and little enough time to do them. She would get one shot at presenting Gray Horse Hill as a premier facility. After that the news would travel fast in the fishbowl of the equestrian world. Good or bad, her reputation . . .

"It is your turn to choose the meal," he said.

"What? Oh." She felt foolishly flustered, disappointingly jittery. "Don't bother cooking on my account. Do you realize we only have a few weeks until the riders arrive?"

"And you plan to fast until then?"

She forced a laugh. "I plan not to make you cook something I'll be too nervous to eat."

He watched while she stacked straw bales, bright as sunflowers and only marginally heavier . . . a thoroughbred's bedding in a mustang's barn.

"You need a break," he said.

She took a deep breath. "It's okay, you know."

"Is it?" he asked.

She turned toward him, flexing her gloved hands. "She's a wonderful person."

His brows lowered. "Is she?"

"You know she is. Bright. Skilled. Kind." She forced a laugh, punctuated it with a shrug. "I'm half in love with her myself."

"I'd feel better if I knew who we were talking about."

"Bravura Lambert," she said and laughed again. It sounded ridiculous even to her. "She's a phenomenal mother."

"Ahhh." He nodded, watching her face. "She is."

"And she's . . . she's pretty. Her hair . . ." Good God, was she waxing poetic about another woman's hair? "It's lovely."

The barn went silent. She tapped her thigh.

"You have much in common," he said.

She stared at him a second, then snickered. "I

think you've been in the sun too long, Hunter Redhawk."

"Determination," he said. "Courage. Caring."

"If you were a horse I'd give you two grams of Bute and call the vet."

"You are not entirely dissimilar physically, either," he added.

"Now I'm afraid you're hemorrhaging from the brain. Vura could probably bench-press this barn." And she had more curves in her wrist than Sydney had in her entire body. But she wasn't jealous. That would be ridiculous.

"You both light up the world when you smile."

"You *are* reaching."

"Your eyes," he said and scowled as he saw hers widen. "They're the exact same color blue."

"You need to eat," she said and laughed again.

"I'll leave something in the oven for you," he said and turned away with a scowl.

Chapter 29

"No!" Sydney said and glanced up. Feather-soft drops pattered on her face. The rain had held off for weeks. Each morning had greeted them with periwinkle skies and popcorn clouds, giving them time to finish a dozen pivotal projects. August had sped past. September was flying by just as fast. Nighttime temperatures were already dropping into the forties. The days, however, had been glorious. Judging by the bubbling thunderheads, though, that trend was about to come to a crashing end; they were not going to finish the jump course today. But they were close; the bullfinch had been covered with brush, the double oxer, much like the one that had caused her injury, looked sturdy and challenging. The sight of it gave her a twinge, but it was just a passing flutter now. Not fatal. Not insurmountable. She was no shrinking violet. She could plant posts, hang Sheetrock, and mount a sixteen-hand horse bareback. In fact, she had done just that the previous night, she thought, and remembered the light in Hunter's eyes as he watched her canter a circle, arms thrown wide, face lifted toward the endless sky.

"We're almost finished," Vura said, and hefting a hammer as long as her torso, swung at the spike holding back the embankment of turf. The combination obstacle would be challenging but not overwhelming, a leap over the ditch in which they currently stood, room for three swift strides, and then a vertical jump. "We can do it."

Sydney picked up the nearby axe, turned the flat head away from her, and focused on the closest spike. Hammering was still not her forte.

Up above, Hunter was wedging a horizontal log between two planted posts.

The rain was driving harder now, striking their bare arms, stinging on contact.

"Let 'er rip," Vura yelled, and grinned through the slashing drops, never missing a beat as every swing hit the spike dead-on.

Sydney struck her target a glancing blow.

"That's it," Vura cheered. "You're doing great."

What she wasn't doing was great, Sydney thought, but there was something about pitting her strength against steel and soil that made her muscles sing. She grinned at the effort, swung again, and missed her target completely. Gritting her teeth, she prepared for another try.

"Your optimism is . . ." Gathering her flagging strength, she tried again . . . a swing and a miss. "Sorely misplaced."

Vura laughed and finished off two more spikes while Sydney battered away at her one.

"It's raining." Hunter, three feet above them, had to raise his voice to be heard above the deluge.

"Really?" Sydney asked. Her hair was dripping down her back.

"I thought you would have noticed," he yelled.

"Guess we'd better get home before your truck deteriorates completely," she said.

He snorted. They grabbed their tools.

"Come on, Petunia," Hunter yelled, and the

little girl, mostly sheltered beneath a tarp erected beneath two bur oaks, galloped after them. The rain was a solid sheet by the time they reached the truck, but they laughed as they scrambled inside.

"Where did that come from?" Sydney asked and slammed the door behind her. It remained ajar, partly due to the fact that four drenched bodies were crammed onto a battered bench seat better suited for three.

"Shut the door," Hunt ordered. "You're ruining my upholstery."

Sydney laughed out loud. "Upholstery's a pretty fancy word for . . ." She slammed the door again, but it still wouldn't close.

"Come on, duchess," he badgered. "A peasant could do better than that."

Lily giggled as her mother squeezed her tight. Their faces, so close together, looked almost identical. "You'd better watch out, Hunt," Vura warned. "Syd's getting pretty good with a hammer."

"Good?" he asked and raised one dubious brow.

"Good enough to hit you in the head with one," Sydney said and finally succeeded in closing the door.

He grinned and started the engine. "Duly warned." His eyes gleamed as his gaze settled on her. "You look good."

She breathed another laugh and brushed back a

few hairs that had come loose from her ponytail. There simply was no time to worry about prim buns and bobby pins. "I bet I don't."

"Don't try your luck at craps," he said.

She glanced away, blushing. His eyes still burned on her face, but he took mercy on her finally, turning back to stare through the windshield as the rain diminished.

Between them, Lily sang about the travails of the itsy bitsy spider. Vura chimed in, doing the motions above her daughter's tiny hands. "Come on," she urged and elbowed her comrades until they joined in.

It was an enthusiastic if off-key quartet that rattled along toward home. Hunter gunned the ancient engine, roaring through a narrow section of Beaver Creek and up the sandy embankment that led into the back acreage of Gray Horse Hill.

"Down came the rain," Hunter rumbled, and pinning Sydney with his molten gaze, motioned toward his own face. "And splashed mud on your cheek."

"What?" She mimicked the motion.

"Out came the sun and dried up all the mud," he said, and shifting into park, turned the key. The truck died a slow, wheezing death.

"I've got mud on my face?" Sydney asked, and throwing her weight against the passenger door, managed not to fall on her head when it sprang open.

"Just a little," he said and nodded toward the side-view mirror.

She took a look. Goo was smeared in a generous arc from her eyebrow to her chin.

Hunter chuckled at her shocked expression as Lily toppled off the seat. Dropping her giddyup bag on the slippery earth, she scooped up a handful of mud. Eyes gleaming with mischief, she lifted the offering to Sydney. Hidden behind the old rattletrap, her actions went unseen. Carefully stifling her grin, Sydney accepted the muck as Vura stepped out of the vehicle.

"You wouldn't," she said, but Sydney nodded.

"Hey, Hunt . . ." she called, and when he turned, launched her gooey missile over the top of the cab.

Maybe it was dumb luck that caused it to hit him square in the ear. Maybe it was endless weeks of sweat and blood and hardening muscle.

Vura rocked back on her heels, belting out her signature laugh. "I warned you about her aim."

Hunter grunted, then, scraping the muck from his ear, lobbed it back across the hood of his vehicle. It struck her chin dead-on.

She gasped in surprise.

"Hey!" Lily yelled, and grabbing up handfuls of muck, tossed them wildly. They soared two feet and plopped onto Hunt's cherished truck.

There was a moment of stunned silence, and then the battle was joined.

It was a free-for-all with no rules. No teams. No real objective but to rejoice in life.

In a matter of minutes Sydney was panting, Lily was giggling, and Hunter, that giant warrior of a man, was covered front and back with enough mud to plant carrots.

Charging around the bumper, he snatched Lily from the ground and shoved her under one arm. She hung there like a programmed missile. In his left hand he held a blob of mud so gooey it dripped from between his fingers like glue.

"Stay where you are," he warned, "Or Goldenrod here gets it."

Lily squealed like a piglet just before his remaining opponents plastered him with grime.

It was then that the sky opened up in earnest.

Hunter laughed, squinted up at the clouds, and raced toward Lily's fallen bag. "Grab it," he ordered and whooshed her toward the ground.

She snatched one handle with a shriek of joy and then they were all running, racing toward the porch like a mischief of sodden rats.

The stairs clattered as they stormed up them, but at the top Lily shrieked in dismay. "My goodies."

Already soaked, Sydney bent to scoop up the child's treasures. A bit of rose quartz, a hank of black mane, a photo of—

Her hand stopped as the others rushed into the house.

"Hurry!" Lily yelled. "Hurry, Sydney."

But she couldn't hurry. Couldn't quite breathe. Instead, she drew the picture from the saturated wooden step and carried it slowly inside.

"Kick off your boots, Lily Belle," Vura ordered and laughed. "You're as wet as a—" She stopped when she saw Sydney's face. Stopped and breathed, hands perfectly still on her daughter's shoulders.

Sydney's fingers felt numb, her heart strangely heavy in her chest. "Why do you have a picture of my mother?"

"What?" Beneath the mud smeared across her cheeks, Vura looked as pale as spring snow.

"My mother," Sydney said, and leaving the door open behind her, took another step into the house. "Lily had her picture. Why?"

"I don't . . ." Vura's voice was strained. She snapped her gaze to Hunter and away. "What are you talking about? That must be something . . . It's probably just something Lily cut out of a magazine."

Sydney glanced at it again. It was a photo of a ballerina. A full shot from a distance. Her dark hair was covered by a feather circlet and her face was in profile. Still, Sydney had been so certain. "I'm sorry." She shook her head, exhaled a laugh. "For a minute I thought . . ." she began, but then Lily scampered over and took the photo from her hand.

"Grandma was as pretty as a song," she said and hugged the picture to her mud-smeared jacket.

The room went silent. Vura's eyes were wide. Hunter's were troubled.

"Lily honey . . ." Vura's voice was very soft. "Go wait in the truck."

"But it's raining and I don't—"

"Go now," her mother ordered.

The girl frowned, turned slowly, then scurried away.

Sydney exhaled carefully and glanced at Hunter, but he did nothing to allay her doubts. She opened her mouth, though she had no idea how to begin.

"I wanted to tell you." The words tumbled from Vura. "Right away. I wanted to tell you as soon as I met you. But you were so distant at first, so . . ." She shook her head. "Not at all like Mom. Not how Daddy described her. And I thought . . ." She shook her head. "I really didn't think it could be true."

Sydney felt as if she were in a dream, some sort of outlandish fantasy. "You didn't think what could be true?"

"Hey!" Tonk stepped inside, clothes dry, grin slanted. "It looks as if I finally got the good job this . . ." His words trailed to a halt. "What's going on?"

Vura swallowed and kept her gaze steady on

Sydney's. "See, the thing is . . ." She shrugged, laughed. "We're sisters." She fisted her calloused hands against her tattered blue jeans. "Half sisters." The words were almost inaudible now, as if they didn't quite dare disturb the silence.

Sydney remained perfectly still, barely breathing, back painfully straight. "My mother died in a car accident."

"Yeah." Vura nodded. "Mine, too."

"She was attending a ballet in Chicago."

"Where she planned to meet Dad."

"That's not true." Sydney felt strangely weightless. "She and my father were happily married. She was the chairwoman of Good Samaritan Charities, director of the Middleburg Theatre for the Performing Arts."

"She had filed for divorce months before the accident."

"You're a liar!" The words snapped through the air like a bullet.

"Sydney," Hunter said and took a step toward her.

She jerked back. "She's lying."

"Just breathe."

"What's going on?" she asked. "Is this a joke? Some kind of practical joke?"

Vura shook her head, expression pained. "I just wanted to meet you. I don't have any siblings. *Thought* I didn't. Always wanted a brother, but . . ." She grinned. The expression was weak and hopeful, but Sydney shook her head.

"You're delusional."

Vura exhaled softly. "I was twelve when Dad first told me about you. I wanted to meet you then, but he didn't think . . ." A muscle jumped in her cheek. "He didn't think you were ready."

"Ready! For what? For lies? For . . ." Sydney waved a stiff hand. "Why are you doing this?"

"I wrote to you once."

Sydney shook her head.

"But your father read it first. Threatened . . ." Vura stopped, winced, hands splayed in front of her like a shield. "I'm sure he was just worried about you. That he just wanted what was best for you."

Sydney turned toward Hunter, mind spinning at a world gone mad. "It's a lie," she said. "Mother never would have done such a thing. She was above reproach . . . a trustee for Ashville Academy."

Their gazes met, ice on amber.

"I wanted to tell you, too," Hunter said.

And the world ended.

"You knew." Sydney's voice was nothing more than an echo in an endless tunnel. "You knew all the time?"

"No. Just for a while. A few weeks, maybe. There wasn't much on the Internet. But the evidence seemed pretty—"

"Weeks! You've known I had a s . . ." She

shook her head, forced a laugh. "You knew for weeks that I had an employee who was mentally deranged and you didn't think it worth mentioning?"

The house was silent but for the beat of the rain. It thrummed out a rhythm of betrayal.

"It's true, Syd," Hunter said.

She huffed a noise, something indescribable. "You're as crazy as she is."

"Dad adored her." Vura's voice was very small. "Worshiped her. She had already left your father when they began seeing each other."

"She would never have done that!" Adrenaline was pumping like toxins through Sydney's system. "She loved us."

"She did! I know she did," Vura agreed and took a quick step toward her as if to ward off the pain, the uncertainty. "She wanted you with her. Tried to take you along, but Leonard Wellesley . . . he's a powerful man and she . . ." She shrugged. "She couldn't bear having her entire life dictated."

Dictated. Sydney winced at the word, remembering the endless constraints, the unbending rules, but she shook her head, pushed away the doubts. "You've no idea what you're talking about."

"I know Dad loved her," Vura said. "I know they were happy together." Her eyes were bright with tears. "And I know she was my mother."

Sydney backed away.

"I was named after her."

The breath caught hard in Sydney's throat.

"Bravura. It's a dance movement. A—"

"This is crazy," Sydney hissed. "*You're* crazy. You're all crazy." She glanced at the trio around her. "You didn't know my mother. She was a paragon. The epitome of style and class. The *Washington Post* said so."

"Syd . . ." Hunter took a step toward her, but she snarled a warning.

"No—" She slashed out with the edge of her hand. "I don't have time for this. For your outrageous lies. For your—" Everything seemed different suddenly. Empty. She'd spent her entire life trying to live up to the memory of her mother. To be the person Winona Begay Wellesley would want her to be. Thinking she wasn't good enough. Thinking . . . She straightened her back, inhaled through her nose. "I have important people coming."

"Important people." Vura let her shoulders drop an inch. "Not like us, then."

"No. Not like you at all," Sydney said, and turning, stepped into the rain.

Chapter 30

"Hello, Father." Even here, standing beneath the cottonwood tree in the farseeing hills of South Dakota, Leonard Wellesley wore a custom-made suit and Italian oxfords.

"Sydney . . ." His voice was cool. She had almost forgotten the precise cadence of it.

"I was hoping you'd be able to come earlier." It was a lie. Or at least a partial lie. Maybe some portion of her had wanted him to come, to see, to ordain before her prospective students arrived. But the rest of her, the cowardly part of her, perhaps, had dreaded this moment with heart-pounding trepidation.

It was October fourth. The first equestrian would step onto Gray Horse Hill within a few hours' time.

"It took fifty-five minutes to get here from that airport." His tone rang with censure, but whether he disapproved of Rapid City Regional or distance in general was difficult to say. He glanced at his watch. "I'll have to leave here within the hour to make my meeting in D.C. So . . ." He lifted his attention to their surroundings. "Let's get started. This is it?"

"Yes." She followed his gaze. Beside the homey brick silo, the barn once again stood proud and true. Stained a rich mahogany, the double doors were open and welcoming. The ancient cupolas, resurrected from a creek bed near a neighboring farm, gleamed atop the roof's wooden shingles. "This is Gray Horse Hill."

"How many stalls?"

"Ten so far." She resisted the urge to fidget. "But I . . . I wanted to talk to you about something else." She had, in fact, tried to call him a number of times. Or, perhaps more correctly, she had *tried* to try to call him.

He turned his scowl on her. She clasped her hands together.

"Were you and Mother planning to divorce?" The words escaped like wild mustangs, squeezing between her lips and galloping into the distance.

His brows dropped low over midwinter eyes. "Where would you get such an outlandish notion?"

Explanations and apologies raced through her mind, but she quieted them. "Were you?"

He drew a long breath through his nose and straightened to steel-rod rigidity. "I did not come here to discuss my personal life with you, Sydney."

"I understand that, but I need to know what—"

"No. *I* need to know," he countered. "I need to know whether you have wasted my money completely or if there is some way to salvage the situation. Now . . ." He scowled at the split-rail fences that separated the house from the endless pastures. A granite-paved pathway wound to the wide, sprawling porch. Beside the flagstones, goldenrod bloomed in the meandering rain garden. Monarchs fluttered about milkweed's pink blossoms. But he seemed to notice neither the butterflies nor the soothing stillness. "Where is the arena?"

"The arena?" She blinked and pulled her gaze from the bench Hunter had placed beneath a gnarled pine. He'd crafted the back from a single plank of asymmetrical oak that had been felled by a recent storm. The knotty wood had been sanded to satin smoothness. The brass plate affixed to one arm said PEACE TO ALL WHO REST HERE. But that peace had been stolen.

Sydney motioned toward the wooden fence located just south of the barn. A full two acres had been devoted to the jump course. Brightly colored standards dotted the carefully groomed sand. "We just completed it. Maybe later—"

"I meant the *indoor* arena."

Sydney clasped her hands together. They trembled slightly. "Funds were insufficient for an indoor."

"And I suppose you expect me to pay for that, too?"

"That's her father?" Vura asked, and just barely managed to contain her wince.

She and Hunter stood in the lea of the barn.

"I believe so," he said.

The pair beneath the cottonwood looked as stiff as T-posts as they faced each other across the gravel drive. Hunter fisted his hands and wished like hell that he had never asked her to call her father. Something had changed the day she'd spoken to him. Something, though he wasn't quite sure what.

"I shouldn't be here," Vura said, but didn't turn away from Wellesley's neatly tailored suit, his rigid form, his disapproving expression.

Hunter watched as well. Sydney had barely deigned to glance his way since the rainstorm. He had tried to talk to her a dozen times, but she had held him off with a hundred necessary details and cool disdain.

"She needs us." He said the words quietly, reverently, but Vura huffed a laugh.

"Are you kidding me? She's been treating us like . . ." She shook her head, ran out of words and drew a shaky breath.

"Mama . . ." Lily pattered up from behind her. "Where's Courage?"

"I don't know, baby." She sniffled and pressed her knuckles to her nose as if discouraging tears. "Maybe she's—"

"She's not in her stall."

"I can't do it," Vura said and wiped her hand beneath her nose. "I came today because you asked me to, Hunt. I came for you, but I won't—"

"Mama!" Lily tugged at her hand. "She's gone."

"I won't bend over backward for a woman who doesn't even *want* family." Vura curled her fingers around her daughter's. "Who doesn't even *try* to—"

"Courage is gone," Lily wailed. "She's gone! She's gone! She's gone!"

Vura glanced at her daughter, then at the empty stall.

Hunter knelt beside the child, heart chilled, stomach twisted. He'd had nothing to do with the mare's release, had been absent when Sydney had turned her loose in the predawn stillness, but that didn't absolve him of guilt. Hardly that. It clung to him like toxic waste.

"Courage is free again, Hollyhock," he said. "Free and happy. Like she should be."

"No." Her eyes were as round as coneflowers in her bright-pixie face. "You said she wouldn't leave until I was here to bless her."

"I'm sorry, Lily. I didn't plan to—"

"You promised!"

"She did it on purpose, didn't she?" Vura ground out the words. "She turned her loose just to spite me. To hurt Lily."

"You know that's not true." Hunter rose to his feet. "Courage was ready to go. We had done all we could for her. If we had kept her longer—"

"And you still defend her." Vura snorted her distain. "Even now."

He glanced at the pair near the cottonwood, felt the cold distance between them. "She has no one," he rumbled.

"I wonder why."

"Her father lied." He would have liked to condemn Wellesley for that, to place the blame squarely at the older man's well-shod feet, but his own failures loomed dark and close. "Her mother left. Think how that would feel."

"Mom tried to get custody. Dad said she missed Sydney like crazy. She'd hired an attorney. They were doing everything they could."

"Tell *her* that."

She snorted a laugh and glanced away. "I'll stay for today," she said. "Finish up what I started. What *we* started. But I'm not doing it for her. I'm doing it for you." Her tone, Hunter realized, was steeped in the kind of pain that can only be caused by love.

He turned away, hoping that love would be enough to heal as well as wound.

Sydney's stomach cramped. Too much coffee, not enough food. It had nothing to do with the fact that she had turned Courage loose without the knowledge of the others. The mustang, after all, had been her responsibility from the very beginning. And the mare had fled. Had tossed her tangled mane and galloped into the trees. Perhaps her gait had been somewhat broken, but she hadn't faltered. Hadn't looked back. And that was good. It wasn't as if Sydney had expected the animal to stay. This wasn't a Disney movie. It had been the best-case scenario. Having such a wild-eyed horse on the property would only have upset her guests . . . and her father. Her father who had barely said two words when they'd toured the barn, who had only grunted at the sight of the meticulously groomed arena and the far-reaching pastures. Even now, as they walked the jump course, he was ominously silent. It was not a hopeful sign. Her stomach coiled tighter, spurring up strangely rebellious thoughts; it wasn't as if she needed his approval. She had made all this happen without him, after all. Had planned and toiled and bled for this rugged piece of land.

Then again . . . Reality nipped at her pride, dragged at her confidence; she would have had no property on which to do any of those things without his money. The truth was, Leonard Wellesley could make or break her future. Could see her dreams come to fruition or crush them beneath the heel of his well-polished oxford. True, she had spent most of her life immersed in the equestrian world. She knew the trainers, the owners, the riders, had sent out a hundred invitations to her peers, competitors, and friends. But it was her father who held the purse strings.

And those same strings, she knew from experience, made the puppets dance.

Sydney glanced across the rolling hills to where Hunter and Vura were, even now, securing the top rail of a triple combination. Lily, ragged rat hugged tight to her purple-sweatered chest, was picking wildflowers nearby.

Sydney pulled her gaze away with an effort, but every view reminded her of a dozen back-breaking tasks she had performed with friends: the Redhawks, Vura and her father, the supportive occupants of the Lazy. Her heart hiccupped in her chest. Friends, she thought . . . had she ever really had any until now? Or had she already alienated those who might be counted among that rare breed?

"The clients are coming today?" Leonard asked, scowl directed at the workers on the distant hill.

"Yes. Late afternoon. The sunsets here are spectacular. We'll walk the course just before—"

"They'll be here within hours and you still don't have the course completed?"

"We're just putting on the finishing touches."

He huffed his disapproval. "What about the winters?"

His tone was somber, his expression pinched, but she had prepared her speech carefully. "Winters can be formidable," she admitted. "But the seasons are part of the beauty of this region. The Black Hills receive an average of fifty inches of snow between October and April, traditionally the off-season for the equestrian world. When on pasture, the horses will benefit from the extra workout they receive while plowing through that snow. Then there are the hills themselves." She scooped an open hand through the pristine air, motioning toward the distant vistas. Her fingers only quivered a little. "Gray Horse mounts will improve their fitness level simply by living in this environment, climbing the terrain, negotiating the streams. They'll develop better balance in the mud and gain confidence in their ability to negotiate uncertain footing. And that's in their leisure time." Her oration had been prepared for prospective students. Even now she was honing it for her well-heeled father. "And I'm sure I don't have to tell you what kind of knowledge can be garnered from Guenter Klimke's tutelage." She allowed a moment for him to absorb the name.

"You got Klimke?"

She resisted wringing her hands. The renowned German instructor had not exactly signed in blood, or signed at all, come to that, but he had assured her that if she got the proper clientele, he would consider her offer.

"Apparently, he's been wanting a base in the United States where he can teach," she said.

"So he's coming here."

"Yes," she said and willed it to be true. "Yes, he will be—"

"Where will they stay?"

"I beg your pardon?"

"Your students . . . if you get any, where would they live while they train?"

She forced herself to breathe, in and out, in and out. "At this juncture I will have to rent a block of rooms at the Sundowner in Pringle. The accommodations won't be—"

"Never going to work." His voice was clipped. "The clientele we're looking for will expect accommodations on the premises. Excellent accommodations."

He had said "we're." As if he was already invested. Already on board. Sydney had no idea whether she should laugh or weep. So she remained silent and trembled.

"We could connect it to the barn, so they have no need to walk outside if we tear down that brick . . ." He paused, scowled. "What is that thing?"

"The silo?" She cast her gaze at the ancient structure built to store fodder. It had been the first thing that had attracted her to this property. Before Beaver Creek had wound its way into her heart, before the red-painted bluffs had seeped quietly into her soul, she had loved the silo.

He nodded. "We'll get rid of it."

"But it's part of the whole package. Part of the charm."

"Charm." He snorted and glanced at his watch again. "What else have you got?"

"Well, I . . ." She moved forward, felt the muscles in her thigh pull tight, stretching tension all the way to her cranium, pushing an ache into her head. He followed her, but in a moment she stopped. "I wanted to show you this," she said and glanced around. Goose bumps shivered over her skin, though she would never know why the sight of the high, rugged plains stirred her so.

"What?" her father asked and scowled out over the hills.

"I believe the students will appreciate the view."

He shook his head. "We'll bulldoze that area." He waved vaguely. "Put in an indoor arena. The parking lot will—"

"No." The single word came out soft but steady.

He pulled back his shoulders another half inch and turned toward her, eyes narrowed. "What did you say?"

She clasped her hands together. They no longer shook. "This is my place. My home."

"Built with my money."

"And my expertise. My vision."

"Vision! What you have is a pipe dream. You don't know the first thing about running a business, about the sacrifices needed to be a success. It would be laughable if it weren't so—"

"Is this why Mother left you?"

The world between them crashed to silence.

"What did you say?"

"Because you undermined her at every turn? Told her she was worthless? Made her feel . . ." She glanced out over the long sweep of hills before turning her gaze back to him. He looked small suddenly. Small and old and bitter. She could almost feel sorry for him. "Because you made her feel like me?"

He gritted his teeth. His eyes looked hard and mean in his pale face. "I gave her everything I had."

She nodded vaguely. "But maybe you had nothing to give."

She never saw him strike, just felt the sting against her cheek. Perhaps it was shock that made her remain where she was, made her stand her ground. Made her lift her chin in silent defiance. He raised his hand again, but it was caught suddenly, snared in a fist as hard as granite. He tried to pull away, but the grip only tightened.

Rage was stamped on Hunter Redhawk's normally impassive face.

"Who the hell are you?" Wellesley snarled.

"I could ask you the same."

"I'm Leonard Wellesley the Third!" he snarled, and yanking his hand away, stumbled backward.

Hunter lowered his head slightly, stalking him. "So you are Sydney's father."

"Of course I'm her—"

"The man who raised her." Hunt took another step forward, shoulders slightly hunched, voice little more than a whisper. "Who carried her against his heart." He spread his fingers across his chest, then curled them into a fist. "Who shaped her into what she is today."

"And what is that?" Wellesley asked. "A person who would—"

"Strong," Hunter interrupted and didn't glance at her when he said the word, but his tone was earnest. Almost reverent. "Kind. Brave."

"This has nothing to do with you," Wellesley snorted. "You don't know the first thing about the—"

"You *are* her father," Hunter said and nodded solemnly. "And therefore deserving of respect. So I tell you . . . respectfully . . . that if you hurt her again . . . if you wound her in any way . . . I will end you."

There was a moment of silence, then sputtered indignation. "How dare you threaten me, you—"

"Where is she?" Vura rasped.

Sydney pulled her attention from the men with an effort. The other woman's face was flushed, her hands shaky. "Vura, what's wrong? What are you—"

"Lily's gone!"

Dread stabbed Sydney's heart, clean and sharp. "What do you mean, gone?"

"Gone! I can't find her anywhere."

"Who is this person?" Wellesley asked, but Sydney barely heard him.

"Did you check the barn? You know how she—"

"Yes! Yes. Of course I checked the barn!"

"Then maybe—"

"I think she went to find Courage." Vura's words were little more than a breath of terror, but Sydney heard. Heard and felt the blood drain from her face.

"No," she whispered and let her gaze meet her sister's for the first time in weeks.

Vura's voice broke. "I can't find her, Syd."

"We will, though. We will." Without thinking, Sydney reached for her sister's hands. They shook in hers. She squeezed her fingers tight and turned frantic eyes toward Hunter.

"When did you last see her, Vura?" he asked.

"She was climbing the big cottonwood beside the . . ." Her voice broke. "Beside the creek."

He nodded once, short and crisp. "I'll get Tonk, call Colt, head west from the bridge," he said, and turning his back to her father, raced toward the house.

"The police?" Sydney asked.

"They're on their way." Vura's voice was strained, her eyes pleading.

Sydney glanced toward the endless acres into which the mustang had fled. It would be dark soon. What happened when the light was gone and the temperature dropped? Panic stabbed, cold and bitter in her gut, but she fought it back. "We'll spread out and search every inch, Vura.

We'll find her. We'll find her any minute. Don't—"

"Aren't you forgetting something, Sydney?" Her father's voice was chill, sending guilt flaring through her.

"Yes. I'm sorry. Father, you can help. Go—"

"I meant your students. They'll be arriving soon."

"Of course." Her voice broke with relief. "You can organize them. Break them into groups. Make sure they call to her. Her name is Lily. She's four years old. She's wearing . . ." She thought about the child's perpetual brightness and felt her eyes sting with tears. "Purple. Sometimes she falls asleep in unusual places, so call her name loudly and often. If you meet anyone, ask if they've seen her. She's small for her age, but she's as bright as a—"

"Sydney!" His tone was sharp. "I don't think I have to remind you what you've got riding on this afternoon."

She stared at him and wondered when she had become such an optimist. Three months ago she never would have assumed he would be thinking of a child he had never met. A child he did not care about.

"Yes." She nodded slowly. "I know," she said and turned back to Vura. "We'll find her," she promised. "No matter what it takes. We'll find her."

• • •

Hunter scanned the canyon below him. She had to be somewhere. She had to be safe. It couldn't happen again. It couldn't, he told himself, but his gut said something else entirely. He had failed again. Had become distracted. Had let the child slip through his fingers. "Lily!" He roared her name. But no butterfly voice answered back, no blossom-bright eyes shone up at him, and the sun was slipping away as if it didn't care, casting ghostly shadows over the valley, over his world. "Lily!" he yelled and ran along the ridge to the north.

Hours dragged by like millennium. The darkness was complete, pierced only by Sydney's flashlight.

"Lily! Lily, where are you?" she screamed, but the words emerged as little more than a squeak of noise. She had long ago gone hoarse. The phone in her pocket had died hours before. Still, she stumbled through the blackness, searching blindly. She was lost, had no idea if she was still on her own land. She might have passed her boundaries long ago, but it hardly mattered. Lily wouldn't know the difference. Wouldn't know if she was safe or headed toward increasing danger. Sydney closed out the panic and stumbled on. Beneath the dark-needled limbs of evergreens, the world was black. Like her heart. Like her soul. How could she have been so idiotic? So cruel? So thoughtless. She knew how Lily loved Courage. Knew. And yet she had released the mare, and in doing so had turned the child away. Like her own mother had turned from her. Like . . .

She closed her eyes to her own gnawing self-absorption; this wasn't about her. For once in her life . . .

She jolted as the earth disappeared beneath her and fell, striking water as cold as death. It splashed into her face, soaked her legs, her chest. She stumbled to her feet and glanced around. She must have circled back. Must have returned to the creek. Or was it another stream? One she didn't know. Turning, she staggered toward what she thought might be north. Calling, calling again.

A light shone up ahead. She gasped with hope. "Did you find her?"

No one answered.

"Do you have Lily?" she yelled and realized suddenly that she was looking at her own barn. She stumbled toward it. Every light was on in the stable, but only the two geldings resided there. They nickered as she glanced inside the stalls, hoping against hope to see a little purple-clad figure asleep in a corner. But luck had abandoned her. She rushed toward the house. Her fingers, stiff with cold, were almost incapable of turning the knob, but she managed to stumble inside.

"Lily—" she began, but Vura was already bursting out of the kitchen, eyes red, fingers curled like talons.

"You must have found her." Her eyes darted from side to side, searching hopelessly. "You must have."

Sydney shook her head and raised her gaze to Hunter, who stepped in from outside. Behind him, the night looked as black as silt.

"Any trace?" His voice was nothing but a growl. "A scrap of cloth? A footprint?"

"No."

His face looked as if it had been craved from stone, but his eyes shone with pain.

"It'll be okay," Sydney said and stumbled toward him, but he backed away and disappeared into the darkness.

Vura looked too drained to cry.

"We all need some rest."

Sydney glanced at the speaker, vaguely aware of the badge pinned to his jacket.

"I'm Officer Lalange."

Quinton Murrell wrapped Vura in his arms, cradling his daughter against his chest. An older version of Colt Dickenson appeared alongside a plump woman with a kindly face.

Sydney skimmed the crowd. "What about the others? They must have found something."

Colt shook his head. "Emily went to pick up Bliss a little bit ago. She'll be back soon. Sophie and Ty are still driving through the pastures, hoping to pick up some sign of her in the head-lights. Casie—"

"Where's Father?" she asked. "And the students." She remembered them suddenly, as if they were part of another world. A less important world.

Colt's expression was atypically sober. "I guess your dad had a meeting he had to get to. He, ahhh . . . he talked to your guests before he left. Told them they would get a chance to see the facilities some other time."

"So they left?" Sydney didn't know what she had expected. Still, she felt dazed, strangely wounded.

"I think he said he'd reimburse them for their flights."

She shook her head, disbelieving. Who would leave while a little girl was in jeopardy? she wondered, but the truth rushed in on her: She might have. Once upon a time, she might have done the same thing, justifying her actions with a thousand weak-kneed excuses.

"We're all exhausted," Lalange said. "We're not going to do any good if we don't get some sleep. I suggest that you folks go home." He nodded toward the Lazy Windmill entourage. "It'll be dawn in a couple of hours. We can meet back here then."

"Vura . . ." Sydney's voice sounded sandpaper

rough to her own ears. "Why don't you lie down in my room? Try to rest until—"

"Lily . . ." Vura's voice trembled. She cleared her throat. "My baby's going to show up any minute. Any second." Fear shone like madness in her eyes. "I need to be here for her."

Colt's mother made a mewling sound. His dad wrapped a protective arm around her shoulders.

"Maybe you folks have some extra blankets?" Lalange suggested.

Sydney shook her head, barely aware of her actions. "Just what's on the beds."

"We'll get some." Monty Dickenson, Colt's father, made the offer. "From the farm."

His wife nodded, face contorted with worry. "We'll put together a few sandwiches. Make coffee."

"All right," Lalange said and rattled off orders, though there was little more to be done. Still, Sydney couldn't bear to remain in the house where the air was heavy with fear.

The lights remained on in the barn. Hunter was dropping hay into Fandango's stall.

"We'll find her," Sydney said.

He turned toward her, anguish edged with guilt in his eyes.

She took a staggering step toward him. "You don't blame yourself for this."

Their gazes met, sorrow on sorrow. Terror on terror.

"Of course not. It's just bad luck. Just like Sara's death was . . ." He paused, gritted his teeth, looked away. His face was tight with pain.

"Don't do this to yourself," she said. "It's not your fault."

"Whose then?"

"No one's. It's no one's fault," she said, but she knew it for a lie. If she hadn't turned Courage loose, Lily would still be safe in her mother's arms. If she hadn't treated her friends like slaves, Vura would have had time for her daughter, time to lavish her with the kind of attention that children needed. But maybe Sydney hadn't honestly wanted that. Maybe she was so damaged, she couldn't bear to witness the kind of love she had been denied. Maybe . . . she thought, but Hunter was already turning away and in a moment he was gone, leaving her alone with her misery.

From the end stall, Windwalker nickered for attention. Retrieving hay like an automaton, Sydney fed him his ration. But a noise from the loft made her freeze in her tracks.

"Lily," she breathed and spurted for the ladder. Up above, it was dark and quiet. "Lily," she called again, but silence echoed around her. Then a marmalade cat streaked from a hidey-hole.

Tears burned Sydney's eyes. Alone and anguished, she curled against the straw bales and cried.

• • •

A noise awakened her. Sydney sat up with a start, fumbling groggily for reality. Dreams and worries had melded in her mind, but in a moment she recognized her surroundings. The hayloft at Gray Horse Hill.

"Oh." Hunter's face cracked as he climbed fully into the haymow. "For a minute I thought . . ."

"Did you find her?" she asked, though the answer was clearly stamped on his tortured features.

He turned away, shoulders bowed.

Sydney staggered to her feet. The sun was just rising, shifting filtered light through the east window. Fatigue weighed her body as heavily as despondency weighed her soul, but the sigh of Hunter made her draw a breath and reach desperately for optimism.

"She'll be okay," she said.

He lifted his tormented gaze to the newly framed windows and made no response.

"She's probably just asleep somewhere. Everyone should be back by now. We'll regroup, split up, and try again as soon as—"

"No," he said.

"No?" Anger flared through her. He had no right to give up. "We've got to—"

"It can't be," he breathed and strode closer to the window. It wasn't until that moment that she realized he wasn't speaking to her. He was holding his breath, gaze welded on a distant hill.

"What is it?" She could barely force out the words as she crowded up beside him. He lifted a shaky hand, pointed. And there, silhouetted against the rising sun, was a dark form. A horse. And on its back . . .

"Lily!" He croaked the name and then he was running, scrambling down the ladder, racing outside.

Sydney jolted after him, but by the time she'd reached the barn door, he had stopped. She gripped his arm in fingers numb with tension.

Moving through the autumn grass, head low, steps steady, came Courage.

And upon her broad, clay-colored back, sat a small hunched child. Her hair was tangled, her purple pants torn.

Across the graveled yard, anxious faces gazed from the porch.

"Lily . . ." Vura cried out and flew down the steps, but Colt caught her as she rushed past.

"Wait! Just wait."

Fifty yards away, the mare jolted to a halt. She tossed her dark forelock. Atop her back, the tiny form shifted. Then Lily glanced up. Her gamine face was haloed by a mess of spun-caramel hair. "Mama?"

"Lily Belle." Vura's voice broke. She raised her hands to her face, smothering her sobs, but dared move no more.

"I found her," Lily called and raised the mare's tangled mane in one grubby hand.

Vura cried a stuttering laugh as her daughter wrapped her fingers in the horse's dreadlocks and dropped to the ground.

They stumbled toward each other. In a moment they collided. Mother and daughter. Vura snatched Lily to her chest, breathed in her scent, cried against her tiny shoulder.

The others swarmed from the porch.

Courage threw up her head and bolted, but she stopped beside the silo to watch the reunion.

Everyone spoke at once. They reached out, touching the child's arm, stroking her hair. All except Hunter Redhawk, who stood aside from the others. Tears slipped silently down his chiseled cheeks.

Lily turned toward him, eyes bright, fingers already twisting in her mother's tumbled hair. "It's all right, Hunk," she lisped. "She'll be okay now that she's home."

Chapter 31

"What are you going to do with her?"

Sydney turned as Hunter approached. His footfalls were all but silent against the gravel. He nodded, motioning past her to the high plains beyond the barn where they stood.

From a rock-strewn hillside, Courage raised her head. The frolicsome wind teased her mane and swept her midnight tail across scarred hocks. Behind her, the red buttes reached like ancient cathedrals for the sky.

"With Courage?" Sydney smiled, pulled her gaze from the soaring scene, and ignored the emotions that tightened like a noose around her heart. "Nothing." She cleared her throat. "I'm putting Gray Horse Hill up for sale. Going back home." But where was that? Where had it ever been if not here where the hills cradled her like a beloved child? Where the rivers whispered of forever and the wind sang of healing? She forced a laugh. "I think I scared my potential students all the way back to the East Coast without ever meeting them."

"There are other students."

"Actually, I'm afraid there might be a shortage

of wealthy, bored kids with hundred-thousand-dollar horses."

"So you're giving up," he said.

"I'm . . ." she began and remembered she didn't have to explain herself to him. He had packed up his truck the night before. He was leaving. "Things didn't work out exactly as I planned."

He exhaled quietly, watched Courage return to her grazing. "Then make a new plan."

A spark of anger burned through her. "And what are your grandiose schemes, Redhawk?"

He looked away from the lone mare. "I've been wanting to see New Mexico. Maybe spend some time in—"

"Don't," she said and laughed out loud. "Don't try to pretend you're not running away."

His eyes caught hers. She felt herself being pulled under and glanced away. "Vura needs you."

"Vura," he repeated, and though she didn't dare look at him, she knew his attention remained riveted on her face.

"And Lily . . ." She said the name softly. She had not yet recovered from the terror of losing her. Nor had she entirely come to grips with the truth about their kinship.

Sydney's mother had left Leonard Wellesley. Left him and his money and his mansion and found another. Someone who would cherish her without smothering her. Who would love her as she was. That much was clear, understandable. But how could Sydney's father . . . the man who was supposed to put her welfare above all others . . . how could he have lied to her for the entirety of her life? How could he have spent twenty years trying to force his only daughter into his skewed image of perfect femininity?

"And what of those who need *you?*" Hunter asked.

Sydney pulled herself out of the past with an effort. "That's the beauty of it. No one needs me," she said, and forcing a smile, turned away, but he caught her arm.

Their gazes clashed. "You're wrong."

She raised her brows at him and felt her breath hitch in her throat. Their gazes fused and held. Silence stretched between them. She tried to tug away, but he tightened his grip and nodded toward the distant hills.

"What will she do when you are gone?"

Sydney swallowed, trying to ease the tension in her throat. "She's a wild thing. Like you said."

"We all need a place, duchess. Even wild things."

"There's nothing I can do," she insisted, but his eyes darkened, calling her a liar.

"There isn't!" She spat the words. "I'm out of money. Out of time. Out of . . . hope." She cleared her throat. "And I don't see the situation changing if I stay here."

"Your father cut you off." His tone was deep and quiet.

"Yes." She tilted her chin, clenched her fists. "But he'll . . . we'll work things out if I . . ." She forced a chuckle and felt herself die a little. "We'll work things out."

"If you do as he says." He scowled. "Live as he demands. Marry as he wishes."

She raised her brows. How surprising that a man like Hunter Redhawk could guess her father's twisted reasoning.

"And you would accept his demands?" he asked.

She thought about it in silence for a second. The memory of David Albrook felt strange in her mind. Not repulsive, exactly. Just tired. Stale. She shook her head. "I'm not the girl I was."

"No," he said and something flared in his eyes. "You are not. But neither are you the woman I thought you to be if you give this up."

"I don't have a choice." Her voice was louder than she had planned.

"There is always a choice," he said, but she would be a fool to allow herself to believe that.

"You're wrong."

He held her with his eyes. There was anger there. And disappointment. He gritted his teeth, then, nodding once, he turned toward his truck.

She watched him go. Watched him pull open his door and step inside. Heard his ancient engine grumble as he turned the key, and felt his departure ache like an open wound in her soul.

He didn't look back. Didn't even glance at her as he drove away.

But in a matter of moments, he stopped. The engine died. Reaching onto the passenger seat, he retrieved something.

Sydney felt her heart hitch as she watched him step out of his vehicle, face expressionless, strides long and purposeful.

For reasons unknown, it felt difficult to breathe as he approached her, impossible to meet his gaze as he shoved a folder into her hands.

She kept her back very straight. "What's this?"

"Look at it."

"I've got things to—"

"Read it," he ordered and waited while she opened the package.

The first photograph struck her like a blow. It was Courage . . . not as she was now, wild and free and unfettered, but as she had been, broken, starved, dying. Sydney pursed her lips and choked back the tears. Fingers slow, she shifted to the next image. The mare was lying down, bandaged legs bent beneath her. She was still scrawny, still broken, but something was different. There was a light in her eyes. A . . .

Scowling, Sydney looked closer, focusing on a messy tangle of hair just above the dark crest of the mare's neck. And beneath it, where the dun's mane hung heavy and long, a tiny scrap of purple, probably unnoticed by the photographer, was visible between the animal's forearm and neck.

"She was in there," Sydney hissed. "Lily snuck in with her."

Hunter nodded.

"But it was locked. The stall was padlocked. It's impossible."

"Perhaps Lily didn't know that." He shrugged, a single lift of a heavy shoulder. "Or maybe the picture was taken before we began locking the stall."

Sydney scowled, unable to speak as she lifted the papers from the folder.

An essay lay beneath a half-dozen more photographs: "Courage," by Ty Roberts. Sydney read through it, blinked back tears when she could no longer see, wiped her eyes when that didn't suffice. It was a simple story and true, written with a cowboy's brevity and a poet's magic. She cleared her throat as she shoved the pages back into the folder. "That doesn't change—"

"You missed a picture," he said.

She shook her head, unable to accept more, to feel more, but he reached into the folder himself. Drawing out a photograph, he pushed it toward her. She lowered her gaze against her better judgment.

It was a distant shot of a clay-colored horse. A

tiny purple-dressed figure was perched on its back. Fog was rising from the canyon below, blurring the image, but you could still see the courage, the will, the bond, tight as a fist, between horse and child.

"Emily took it from the upstairs window while Bliss slept that morning."

Sydney shuddered a little sob, but allowed herself no more. "This doesn't change anything."

"Really?" He huffed a laugh, shoved his hands into the pockets of his jeans, and glanced at the distant hills. "These pictures . . . these words . . ." His river-agate eyes were bright. "What will they do to others if they can make a duchess cry?"

"I'm not crying."

"Then your eyes are melting."

She stifled a laugh and shook her head, but he spoke before she could.

"If the story was published . . . if people saw that horse . . . if they knew there were others like her . . ." He let the words fall into the quiet of the morning, but she could not let them lie.

"They'd . . ." Against her will, a sliver of excitement slipped through the fog of defeat. "They'd want to help. They'd do what they could to help fund the project."

"Ai. If they have a soul, they would."

"I could . . ." She kept her body very still, lest she move and lose the magic. "I could take in more mustangs."

"You've got the land."

"We could educate people. Make them understand. About . . . about the need for wild things. For wild places."

He nodded once, but she barely noticed. "They could see the horses in their natural habitat. Pay extra to ride through the hills. We could bring in local artisans." She thought of the horsehair vase Tonk had given her. "Sell . . ." Her mind was soaring. "Pottery and watercolors and jewelry, take a commission to pay for taxes and—"

"There she is." His eyes burned into hers.

"What?"

"Welcome home, Sydney Wellesley," he said, and nodding once, turned away.

She felt the dream being ripped from her soul. Felt the possibilities roll away like mist in the wind.

"I can't do it," she said.

He stopped, turned. Anger and disappointment lay like a blight on his striking features.

"Not alone," she added. There was a plea in her voice so soft and earnest, it all but ached. But she didn't care.

She watched his brows dip lower, felt his fear. It would be so much easier for him to run away. So much simpler. But she had no desire to make his life simple.

"I'll need . . ." She paused. She had no idea what she was going to need. "Safe fencing and more hay and . . ." Their gazes clashed and held. You, she thought. I'll need you. But even now she couldn't force out the words. Couldn't take the chance. But neither could she let him go. Not without trying.

"I need your help," she said.

He watched her in silence for a small eternity, and then he smiled. The expression was gentle and strangely proud. "You do not need anyone."

She let the warmth of his faith soak into the core of her being. "Then maybe I just want . . ." The truth was so close. So close, but still unreachable. ". . . your help."

Seconds ticked away. "Do you always get what you want?" His voice was low and cautious.

"No." A smile tugged at her lips. Happiness called. But contentment, that rare, fragile bird, was already fluttering quietly onto her shoulder. "I'm considering starting a new trend, however."

He waited, uncertain.

"Do you want me to beg?" she asked.

He snorted. Humor shone in his dark-magic eyes. "I do not believe you capable of such a thing."

"Somebody once told me I could do anything. Who was that?" she asked, and turning her eyes sideways as if in thought, tapped her cheek. "Oh yes . . ." She looked back at him abruptly. "It was you," she said, and holding her breath, dropped to one knee.

He jerked back in surprise, but she had snagged his sleeve.

"Hunter Redhawk . . ."

"What the devil are you doing?"

"Please," she said.

"Get up."

"Stay."

He glanced around as if expecting a film crew to pop up from behind a boulder. But the paparazzi had not shown up. Sydney Wellesley, as it turned out, was of no particular interest . . . just your average farm girl, struggling to make ends meet. Contentment took a sharp bend toward unfettered joy.

"Stand up!" he demanded, but she remained where she was.

"For Lily," she said.

He shook his head and tried to back away, but she tightened her grip on his arm.

"And Vura, and Courage, and . . ." She swallowed, searching for her own courage, and he froze, watching her, unbreathing, unmoving. "And me."

An eternity passed. Her chest ached with the wait. Her thigh throbbed with tension, but it was just pain, no longer debilitating.

"If I do . . ." Was he glaring at her? "Will you promise never to beg again?"

She laughed. "But I'm just getting the hang of it, and I think . . ." She canted her head at him, thrilled by his grouchy expression, amused by his obvious discomfort. "I think it might be an extremely useful tool. Please . . . please . . ." she said, and managed, somehow, to sound more pathetic each time. "Please stay."

"Fine! All right. Just . . ." He glanced around again. "Get up. You're creeping me out."

She smiled at him, heart singing. "I would," she said. "Really. But my leg went numb."

"Oh, for pity's sake," he said and, lifting her carefully into his arms, cradled her against his heart.

Epilogue

It was the perfect day for a wedding. If you liked fog . . . which Sydney did . . . with a spritz of rain, which was okay, and threats of snow, which was a little less delightful.

Lavender clouds unfurled like blossoms in the east, rolled over evergreen hills, and scattered sparkling droplets onto the honored guests. Behind the Lazy Windmill, bur oak and golden aspen provided a fiery backdrop for the ceremony.

The bride arrived on a bay stallion that arched his mahogany neck and pranced with princely strides. The scuffed toes of his rider's weathered boots peaked out from beneath her snow-white gown. The elegant lace and smooth satin looked pristine against the deep luster of the horse's burnished coat. Beside her, young Ty Roberts accompanied her down the aisle on his beloved Angel. Even the ancient mare jigged a few steps. Orange butterfly weed adorned her mane and tail. Beside the cocky stallion, she danced a little, flirting. Her rider placed a work-roughened hand on her neck, soothing, steady.

Sydney felt her chest tighten. She had never been a sucker for weddings. Had not planned that Cinderella day as many had, but there was something about the unbridled joy in Casie Carmichael's eyes that made her throat tighten up. Something about the loving care in Ty's touch that made her eyes sting. And that was even before the bridegroom topped the hill on his penny-bright palomino.

Sydney couldn't help but notice that Colt Dickenson's cocky grin was notably absent or that his hands, those callused hands that had grasped a thousand ropes, were not entirely steady on the reins. And when he spoke, his voice trembled just a little.

Their vows were simple and reverent, their gazes only for each other. Emily Kane wept openly and cuddled Baby Bliss to her chest. The lanky young man beside her wrapped an arm around her shoulders and whispered in her ear until she laughed soggily.

Vura propped her tiny daughter atop Fandango as her father led the old gelding between the well-wishers. With her gossamer hair wreathed in a circlet of autumn leaves, Lily laughed and tossed petals into the crowd.

Dressed in a beaded vest and dark trousers, Tonk watched their progress with a dark-eyed scowl.

And then the newlyweds were gone, slipping hand in hand past the crest of the hill and into forever.

A little sniffle was heard, but it wasn't Sydney's. She turned toward Hunter. His expression was stony, but his eyes were suspiciously bright. Stifling a smile, she handed over a tissue.

He cut his gaze to hers and raised an insulted brow. "Hunkpapa do not cry."

She met his gaze steadily. "How about the Hessians?"

"They sob like babies," he said and snatched the Kleenex from her hand. "God in heaven, are you going to let me cry alone?"

She laughed a little, but it sounded more like a sob.

"You're not alone," she said and, reaching out, folded her slim, pale fingers around his.

Center Point Large Print
600 Brooks Road / PO Box 1
Thorndike, ME 04986-0001 USA

(207) 568-3717

US & Canada:
1 800 929-9108
www.centerpointlargeprint.com